Absent Friends

Also by Gillian Linscott

A Healthy Body
Murder Makes Tracks
Knightfall
A Whiff of Sulphur
Unknown Hand
Murder, I Presume

Featuring Nell Bray

Sister Beneath the Sheet
Hanging on the Wire
Stage Fright
Widow's Peak
Crown Witness
Dead Man's Music
Dance on Blood

Absent Friends

Gillian Linscott

St. Martin's Press
New York

Library of Congress Cataloging-in-Publication Data

Linscott, Gillian.
  Absent Friends / Gillian Linscott.
    p. cm.
  ISBN 0-312-20765-4
  I. Title
PR6062.I54A63 1999
823'.914—dc21
                                          99-13681
                                          CIP

First published in Great Britain by Virago, a division of Little, Brown and Company (UK)

First U.S. Edition: May 1999

10 9 8 7 6 5 4 3 2 1

Seventeen women stood as candidates in the first general election in which women voted, December 1918. The author hopes that they might have forgiven her for adding a fictional one to their number.

Acknowledgements

The author would like to thank the staff of the Imperial War Museum for their patient help; Graham Probert for his advice on motor cars; Nigel LeFeuvre, piano tuner of Leominster, for working out how to put a ghost into a piano.

Chapter One

❧

From inside my living room, typing a letter, I heard the feet going uphill, hundreds of them. Not marching. We'd had too much of marching. If there was a rhythm, it was more a kind of skip and shuffle, like people who were bent on celebrating but still not quite able to convince themselves that it was allowed. I tried to block it out and concentrate . . . *believe it is essential that as many woman candidates as possible stand for election. The fight to get the Vote is pointless unless we use it as a force for change. My qualifications* . . . Skip and shuffle, skip and shuffle, getting louder. The crowds had started moving uphill even before it got dark, and on a cloudy afternoon in the middle of November, darkness came early. They were being drawn to the heights of Hampstead Heath, as Londoners tended to be at times of celebration. The truth was, I was ready to be distracted. This was the fifteenth time that afternoon I'd typed the same words and confidence was waning with each repetition. But with another eleven to do before the last post on Sunday I couldn't afford doubt or modesty. *My qualifications include almost fifteen years campaigning for the Vote as a member of the Women's Social and Political Union. I am the co-author of a report into* . . . Some distant cheering now, from down the

1

hill towards the underground station, the sound of a brass band playing 'Soldiers of the Queen'.

Four days before, on a drizzly night, I'd stood shoulder to shoulder with thousands of people in Fleet Street, to see the first editions of the newspapers come out and confirm it was peace at last. Victory too, if that had any meaning left, but above all an end to four years of war. Then, two days after that, I'd sat with my friends in the Ladies' Gallery of the House of Commons and heard Lloyd George call a general election. That marked an end of an even longer war. In this election women would be voting for the first time. More than that, some would be standing for election including, I hoped, Nell Bray. As I was pointing out in the letter, I had ideals, policies and experience. There were just three small problems. I had no constituency, no party machinery, no money. True there was something calling itself the Women's Party, but since that mainly consisted of Emmeline and Christabel Pankhurst yelling for revenge on the Germans I'd have as soon stood as a Tory. Or almost. With a month to go to the election I'd made a list of the twenty-six constituencies I knew best and was writing to friends or contacts in all of them looking for a political fairy godmother . . . *above all, to make sure this is the last world war by supporting the League of Nations and* . . . Damnation. Skipped a paragraph. I tore the sheet out of the typewriter, screwed it up, threw it in the grate and went over to the window.

At the end of the street the crowds were streaming along, coming thick and fast. Even through the glass and half a street away, their urgency got to me. I grabbed my coat and hat and went out into the damp, brass-thumping night. By the time I got to the end of the street I was almost running with the need to join them and catch this germ of celebration. A man in a flat cap and a boy with a cardboard trumpet stood back, grinning, to let me in and I was part of the impromptu procession. Odd, after all those years, to be in a procession without a banner in my hand. We walked, all strangers to each other, elbows brushing, catching each other's eyes and grinning in a way that was half shame-faced, half thrilled with ourselves like children playing truant from school. There wasn't far to go. At the top of the hill the crowd had mostly come to a halt around Whitestone Pond and the flagstaff, where a Union Jack flattered damply in the breeze. To the north of the pond the crowd bulged out around Jack Straw's Castle, with the lights of the pub glinting on beer glasses and waiters trying to push through with loaded trays. Most people were looking back down the hill and the brass band's music was getting louder.

'Eh missus, can you see them from up there?'

I was wedged in by a large family party and a couple of urchins were tugging at my sleeve. I was too used to jokes about my height to resent it, even if it had been a time for resentment.

'See what?'

'The torches.'

And I could see them, a line of flaming torches coming up Heath Street, then more torches behind them, until the whole road was picked out in regular points of flame with serious male faces behind them. They came to a different rhythm, no civilian shuffle and hop but a regular march. A ragged cheer went up, and got louder as the first ranks of torches came level with the crowd by the pond, illuminating the khaki uniforms of the Army Service Corps. The band came past, drowning the cheering, then there was an outbreak of booing, hissing and laughter. Four of the marching men were carrying a figure like a Guy Fawkes by its floppy legs and arms, a cardboard Prussian helmet tied to its stuffed pillow head.

'Kaiser Bill. They're going to burn Kaiser Bill.'

Most of the crowd fell in behind them along West Heath Road, some carrying their own makeshift torches of screwed-up newspapers, with flakes of burning paper floating off to the dark heathland, left and right. Some of us stayed there by the flagpole. The bonfire was on the West Heath, just below us, so we had a good view as the flames ripped into the sky and heard the cheers as Kaiser Bill burnt. There was singing too, 'Rule Britannia' 'God Save the King' 'It's a Long Way to Tipperary'. I heard a gulping sound to one side of me, looked down and saw a plump, elderly woman in a felt hat. I'd been conscious of her singing, rather out of tune, but now tears were streaming down her face. She was trying to say something, out of lips locked together and a gulping throat and a look of misery in her eyes that seemed to go down to the centre of the earth. I put my arm round her. She collapsed against me and a few words came.

'Can't help thinking . . . Can't help thinking . . .'

That was all. She leaned against me for a while, shaking, then pushed me away as if somehow I'd been the cause of it and walked off, sobbing but trying to sing at the same time.

She was right, though. You couldn't help thinking. Standing up there by the flagpole, with the bonfire flaring, the crowd singing and cheering and the lights of London stretched out below us, I thought of friends who were gone for ever and of other friends, still alive as far as I knew, but taken so far away by war that they seemed almost as distant as the dead. There was Bobbie Fieldfare, driving ambulances in France, probably as recklessly as she'd galloped horses over fences or thrown stones through shop windows in Oxford Street. Simon Frater, classicist – also somewhere in France. That had been one of the surprises of the last four years. I'd expected that a quiet academic like Simon would have been a pacifist, but there he'd been, as soon as war broke out, clamouring to be enlisted. In his case, it wasn't even bloodthirstiness or simple patriotism but an extension of his classical studies. The city states of ancient Greece had survived because it was their citizens' duty to fight for them. Socrates himself had been a soldier. So Simon Frater answered the call and severely perplexed some poor recruiting officer. The fact that he was short-sighted, incurably clumsy and a potential danger to anyone but the enemy when in possession of a firearm made him hard to place. After several unsuccessful experiments, somebody realised that a mind that could manage Greek poetry might have its uses in breaking enemy codes. The last I'd heard of him he'd been attached to the intelligence staff of a general and was based in a chateau. He should, with luck, have survived the war but I didn't know. Nobody knew. Then there was a barrister named Bill Musgrave. Or rather, there had been a Bill Musgrave, but there was now Captain William Musgrave. I hadn't seen him for nearly three years. There'd been an opportunity a year before when he was home on leave, but I'd deliberately missed it because by that time I was breaking the law again, trying to help men who were refusing to be conscripted into the Army. Harbouring deserters hardly made me fit company for an Army officer, or him for me.

I found I'd started walking and moved away from the crowd. After that first warm feeling, celebration hadn't been as infectious as I'd hoped. I walked round Whitestone Pond, picking my way through the people overflowing from Jack Straw's Castle, across the road to the main part of the heath. Even though I'd had enough of crowds, the idea of returning to my cold room and the letters wasn't appealing. I thought I'd walk over to Highgate Ponds and back, then with any luck I'd be tired enough to sleep. The paths over the heath were so familiar to me that my feet knew them in the dark. I left the gaslights and the pavements behind me and turned on to a path among the bushes. For the first few hundred yards I was conscious of giggles and whisperings of couples I'd disturbed and walked on as quickly as I could, not wanting to spoil their night. Then I was out on the open heath. It was quieter there, but not as quiet as the heath usually is at night. From behind me I could still hear, faintly, the shouting and singing from the bonfire on the West Heath. To my right the ground sloped away to London, a glimmer of lights all the way down to the Thames. I could see more bonfires and a softer and more distant wave of sound came up from the whole of the city, cheering, singing and shouting merging into what sounded like a great repeated sigh of relief.

Listening to this, I became conscious of a closer sound – footsteps following me. At first I thought it was just somebody like myself, wanting to get away

from the crowds. They were heavy male steps, whoever it was walking faster than I was and on the same
path. I wasn't alarmed. Even if it happened to be some
drunk wanting confrontation, I'd dealt with worse
than that and didn't intend to be deprived of my walk.
I deliberately kept to the same easy pace and didn't
turn round, intending to step aside and let him pass.
The steps came within yards of me so that the back of
my neck was prickling, then slowed to my own pace.
Whoever it was didn't intend to pass after all. For a
minute or so we went on like that, then I got tired of
the game. I stopped, stepped sideways on to the
grass. The steps stopped as well. I could hear his
soft breathing.

'Do go past me,' I said.

A pause, then his voice. 'Nell?' Then, more formal.
'Miss Bray? It *is* Nell, isn't it?'

Bill Musgrave's voice. Bill, who should be somewhere in France, standing there a step away from me.
I could even smell the damp wool of his jacket and a
whiff of pipe tobacco. For a moment I couldn't
answer, thinking that I'd summoned up his image
from loneliness. Or Bill must be dead, and this was the
ghost of him.

'I don't believe in ghosts.'

I must have said it aloud, because he laughed.

'You don't have to.'

I took a step towards him, almost touching him to
make sure he was real, but not quite.

'What are you doing here?'

'Looking for you. I went to your place but there
was nobody there but the cats. So I came up here and
saw you striding off as if you were going for a ten-mile
hike. May I join you?'

7

I couldn't see his face in the dark, but his voice was cheerful and matter-of-fact as if we'd been only a few days apart.

'Why not?'

We still hadn't touched, not even hands, but as we started walking again I accidentally brushed against his left elbow. He drew away and then apologised.

'It's why I'm home. I came over on a hospital train three days before the Armistice and they sent me straight to hospital in Oxford.'

'What happened?'

'We'd heard there was a stretcher party under fire. I was going back with a sergeant to try to hurry it along when a stick grenade came hurtling in. He lost most of his hand. I was lucky.'

'Bill, you'd better know this. I've been working with deserters, campaigning against conscription.'

'Well, of course you'd be campaigning against something. Don't worry, I know.'

'How?'

'We weren't as cut off as you think. I met somebody who'd been with you in that business in Wales last year.'

'Who?'

'Can't remember his name. Anyway, it didn't surprise me.'

'Did you mind?'

'Mind?' He stopped. 'Oh, I see. I'm one of the enemy, am I?'

'Not enemy. Of course not enemy. But it's why I didn't see you, stopped writing.'

He started walking again and I walked beside him, being careful of the elbow and of something that felt even more fragile.

8

'Nell, believe it or not, I did what I could in my own way. You know what they mean by Friend of the Accused?'

'Somebody who speaks up for the prisoner at a court martial?'

'That's right. Well, a couple of poor devils accused of cowardice knew I'd been a lawyer in civilian life and asked me to speak up for them. One of them – it didn't do him any good because they shot him anyway. The other got off, so he might have been there to hear the guns stop provided the enemy didn't shoot him first.'

We walked towards the edge of one of the Highgate Ponds then turned back. After a while, talking came more easily. He asked what I was doing and I told him about the letters.

'Can't you just choose a constituency and go and stand?'

'You need more than a megaphone and a wagonette for a general election. Posters, leaflets, hire of halls – not to speak of a hundred and fifty pound deposit which I shall almost certainly lose.'

After a few steps he said, 'You know, you don't get much chance to spend in the Army. I must have nearly two hundred pounds saved up from—'

'No.' I felt like laughing and crying together. He'd never been the rich variety of barrister and that money would be all he had in the world. 'I can't take it from you. You don't even care about politics very much.'

'I'd like you to have what you want.'

'Thank you, but no.'

When we got to the Hampstead side of the heath I invited him back to the house but he said he had to catch the last train for Oxford. He was still a soldier and an officer, after all, and wasn't supposed to be out of the hospital, though discipline had slipped a little in the general celebrating.

'But I'll get a few days' leave as soon as I can. There are months owing to me. Then we'll get together and plan your campaign.'

As we paused for a last look down on the London lights a great red-and-white rocket went up, probably from the official Ministry of Munitions fireworks display in Hyde Park, and seemed to hang in the sky over the whole city.

It was probably at much the same time, at another victory celebration in a shire a long way from London, that Mr Charles Sollers, button and buckle manufacturer, stepped forward to light the touch paper on another firework and was blown to smithereens.

Chapter Two

⊲

Over the next two weeks, the word that came back from twenty-six constituencies wasn't encouraging. There were plenty of goodwill and good wishes, people willing to work with me but no money available for hopeless causes. The nature of the election was part of the problem. The Coalition – of Tories and Liberals – that had run the war was determined to hang on together into the peace, so they were putting up Coalition candidates and not fighting each other. They hoped that would give electors a simple choice: are you voting for the men who won the war or do you insist on being ungrateful and unpatriotic? I could swallow my own disappointment. What hurt most, after all the work, was the growing knowledge that with around eight million women eligible to vote for the first time, only a handful would have a chance to vote for other women. As far as I knew, out of 707 constituencies fewer than twenty would have a woman candidate. The only one of those who had a ghost of a chance of being elected was Christabel Pankhurst, because she had the support of Lloyd George in return for wartime recruiting by herself and Emmeline. As far as I was concerned, Christabel and Lloyd George deserved each other. The Prime Minister still tended to back behind the nearest policeman at the sight of me. It looked as if my role in the election would be campaigning for somebody else and I'd more or less decided on Charlotte Despard who – at the age of 74 – was standing for Labour in Battersea. It was probably another hopeless cause, but then I'd been brought up on them. When I was no more than a toddler I'd had a rosette pinned on my coat and was taken out to campaign for my father around the poor streets of Liverpool. He never got elected either. This resolution to work for Charlotte wavered a little when I got a letter from my friend Rose Mills in Lancashire. Only not Rose Mills any more, Rose Kendal now. Near the start of the war, she'd married a cotton-town trade unionist, Jimmy Kendal, then seen him go away to the Machine Gun Corps. But he'd survived. The Army, so reluctant to let go of its men even now that peace was here, had been forced to release him because he was standing for parliament in his home town. He had an excellent chance of being elected and Rose was full of excitement, inviting me to come up and stay with them and join his campaign. I was tempted, even though Jimmy had never quite forgiven me for once suspecting him of a murder for which his brother was very nearly hanged.

Over the two weeks of getting back regretful replies there was just one glimmer of hope and that had come from such an unlikely direction that I didn't take it seriously. I was at a sale of arts and crafts, helping to raise money for somebody else's campaign, when a sculptor friend named Moira came up to me at the coffee stall. She'd married a stonecarver and now lived and worked in Herefordshire, not far from the Welsh border, and had come up to town with some of her work to sell.

'Where are you standing then, Nell?'

12

I bought her a coffee and explained the money problem. Not that she could help there. As an artist, she was even poorer than I was.

'Have you thought of Duxbury?'

I ran through my list of possible constituencies and couldn't place it.

'Where I live. North Herefordshire.'

I hadn't looked at rural constituencies because most of our support tended to be in cities. When I said that, Moira got annoyed.

'Aren't people in country constituencies worth bothering about?'

'Of course they are, but they're not very radical. I don't suppose your Duxbury's any exception. My vote would hardly get into three figures.'

'We're not all Tories. Our friends would vote for you – or most of them.'

'Making?'

She started doing a count with thumb and fingers of one hand, on the side of the coffee cup. I made it seventeen before she gave up.

'Dozens.'

'Overwhelming. Could any of those dozens help with my campaign funds?'

I expected her to confess that no, they couldn't, but an odd look came over her face.

'Well, not as such. But it is an unusual situation. The Coalition candidate got killed so they had to find another one in a hurry. The Liberals were supposed to be standing down, but there's a rebel group that won't and so—'

'I don't see how that helps. I wouldn't stand as a Liberal even if they wanted me.' Not even to make Lloyd George choke on his tea.

'No, it's not that. Supposing I could find somebody in Duxbury to pay your campaign expenses, would you stand as an independent?'

'If they gave me a free hand with policy, I'd consider it.'

I thought I was safe in saying that because it seemed about as likely as rain falling upwards. Moira was probably only saying it because I'd been rude about her rural radicals. She said mysteriously that she'd see what she could do, then shot across the room after somebody with a reputation as an art patron. As for the reference to the Coalition candidate being killed, I hardly gave it a first thought, let alone a second one. A lot of people had been killed. The conversation went out of my mind completely while I chased my flock of political wild geese and didn't come back into it until the morning when I found in my post a letter with a Duxbury postmark. It arrived quite out of the blue – or out of the mauve perhaps, since that was the colour of the stationery – and came from a woman I'd never heard of in my life.

> *Whitehorn Hall,*
> *Near Duxbury,*
> *Herefordshire*

Dear Miss Bray,
I have heard about you from a friend. I wonder if you would be interested in helping to put right a very great injustice by being a candidate in the Duxbury constituency in the forthcoming election. The man standing as a Conservative/Coalition candidate has done a very great wrong, which I cannot write about but will tell you when we meet. I am acting with the approval of my late husband. I would be responsible for all

your election and travel expenses. Please send a tele-
gram and let me know when to expect you.
Yours in hope,
Lucinda Sollers

Please, please do this. I don't know where else to turn.

The letter was written in a beautiful, flowing hand in shiny black ink. The words 'very great injustice' and 'very great wrong' were underlined. It arrived on Friday, 29 November, just five days before nominations had to be in and when I'd given up hope of being able to stand. The reason why I didn't do as she said and telegram immediately was the whole thing smelled wrong. I'd wished for a political fairy god-mother and now one had arrived in a flutter of gauze and spangles. Not a word in her letter about policies or even about women voters. Her name meant nothing to me, and if there'd been a supporter of women's suffrage in a country area so dedicated that she was willing to spend hundreds of pounds on the cause we'd have heard of her by now. Crank, I thought. And yet Moira, who was far from stupid, had given her my name and seriously expected something to come of it. I decided to sleep on it and still hadn't made up my mind what to do on Saturday morning, when Bill was due to visit. He'd written to say he'd got six days' leave, would take an early train from Oxford and hoped to be with me by mid-morning. It was a greasy, drizzly day, but I had the fire going in the kitchen with a week's supply of coal that I'd been saving, both cats on the rag rug in front of it, the kettle steaming and the whole room fragrant with freshly ground coffee. I'd managed to scrounge a few ounces of coffee beans in spite of wartime shortages and the smell was the whole of Europe opening up again. It meant a table outside a café in Paris with pigeons pecking round for croissant crumbs, the glint of the Mediterranean through pine trees, the black wings and pink feet of snow choughs against Alpine glaciers. One more campaign and then I'd go and see that it was all there still. Bill could come too, if he liked. Once I'd have been quite sure that he'd have liked, but that was four years and a war away.

A knock on the front door. When I let him into the narrow hallway and he took his hat off I noticed that there was grey in his hair and the planes of his face were sharper. But the smile was the same, and when he was settled in the chair by the fire with a big cup of coffee in his hand he stretched out his long legs and sighed.

'I feel as if I haven't relaxed since the last time I was here.'

We talked about life in the hospital. The hospital was my old college, requisitioned by the Army medical authorities. It was odd to think of Bill and other wounded men walking in the grounds where we'd played tennis or sat on the grass revising for finals. Everybody was aching to get back to civilian life, he said. It was a kind of limbo, with the war over but the Army still insisting on its rituals. I gave him the news about Rose and Jimmy, asked after the big deerhound that used to lie under his office desk in Manchester in the days before the war.

'Oh, Roswal's fine, as far as I know. I left him with some friends. I'll get up there to see him soon, I hope.'

'You mean you came to see me before Roswal?'

I hadn't intended to be sarcastic, but he looked at me as if I had been, quite sorrowfully. Caught off balance, I brought up the subject of the letter before I'd intended and showed it to him. He read it at a glance and then a second time more slowly, frowning.

'Well?' I said.

'I distrust people who use tinted stationery. And what does she mean, "approval of her late husband"? How can he have an opinion if he's late? What do you know about Duxbury?'

'Not much. Before the war it was held by the Tories with a strong Liberal challenge.'

'A country constituency. They'll probably throw eggs at you.'

'At two shillings a half-dozen they couldn't afford to. Anyway, people in rural constituencies must want peace and work and good housing as much as in cities.'

'It sounds as if you're writing your campaign speech already.'

'If I thought it was a genuine offer, I'd be very tempted. But there's something not right about it.'

'We could go and see her, if you like.'

'We?'

Nothing had been said about how much of his leave he'd spend with me.

'Unless you don't want me.'

We walked together down the hill to the post office and queued to send off the telegram, a short one: EXPECT ME MONDAY AFTERNOON STOP NO COMMITMENT STOP BRAY. All afternoon we strolled on the heath and spent the evening by the kitchen fire, talking. At about nine o'clock Bill stood up and said he should be going to find a hotel.

'Why can't you stay here?'

'If you're going to be a candidate, you'll have to be careful of your reputation.' He was smiling, but partly serious.

'It's past praying for.'

He stayed. In the morning, after a flurry of arrangements with a neighbour about the cats and notes to friends, we took a cab to Paddington. The station was crowded with soldiers and civilians. Peace had set people free to travel again but it still felt like war under the glass and wrought-iron canopy, with a trainload of wounded men arriving, the nurses and the women with tea carts. Our train left late. I had only an overnight bag with me because I was still more than half-convinced that we'd be back by Tuesday, having found that Mrs Sollers was worse than a wild goose.

'Tell me something – why are you encouraging me to see her?'

'Would you have settled otherwise? After all, you've been working for this for most of your life. What else would you do?'

Bill said it lightly, so I could take it as a joke, but I knew him well enough to hear the undertone of wryness as though the joke were in some way against him. As the train chugged on into the Cotswolds and he read a paper I looked out of the window at the damp pastureland and thought about what he'd said. I think we'd felt the Vote would come with fanfares of trumpets, dancing in the streets and a new age starting. The war had done away with that dream like so many other things. Later, as we ran on through the fertile flatlands of the Vale of Evesham, we shared his soldier's ration of chocolate and tea from my flask.

When I looked out of the window a man in a black overcoat that reached to the ground was picking Brussels sprouts. Row after row of greeny-blue sprout plants cut across the view, with smoke and cinders blowing back from the engine, then orchards with bare trees looking black from the damp, an occasional brick-built house on its own in flat fields. Soon after that the spires of Worcester came into view. We changed there, after a long wait and cups of tea from the buffet, on to a local line that ran over the wide Severn, then took a winding course between low hills. Even in the middle of winter, with the trees bare and the grass green-brown, it looked good easy country. There were orchards, the high bare poles of hop yards, small settlements of black-and-white cottages clustering around barns or churches. Sheep were everywhere.

'I hope you're strong on agricultural policy,' Bill said.

Then, just as we were getting used to the easy rhythm of this part of the journey, the train stopped and the platform sign read Duxbury. It was past three in the afternoon, and dusk was already falling. We were the only people getting out. It was a larger station than I'd expected with five platforms, a bookstall and another train waiting on the opposite side. As we got off, porters began loading wicker baskets into the guard's van of our train for the journey back to London, the copper and rainbow feathers of dead pheasants visible through the gaps. Another elderly porter carried our bags across the bridge and out to the station yard. It was deserted, apart from a flat cart turned on its end and a boy of about twelve kicking a stone. Across the yard was nothing but a road and a hedge. Bill and I looked at each other.

'Is there a cab?' Bill asked the porter.

'There would be, sir, but 'e's gone down to 'ereford and not come back yet. Where were you wanting to go to?' The accent had something of the lilt of Welsh in it. The old porter was grinning, quite good-natured but with an obvious curiosity to see what these strangers would make of it.

'Well, the town.'

'Oh, the town. You don't need no cab for that, sir. Straight up the road and you're there. Will you be looking for somewhere to stay the night?' We said we were. 'The best you could do would be Mrs Hincham at the King's Head. Just on the corner of the market square it is. The boy will show you.' He beckoned over the boy, who'd stopped kicking his stone and was staring at us. 'You take the lady's bag and show her and the gentleman to the King's Head. Thank you very much, sir.'

We followed the boy round a bend in the road and the first buildings of town appeared, a terrace of Victorian brick cottages. They were small but decent looking, with lamps already lit behind white lace curtains. In spite of the uncertainty, I felt a surge of excitement at the thought that these weren't just any cottages. The people behind the curtains were voters – perhaps my voters. Nearer the centre of the town the houses were a storey higher and a century older, with symmetrical eighteenth-century fronts and ornate carved doorways. Then we turned into a main street with a row of small shops, a butcher, an iron-monger, a saddler with harnesses hanging on hooks outside and a man stitching at a bench by the window. We passed at least four public houses before we saw the King's Head. The sign – of Charles II judging by the wig – hung out at the corner, just above head height, on a building with black beams and clean white walls that bulged outwards like a badly set blancmange. The sign above the door announced that Mrs Marian Hincham was the licensee. The boy planted my bag just inside a wood-panelled hall, accepted a shilling and disappeared. A door open to the left showed a fire blazing and a shiny wooden bench with its back to us. There was a smell of baking pastry and burning logs.

'Good evening, sir. Good evening, madam. Can I help you?'

A large woman had appeared from a door at the end of the hall. She looked both comfortable and formidable, probably in her fifties, in a brown serge dress and blue canvas apron well-dusted with flour. Her face was round and had a doughy look to it, like an uncooked currant bun, but her eyes were intelligent.

'Mrs Hincham? We wondered if you had two rooms for the night?'

'Only for the one night?'

'As far as we know.'

'We can manage that for you. Will you be wanting to eat?'

'Yes,' said Bill.

I explained that I had to go out again as soon as I'd tidied up. Bill and I had agreed on the journey that I should see Mrs Sollers on my own. It was hard on him because he was as curious about her as I was, but I didn't intend to start my possible electoral career with a man as chaperon, not even Bill. Mrs Hincham led the way up to the first floor, lit a gas lamp on the landing and opened two doors.

'It might strike a bit cold, because we've had nobody in them since October. But we'll make up a bit of a fire for you and put a bottle in the beds. I'll send the girl up with some water for you to wash.'

I shut the door of my room and heard Bill moving about next door. The only light came through the window from a gas lamp in the street below. I looked out and saw the market square, almost empty apart from a cart unloading barrels at a side door of the King's Head. There were shops and offices along two sides of the square and at the far end a stone building with columns and a balcony. Town Hall, probably, where nomination papers would have to be handed in the day after tomorrow. I found a candle beside the bed and lit it. There was a timid knock on the door and a child who couldn't be much older than ten lurched in with a metal jug almost as large as she was, gave it to me, gasped as if she'd been told to say something and forgotten her lines and backed out before I could thank her. The water was warm. I poured it into the big china basin on the washstand, sorted out soap and hairbrush from my bag and tried to make myself look respectable enough for tea with the woman who wanted to be my political fairy godmother.

Before I'd finished Bill called to me that he'd see me downstairs. When I got down he was sitting in the room with the wooden settles and the log fire, a glass of whisky and water in front of him.

'Mrs Hincham decided you'd prefer tea. She's making you some.' She arrived soon afterwards, with a large brown pot on a tray, two cups and a plate loaded with slices of fruitcake of a positively prewar succulence. While she was unloading the tray, I asked her how far it was to Whitehorn Hall.

She stopped what she was doing and looked at me, surprised.

'About a mile.'

'That's good, I can walk there.'

'You don't want to do that in the dark. I'll get young John to put the pony in the cart and drive you up there.'

She went out and came back while I was pouring the tea. 'He'll have the cart outside for you by the time you've finished. Are you going to call on poor Mrs Sollers?'

'Yes. Do you know her?'

'Just to speak to. She came in here once with him, when they had a political meeting upstairs.'

'With Mr Sollers?'

'Yes. Terrible about what happened wasn't it, poor man?'

'What exactly did happen?'

She stared at me, taken aback. 'You didn't know?'

I shook my head.

'Blown to bits, he was, poor man.'

So, I thought, Mrs Sollers was a war widow.

'How long ago was that?'

Her eyes went wider. She was looking at me as if I'd arrived from another planet.

'Just over two weeks ago.'

'How terrible. That must have been practically on the last day of the war.'

The irony of surviving so much then being cheated of life at the end made these last war casualties seem even worse than the rest. Mrs Hincham was still giving me that astonished stare.

'Oh no, Mr Sollers wasn't killed in the war. He was never in the war. It happened here.'

'Here?'

'Where you're going, Whitehorn Hall, at least in the grounds of it. It was at the victory bonfire party. A firework went off too soon and killed him.'

She could tell from our faces that she'd launched her own bombshell.

'Just as well you knew, wasn't it, before calling on her.'

She put a log on the fire and went, telling us to ring the bell on the mantelpiece if we wanted more tea. Bill and I stared at each other.

'Well!'

'Bill, this is terrible. The poor woman's obviously unbalanced by grief. I can't take advantage of that, however much I want to stand.'

'It sounds like it.'

'The only decent thing to do is to write her note of condolence, send it out by the pony cart and go back to London by the first train tomorrow.'

'And not even see her?'

'What's the point of that? I don't know her. I can't do her any good.'

'She seems to think you can.'

'I don't suppose she knows what she's doing.'

We talked about it for a while and eventually came to the conclusion that, having sent the telegram, I was committed to keeping the appointment. But as I bowled out of town in the pony cart, with young John driving and a dim lamp on the front picking circles of bare hedges out of the darkness, my hopes of fighting my own campaign had sunk almost out of existence.

Chapter Three

◈

After a while we turned on to a rutted downhill track and there was the dark bulk of a house below us, hunched against a hill. It seemed a haphazard shape, with a squat tower at one end and a roofline at several different levels. Lights from windows on the ground floor reflected in a dark stretch of water that might be a moat. Young John drew up on a semicircle of gravel, near an abrupt stone bridge that arched over the water to a wooden front door with leaded windows on either side, lights on and curtains drawn back. There were smells of pondwater and cows mooing from somewhere not far away. I was bothered about young John and the pony having to wait in the cold, but he said he knew someone round the back who'd see him alright and drove off. I crossed the bridge and pulled at a thin rope beside the door. A bell inside made a tinkling sound like something from an eastern temple, at odds with the mud and the farm smells. The door was opened almost immediately by a young woman in a green woollen dress and white apron who took my hat and coat and led me along a dimly lit corridor. She opened a door, announced, 'Miss Bray, ma'am,' and left.

The brightness of the room after the dimness outside felt like diving into a big warm aquarium. It came from dozens of candles all over the place, on the mantelpiece, tables, windowsills, hanging in wrought-iron circles from the ceiling, their wavering light reflected in a multiplicity of mirrors, and mirrors reflected in mirrors. There were a lot of blues and greens in the curtains and upholstery, increasing the water effect, so that Mrs Sollers seemed to swim towards me, mermaid-like. The hand that took mine felt light and cold, and I'd have hardly been surprised if her fingers had left damp trails. She was probably in her mid-thirties, tall and slim, but gave an impression of bonelessness like a victim in a Pre-Raphaelite painting. I'd expected black, for a woman so recently bereaved, but she was wearing dusky purple, with heavy copper bracelets on her wrists and a slab of polished malachite hanging from a copper chain round her neck. Her hair was reddish brown, rather crinkly, caught up at the back by a pewter comb of Celtic design. She let go of my hand and, with a little floating movement of the fingers, indicated that I should sit down.

'I'm so very glad you're here.'

Her voice was low, her eyes big and dark in a face as pale as the bark of a silver birch. I sat down by the fire on a chair upholstered in pale blue slubbed silk and said I was sorry to hear about her husband's death. Her eyes were on me, concentrating on my face rather than the words.

'Yesss.'

It came as a long exhalation, then there was a silence. I could hear movement in the hall outside, the creak of trolley wheels. She seemed to have nothing else to say, so it was up to me to get us both out of the situation.

'I can understand that soon after the accident—'

What I'd intended to say, as tactfully as I could manage, was that she must be in a state of shock, in no position to take political decisions. But she cut me off, quite composedly.

'Oh, it wasn't an accident, Miss Bray. His friend Jonas Tedder murdered him.'

'Who's Jonas Tedder?'

'The man who's trying to take his seat. He'll do it too unless we stop him.'

'When you say seat, you mean parliamentary seat?'

'Yes. Charles – my husband – had been chosen to stand as Coalition candidate. He was certain to be elected. Jonas Tedder was the only other man up for consideration, but he didn't stand a chance. So he murdered Charles and now he's standing instead.'

She looked and sounded entirely calm, except that she was gripping the copper bracelet on her left wrist in the fingers of her right hand, twisting it so that it must have been biting through the fabric of her dress and into her wrist. There was a tap on the door. The housekeeper wheeled in a tea trolley and withdrew. Lucinda Sollers wafted upright and poured two cups of what smelled like Earl Grey, apologising for the absence of a lemon.

'I understood that Mr Sollers was killed by a firework.'

'Yes, a firework that had been stuffed full of explosive by Jonas Tedder.' She put the tea on a small table beside me and sat down again, the purple folds of the dress settling gracefully round her long calves.

'What party is Mr Tedder?'

'Oh, Conservative too, like Charles. Except we're all Coalition now.'

27

'Have you told the police about your suspicions?'

'They're not suspicions, it's fact. There would be no point. Jonas Tedder is a magistrate. And if we don't do something, he'll be a Member of Parliament and it will be too late.'

'Even MPs can't get away with murder.'

'He will, unless something is done about it. That's why we decided to write to you.'

The last of my political optimism flapped a defeated fin and sank. It had been because of my unsought detective reputation, not my politics, that she wanted me.

'What do you expect me to do about it?'

'Stop him being elected. He'll never stand trial, we know that. He has too many friends in the county. But he shan't go to parliament and take the seat that should belong to Charles.'

I didn't like the implication that parliamentary seats were anybody's rightful property, like armchairs or golf clubs, but let it pass.

'How would I stop him? You do realise, I'd have very little hope of being elected here?' That was putting it mildly. No chance whatsoever.

'You could make speeches, talk to people.'

'I couldn't stand up in the town square and accuse an opponent of murder, even if I thought he'd done it.'

She let go of the bracelet. Her right hand came up in a claw and scored along the arm of her chair, making a sound on the slubbed silk like skin ripping. 'He's allowed to kill Charles, but nobody's allowed to say it.'

'Is there any evidence at all for this?'

'Who else would do it? Charles had no enemies.'

I thought, but didn't say, that a politician with no enemies never existed.

'If I were to investigate, I couldn't start with the assumption that it was murder, let alone that any particular person did it.'

'I've told you what happened. I'll *show* you what happened.' She stood up and floated to the door. I put down my tea and followed. She turned left into the corridor, away from the front door, and led the way to a room at the back of the house with a French window looking out on to the garden. As far as I could see in the dark it was the kind of glory hole you get in country houses, with outdoor clothes for gardening and sagging old chairs for dogs to lie on.

'We didn't bother to get the electricity put in here.'

She took a coat off a hook, threw it round her shoulders and unhitched something from a nail. A flare of a match showed a big paraffin lantern. After she'd made several unsuccessful attempts to get it going I took it from her and lit it. A glow spread round the room, revealing dead geraniums in pots, croquet mallets, boots. A line of wooden boxes, like ammunition boxes, stood against a wall. She touched one of them with her grey suede shoe.

'The fireworks were in those. He must have come in here to do it. The door's never locked.'

She opened the French window and I followed her out on to a terrace. She hadn't offered to get my coat and the air struck cold and damp. A tawny owl hooted from the woods and a more distant one replied. She led the way, holding the paraffin lamp, down a few steps and along a stone-flagged path round the back of the house to the left. The flagstones were slippery from the wet, but she went confidently and silently. The path slanted away from the corner of the house, across a tussocky lawn with a sundial, then

29

to another bridge, broader and lower than the one to the front door, over a wider stretch of water. We crossed the bridge on to another expanse of grass, more meadow than lawn. Beyond it, woods sloped up into the darkness. There was the faintest smell of burning in the air.

'It was the tennis court before the war. We had the bonfire here. The grass would have to have been dug up and re-seeded in any case.'

She walked, more slowly now that there was no stone path, towards the middle of the field and crouched down. She put the lamp on the ground beside her and its light spread over a circle of grey ash, with a few charred branches.

'This was the bonfire. Most of us were standing round it, or on the bridge. Charles insisted that the fireworks should be let off right over there, at the bottom of the bank. He was a careful man.'

'And he was letting off all the fireworks himself?'

'Yes, he'd planned it all very carefully. He knew what order he wanted them in and didn't trust anybody else to do it. He liked to do things for himself.'

'Was anybody near him when it happened?'

'No. Our old gardener had been helping, but Charles had just sent him back to the house to tell cook to put the soup on.'

'How many people were there?'

'Oh, dozens and dozens. We'd invited all the children from the school, the people from church and their families, his friends from the Conservative Party.'

'Including Mr Tedder?'

'Yes. And I'll tell you something that might convince you. They left early, before it happened.'

She was still crouching, her pale face and wide eyes lit from below like a mask floating just above the ground.

'They?'

'He and his wife, Felicity. She suddenly had a headache – he said.'

'But if they left early, how could he put the explosives in the firework?'

'He could have done it before the party started, or even the day before. He came out here on the Friday to collect Felicity from a meeting of the wives' Christmas bazaar committee. Easy. We never locked the garden room and everybody knew the fireworks were there.'

She straightened up and we began to walk across to the rising ground where she said he'd let off the fireworks. There were still cardboard cylinders wrapped in scraps of coloured paper strewn in the grass, the remains of rockets and Roman candles. From the bank we could see the lights of the house glimmering on the water, even make out the pale circle of bonfire ash.

'There were a lot of people watching then, when it happened?'

'Yes. We got all the children away as soon as we could. But they knew. They couldn't help knowing.'

Out here in the dark with her, with the smell of the bonfire still in the air, the thing had more reality. Even if I didn't accept her theory, it was a fact that her husband had died here on this bank. She stood like a statue, her calmness eerie.

'What did you see of it?'

'Everything. I was watching from the bridge. I knew there was one last firework to go. It was the

31

biggest one, Prince of Wales feathers in red, white and blue. After that we were going to sing "God Save the King" and go into the games room for soup. I could see him, striking a match, bending down to light it. Then it happened.' She went quiet for a while then said, very low, 'We found one of his hands up there.'

She pointed to a gnarled hawthorn tree further up the slope, near the edge of the woods. I said nothing. Her head drooped and she began walking slowly back across the grass, taking the lamp with her. I followed, thinking hard. Surely no firework, however defective, could have blown a man apart, and yet that was what had happened. I had the word of the landlady at the inn for that, as well as Mrs Sollers', and there'd been dozens of witnesses. By the time we were back in her warm sitting-room I wasn't quite so ready to walk away as I had been half an hour before. She was lying back in her chair by the fire, with the reflected candles shimmering all round her, eyes closed, the suede shoes soaked to the colour of charcoal and clotted with mud and ash.

'Well, will you do it? Will you stand against him?' She opened her eyes, staring at me.

'I want to know more before I decide. Is there anyone you trust I can talk to?'

'There's his solicitor, Mr Rees. His office is opposite the town hall.'

'If I do agree to find out what I can, you must accept that I'm doing it without any preconceptions. As far as I'm concerned, anybody might have tampered with that firework or it might have been a terrible accident.'

Her head rolled from side to side against the chairback in a weary 'no', but she made no other protest.

'Also, I'll need your authority to talk to anybody, your staff, any of your household.'

'There's only Peter and me.'

'Peter?'

'Charles' nephew. He's home from Shrewsbury School for the Christmas holidays.'

'Was he here when it happened?'

'No.'

'As for standing, I'd be delighted to have the chance of fighting this constituency as an independent candidate, but not as a vendetta against Mr Tedder or anyone else.'

'You must stop him being elected.'

'I shall be doing my level best. But you must understand that the Coalition candidate is in a very strong position.'

'You can have as much money from us as you want.'

'It's not that simple. There are limits to what every candidate is allowed to spend. If you're going to back me, you should know something about my platform. I support the League of Nations.'

A nod.

'The peace agreement with Germany must be an honourable one for both sides. You can't build peace on vengeance.'

A sigh.

'On home policy, the priority must be full employment, for returning soldiers and everybody else. Improved old age pensions. Government allowances to mothers with children. Free compulsory schooling up to the age of fifteen.'

She was nodding to all of it. I threw in national ownership of the mines and railways. No resistance there either.

'And of course, a full and equal franchise. It's nonsense that women under thirty still can't vote, or women living in furnished rooms.'

She agreed to it all. I think if I'd proposed caviare for all on Friday nights and a motor car in every working man's front yard her reaction would have been the same. She made only one stipulation.

'Your campaign colour will be purple. It's his favourite colour.'

A little showy for my liking, but then I'd been campaigning for years under the suffragette purple, white and green and she was entitled to that much choice for her money. I noticed that she still spoke of her husband in the present tense, but for a widow of just over two weeks that was hardly surprising. The determination to show me exactly where her husband had died seemed to have taken the last of her strength. Still, she managed to ring for the housekeeper to tell her to have the pony cart sent round and stood up to see me out. As we went into the hall, I heard a door opening quietly upstairs.

'I'll come back tomorrow, to let you know what I've decided.'

'I'm not mad. I know he did it.'

Slippered footsteps coming down carpeted stairs.

'How can you know for sure?'

'He told me.'

'*Tedder* told you.'

'No, he did. Charles did.'

Then a man's voice from the bottom of the stairs, a very young man's voice. 'Lucinda, who's this?'

I turned and saw a face that looked like a cross between a faun and a choirboy. His hair was black and curling, longer than conventional, his eyes

34

blue-grey under arched black eyebrows. He was wearing a dark blue smoking jacket with black cord trimming and a blue cravat. Mrs Sollers jumped and seemed flustered.

'This is Miss Bray. She's going to fight Jonas Tedder.'

The look he gave me was a fraction too long for politeness and too short for impudence. The raising of the eybrows would have infuriated me from a grown man. In fact, it did infuriate me and I had to tell myself that this was no more than a schoolboy.

'Miss Bray, this is my husband's nephew, Peter Chivas.'

He shook my hand. 'Enchanted.'

On the way back in the pony cart, I tried to work out why the eyebrows and that affected 'enchanted' had annoyed me so much. I decided it was a bad mental habit. For years when I'd met lads of his age the thought had been in my mind: In a few years that puppy will have a vote without having to do anything for it, and I don't have one in spite of everything. That wasn't true any more, so I could stop raising my mental hackles. Still, there was a much more immediate reason for annoyance. If he hadn't spoken at that exact moment I could have asked Lucinda Sollers about her extraordinary statement that her late husband had accused Jonas Tedder of his own murder. I was glad I still hadn't committed myself. Not quite.

35

Chapter Four

⊗

'So do you think she's mad?'

Bill and I were in the snug at the King's Head beside a fire of apple wood logs that bubbled pale amber-coloured sap as the flames crept along them and hissed like live things. We were the only occupants, apart from a fat tabby cat asleep on the most comfortable chair.

'She sounded perfectly rational most of the time.'

'So did the craziest clients I ever dealt with.'

'I'll have more of an idea after I've seen her solicitor tomorrow. If he thinks his client isn't *compos mentis*, would he have a duty to tell me?'

'More than that. He'd have a duty to stop her throwing her money away on things like election expenses for a candidate without a cat in hell's chance of winning.'

'In which case, we could be on the train back to London by lunchtime. Would you be relieved if that happened?'

'Not necessarily.' Bill took another sip of whisky and water. 'Suppose he doesn't tell you she's mad, and you're in for it. Have you thought about organisation? You'd need an agent for one thing.'

That had occurred to me. I'd thought of sending a telegram to one of my friends in the movement, but all the most experienced ones would already be tied up in other people's campaigns. Mrs Hincham put her head round the door.

'Do you want your dinner in there by the fire? It's warmer than in the dining-room.'

We opted to stay where we were, and she came in with two savoury platefuls. 'It's only rabbit pie. If I'd known we were having guests I'd have made something special. Would you like a glass of cider with yours, sir?'

'Two glasses,' I said firmly, before Bill could answer. Young John of the pony cart brought them in, his raincoat exchanged for a brown beer-stained apron. The cider was the colour of a fox in sunlight, sweet at first taste, then with a crisp bite to it. The rabbit pie came with floury potatoes to mop up the thyme-flavoured gravy. For a while we just ate and drank.

'Do you want me to come with you to see the solicitor tomorrow?'

'No thank you. Once he knew you were in the same profession he'd talk to you instead of me.'

We finished the cider by the fire and went upstairs to our separate rooms.

I had no trouble finding the solicitor's offices the next morning. Out of the door and turn right into the square, said Mrs Hincham. I couldn't miss it. It was a grey day, with rain in the air and the pavement slippery underfoot. There were a few people around in the market square, a butcher's boy with a delivery bike, two elderly women chatting in front of a grocer's shop, a very old man holding the reins of a battered pony cart. They all looked at me as I went past, with no obvious hostility but a deep curiosity, as if trying to slot me into the scheme of things. I guessed that strangers were an unusual event, especially in the depths of winter. I said good morning to the women and the old man. In all cases there was a little pause before they replied, kindly enough but with some puzzlement. The old man added something about the weather which I didn't catch probably because he had just one tooth and it waggled when he talked. The solicitor's office was in a line of flat-fronted red-brick buildings with stone facings that closed off the square, facing the town hall across an expanse of cobbles. The brass plate outside said Thomas Rees, Solicitor and Commissioner for Oaths. The edges of the letters were blurred from many polishings. I walked up two sandstone steps to the front door and pulled at the bell. After a wait, the door was opened by a woman in her twenties, in black skirt and grey cardigan with her hair pulled tight in a bun. I gave my name and explained that I wanted to see Mr Rees, had no appointment, but Mrs Sollers had suggested I should call. She seemed startled.

'Would . . . would you come in and sit down, Miss Bray. I'll go and see if he can see you.'

She showed me to a chair in a room with two desks, an Underwood typewriter and wooden filing cabinets, all very neat and orderly. A small fire was burning in the grate, but at this time of the morning it hadn't done much to warm the room. The secretary disappeared into an inner office shutting the door behind her. I heard her voice, words indistinguishable, then a man's voice.

'Show her straight in.'

Encouraging. It was a warm voice with a Welsh accent. Before I saw him, I imagined him singing bass in the back row of a male voice choir. When I was shown in he turned out to be more of a candidate for the front row as far as stature was concerned, short and plump, bald on top with smooth silver hair round the sides and a cheerful red face. He shook my hand.

'Miss Bray. I've just been reading a note from Mrs Sollers about you. She says you're standing in the election.'

'She's written already?'

'Sent a boy down with it as soon as we opened. Sit down. Shall I take your coat or would you like to keep it on?'

His fire, like the one in the outer room, still hadn't won the fight with the damp air. I kept my coat and sat down on the chair facing his desk, while he settled behind it.

'May I ask what Mrs Sollers said?'

'That I'm to advance you any money you need for election expenses and to help you in . . .' He hesitated for a moment. I guessed he wasn't a man who often hesitated. 'In the other matter.'

'The other matter being the death of Mr Charles Sollers?'

'Quite so.'

We looked at each other. His face had a rueful look.

'You must find this very irregular.'

'Indeed I do, Miss Bray. But then, it's hardly very regular to have a client blown to pieces in front of your eyes, is it?'

'You were there when it happened?'

'I was indeed.'

'To be honest, Mr Rees, I half-expected you to tell me that the kindest thing I could do for Mrs Sollers was to go away and not add to her troubles.'

He considered. 'Is that what you feel?'

'It isn't the impression I had last night, but you must know her better than I do. What's your opinion?'

It was the best opening I could give him if he needed it. Again, a hesitation.

'Mrs Sollers is a sensitive lady. She had what you might call some unconventional ideas, even before this happened. But she's a determined lady too. I should say that once she had an idea in her head, it wouldn't be easy to shift it.'

'The idea she's got in her head is that her husband was murdered. Do you think she's right?'

He picked up a polished wooden paperknife and concentrated on balancing it exactly across his forefinger. It took some time. When he'd got it right he stared at me thoughtfully across it.

'Until this time last week, I should have told you it was a terrible accident.'

'What happened this time last week?'

'The opening of the inquest. I attended it as Mrs Sollers' representative, quite expecting to hear that there had been some carelessness over the firework. The director of the firm that made the thing was there. Naturally they were concerned for their reputation. He gave evidence.'

'Saying, I suppose, that one of their fireworks couldn't possibly have killed anybody.'

'As you'd expect. But the thing was, I have a very strong impression that the coroner believed him and to my certain knowledge the police are inclined to believe him. For what it's worth, so am I.'

The paperknife tilted and slid off his finger. He didn't try to re-balance it.

40

'Could you tell me about his evidence?'

'The fireworks company is in Wolverhampton. Naturally, while the war was on, there was no call for fireworks and they switched to making detonators. But in the last few weeks, when they knew peace was coming, they got permission from the Ministry of Munitions to re-open just a small production line to make fireworks for the victory celebrations. They had to train some of the younger workers and the women who hadn't made fireworks before, so according to this director the whole operation was very tightly controlled. Every single firework that went out of that factory was made and packed under the personal supervision of the director or a foreman who'd been with them since Queen Victoria's time.'

'No system's perfect.'

'Indeed. But then we come to a matter of science. It was put to the director, just suppose somebody had made a mistake and put high explosive from the munitions production line into a firework casing by mistake. Wouldn't that account for the accident?'

'And he said it couldn't have happened?'

'He said it couldn't have happened, but that even if it had happened – even if that firework had been packed from base to apex with explosive – it couldn't have done what that firework did.'

'Why not?'

'It's a matter of physics. Are you good on physics, Miss Bray?'

'Adequately,' I said. I suspected my grasp was no shakier than his.

'It depends on compression. Apparently for explosive to go off with enough force to blow a man to pieces, it must be compressed in a small airtight space

41

when you set light to it. A cardboard firework cylinder wouldn't have the same effect at all. According to this director, you'd have to replace the inside of the firework with a metal cylinder stuffed with explosive. There was no possibility that this could happen accidentally on their production line.'

'Or deliberately?'

'Or deliberately,' he said. But in any case, to what purpose? If somebody had tampered with that firework on the production line, he couldn't have known who'd buy it. The director was asked about sabotage. He said if they'd got through a whole war making detonators without anybody sabotaging them, why should it happen when they'd gone back to fireworks?'

'How did the fireworks get from the factory in Wolverhampton to Whitehorn Hall?'

'Mr Sollers collected them himself and drove them back here.'

'Why? Surely he could have had them put on a train.'

'Mr Sollers always liked to keep the reins in his own hands. He'd only managed to get the fireworks in the first place because the director of the firm was a business acquaintance of his.'

'So the director knew that particular firework would be coming to Mr Sollers?'

'No. He'd only given orders to the foreman that a certain number and certain types of firework were to be ready for collection. The foreman picked them out and packed them. Mr Sollers drove up in his motor car and collected them.'

'When?'

'The Thursday the war ended. The party was on the Saturday.'

'Was anybody else in the car with him?'

'Not as far as I know. The evidence we heard at the inquest was only about what had happened at the factory up to the time that the fireworks were loaded into Mr Sollers' motor car. At that point the coroner adjourned the inquest for further inquiries by the police. That's how it stands still.'

'You said the police were inclined to believe the director of the fireworks factory. Why?'

'We come back to that business of the metal casing. Miss Bray, I hope I'm not making a mistake here, but I'll tell you something strictly in confidence. I happen to know the inspector of police. I know from him that fragments of metal were found in Mr Sollers' body. They didn't appreciate the significance of that at first. After the evidence at the inquest they went back and searched the place where it happened and found more fragments of similar metal there. It looks very much as if somebody deliberately tipped out the contents of that firework and put what amounted to a small home-made grenade inside.'

From the outer office, the Underwood went tap tap. Mr Rees stirred in his chair, keeping his eyes on me.

'How could anybody know that Mr Sollers would be the one to light it?'

'As I said, he liked to keep the reins in his hands.'

'I asked Mrs Sollers if he had any enemies. She said he hadn't.'

He nodded. 'I should say he was popular. His business interests are in the Midlands – mainly a family firm making buttons and so on. They got a government contract making belts and buckles for Army uniforms.'

'So he did quite nicely?'

'Oh yes. But he was a generous man, always ready to take out his cheque book for a local good cause.'

'Has he any business interests in this part of the world?'

'Soon after he moved here about ten years ago he bought the farm next door to him, which he runs through a manager. They breed pedigree Herefords.'

'Had he connections with this part of the world before he moved here?'

'Not as far as I know. He was looking for somewhere in the country, but not too far from the Midlands by motor car.'

'What about his wife?'

'She comes from near here. Her father was a clergyman. A little eccentric, some people said. Quarrelled with his bishop about the vestments or altar cloths and resigned his living. Private income.'

'So Charles Sollers married Lucinda after he moved here?'

'Yes, about five years ago. He was a widower when he came here. His first wife died in childbirth. Lucinda Sollers was younger than he was.'

'Would you say it was a happy marriage?'

'They always struck me as ideally happy.'

For me, that phrase usually rings a warning bell, but he used it without irony.

'Was there any surprise when the Conservatives adopted him as their candidate?'

'I don't think so. He'd been very active in the Party since he moved here. Perhaps there were a few who might have preferred a local man, but with his character and business experience he was an obvious choice.'

'More obvious than Jonas Tedder?'

Mr Rees sighed a long sigh and leaned back in his chair.

'I wondered when we'd be coming to that. She's been talking about him, has she?'

'Yes.'

'I know Jonas Tedder quite well. He's a local farmer and potato merchant, like his father and grandfather before him. Not as energetic a character as Charles Sollers, but he does well enough.'

'With that local background, wouldn't he have been first choice as candidate?'

'To tell you the truth, I don't think he cared too much about it. He was persuaded to stand against Charles for the nomination by a few people who wanted a local man, but the two of them stayed on good terms and he took it very well when Charles got it.'

'Except that Mrs Sollers thinks he blew Mr Sollers to pieces.'

'She came right out and said it, did she?'

'Several times.'

He made a face. 'I'll have to speak to her. Tedder's been very tolerant so far, but there is such a thing as slander.'

'Jonas Tedder knows she's accusing him?'

'Oh yes, but what can he do? You can't go up and argue with a woman who lost her husband two weeks ago.'

'You're convinced Tedder didn't do it?'

'Yes.'

'Have you any idea at all who did?'

'No more than you have – and you got here yesterday, I take it.'

'What about the police?'

'Again in confidence, the same applies to them.'

'But they're investigating?'

He seemed ill at ease.

'Up to a point, but you must remember that until the opening of the inquest last week, everybody thought that it was a terrible accident. Of course, they're short-handed with so many of their men still in the Army and they have to see what comes up from the Wolverhampton end.'

'From what you've told me about the evidence, it's more likely that the firework was tampered with after it left the factory.'

A reluctant nod. I had the impression that Mr Rees was a little embarrassed on behalf of his friend the police inspector.

'Have the police questioned the people at the house?'

'Oh yes, soon after it happened.'

'How many people are there at Whitehorn Hall?'

'It was simply Mr and Mrs Sollers. There were no children from either marriage. There's an orphaned nephew, Mr Sollers' sister's son. He stays with them in the holidays.'

Until that point he'd been chatting away happily, but when he mentioned the nephew his voice went more cold and formal.

'Peter Chivas? I met him last night.'

He picked up the paperknife and started his balancing act again. 'What did you make of him?'

'Very self-possessed, for a schoolboy.'

'I don't think young Chivas thinks of himself as a schoolboy. He's only got two more terms then he'll be off to university. Not before time. I know that was Charles Sollers' opinion as well. He was Peter's legal guardian. The lad's parents were killed in an accident when he was quite young.'

'Did he and his guardian get on well?'

He pursed his lips, staring at the paperknife. 'I suppose there are always frictions when young men start testing their wings. Peter's money from his parents is in trust until he's twenty-one, and his uncle was one of the trustees. But I'd say they got on as well as most in the circumstances. Certainly young Peter had nothing to complain about.'

'What about the staff at Whitehorn Hall?'

'Like everywhere else, a lot of their men have been called up. There's a housekeeper, a cook and a couple of maids who live in. Outside there's an old gardener who does what he can to keep the place together and a manager and a few more old men and lads to run the farm.'

'Were all the staff at the victory party?'

'Oh yes, and their wives and children. Half the town were there. I went with my wife and two of the grandchildren.'

'Can you tell me what you saw?' If nothing else, it would be a useful check on the story I'd had from Mrs Sollers.

'We all stood out on the old tennis court and watched the bonfire. There were baked potatoes, punch for the grown-ups, cocoa for the children. They really did things very well. When the bonfire had died down, Charles and his gardener started letting off the fireworks on the bank.'

'Were the fireworks set out ready when you got there?'

'No. They'd have got damp on the grass. When they were ready to start, the old gardener and a couple of the lads carried them out in boxes from the house and put them at the bottom of the bank. Mr Sollers was telling them what to put where.'

'He was in charge of the whole thing?'

'Oh, very much so. Nobody was allowed to light any of the fireworks except him and the old gardener.'

'Mrs Sollers says Jonas Tedder and his wife left before the fireworks started. Did you see them go?'

'Yes. We were standing with the children on the bridge over the moat. Mr and Mrs Tedder came past, going back towards where we'd left the motor cars, and I said weren't they going to stay for the fireworks? Mr Tedder said Felicity had a headache and the bangs would make it worse. She didn't look well, very pale. Just after that the fireworks started. We had the ordinary ones first, the golden rains and volcanoes and some rockets. I knew he had some big ones he was keeping for last.'

'How did you know that?'

He wrinkled his forehead. 'He must have mentioned it when he invited us. Anyhow, we all knew it. The children were on tiptoe waiting.'

'How close were you when it happened?'

'Quite a long way off, thank God, still on the bridge. We could see him by the light of the bonfire bending down on the bank to light something. There was a second or two when I thought it wasn't going to go off, then the bang and a terrible silence. I can still hear that silence, if you understand what I mean. At first we thought it was just the firework, then somebody screamed and everybody was running and screaming, all over the grass and the flowerbeds. Our first thought was to get the grandchildren out of the way. We were back at the front of the house when somebody came running round to say Mr Sollers was dead.'

'Was anything said at the time about murder?'

48

'No. Not a word. We all thought it was the firework gone wrong. I left the grandchildren with my wife and went round the back to see if there was anything I could do, but I met somebody on the way and he said it was all in hand and the best we could do was get the women and children home, which we did.'

'How soon afterwards did Mrs Sollers start accusing Jonas Tedder of murder?'

'The first I heard of it was about a week later, when the Party adopted him as candidate. They had to move fast, you see, because of the election coming up.'

'Does anybody apart from Mrs Sollers think Tedder murdered her husband?'

'Nobody. They're sorry for her at the moment, but the Tedders are a respected couple and if she goes on like this she'll be making it very difficult for herself to live here. Believe me, if you are going about things in the belief that Jonas Tedder killed Charles you are doing Mrs Sollers no favours. The sooner the poor lady can get that out of her head, the less damage she'll do herself.'

'If so, the best way of getting it out of her head is by finding out who really did kill him.'

He nodded.

'And you really have no idea at all who might have done it?'

'None whatsoever.'

I sat back in the chair and thought. By noon next day the nomination papers would have to be in. I had to make a decision before leaving his office.

'You know that Mrs Sollers wants me to stand to stop Tedder getting in?'

He nodded. 'I have to say that your chances—'

'Would be as hopeful as a snowball's in Hell. I've told her that, not quite in those words. If I stand, it will be on my own policies. I've also told her that if I do look into her husband's death, it will be without any preconceptions.'

'She'd have to accept that.'

'She seems to value your judgement at least. Tell me, as her friend and her legal adviser, am I making things better or worse for her if I do what she wants?'

He sighed. 'It's hard to see how they could be much worse.'

It was as much as I could expect from him.

'I'll do it. I'll keep the election expenses as low as I can for her.'

'She said in her note that I was to advance you whatever you needed, for the election or the . . . um . . . investigation.'

'I won't take her money for investigating.'

We stood up and shook hands. He wished me luck. I stood on the steps of his office feeling as if I were on the edge of a cold bathing pool. Nothing for it but to plunge. I took a deep breath, walked across the cobbles – still observed by the old man with the waggly tooth – up the steps to the town hall and asked a clerk at a reception desk to direct me to the returning officer.

Chapter Five

F ive minutes later I came down the steps, leaving a
few surprised faces behind me, with the precious
piece of paper in my hand. It needed ten signatures of
Duxbury electors, which was a problem since I didn't
know ten people. Still, when in doubt, keep going. On
my way across the square I'd glanced down a side
street and noticed a sign hanging outside an office,
'The Duxbury Chronicle'. I turned into the side street.
It was cobbled from side to side, no pavement, and at
least a century older in its architecture than the town
square. White plaster walls bulged out on either side,
so that at second-floor level they were almost meeting
overhead, leaving no more than a strip of grey sky.
There was a cobbler's shop with a row of mended
boots in the window, a men's barber with no customers, a greengrocer with nothing but potatoes, turnips and cabbages on display. Halfway down the left-
hand side was the sign I'd noticed. Under 'The Duxbury Chronicle' it said in smaller letters '& Bennington Intelligencer. Est. 1792'.

As I pushed open the door and walked in, the
familiar reek of printer's ink hit me and for the first
time since coming to Duxbury I felt on home
ground, with memories of long days and nights
printing posters and handbills. Behind a battered

counter a lad was operating a small flat-bed press of a type I knew well. He had a paper cap on his head, a smear of ink on his nose and a frown of concentration. He stopped what he was doing and came to the counter.

'May I speak to the editor, please?'

There was the pause of a few seconds that I'd already noticed as characteristic of Duxbury. It wasn't slowness of mind so much as a determination not to be hurried. Then he disappeared into a back room.

'Good morning, I'm the editor, Alexander Jones. Can I help you?'

He was in his early thirties, with a voice that didn't come from that part of the world. One glance at him answered the question that you couldn't help asking yourself at that time about men of fighting age – how he'd managed to avoid the Army or prison. He wore glasses with lens as thick as lemonade bottles and walked to the counter with a limp, dragging one leg. But the eyes behind the glasses were lively and there was a hint in his voice that he didn't take things too seriously. I introduced myself and said, as levelly as I could manage, that I was standing as an independent candidate for Duxbury. His eyes went wide, then he laughed, not derisively.

'Here's a turn-up for the book. I've heard of you, haven't I?'

'Quite possibly,' I said, hoping that it was my activities for the Vote or against conscription, rather than other events. I intended to keep my electioneering quite distinct from the question of Mr Sollers.

'What in the world possessed you to come to a place like Duxbury? Have you any connections here?'

I said, quite truthfully, that it was important that people in as many places as possible should have the chance to vote for a woman.

'Even if I'm not elected this time, a few thousand votes for a woman in this election will be tens of thousands in the next one and sooner or later Duxbury will have a woman representing it in Parliament.'

That was for quoting, of course. I knew perfectly well, as he did, that I'd be lucky to get even one thousand votes. Still, the rest was true. Also for publication, I gave him my platform: League of Nations, a fair peace, jobs and houses, allowances for mothers. He was making notes by then, in fast longhand.

'Who's nominating you?'

A difficult one. The only names I was sure of were Moira and Lucinda Sollers, and news that the widow of the late Tory candidate was supporting me could keep until later. I said grandly that I'd let him have the list the next day, after the nominations went in. From the look in his eyes, I think he saw through the bluff.

'Make it as soon afterwards as you can. Most of the paper goes to press on Wednesday afternoon and we'll be carrying addresses from the candidates when we come out on Friday.'

'Excellent. I'll make sure you have mine first thing tomorrow morning. Eight hundred words?'

'Five. I'll have to find some extra space now that there'll be three of you.'

This was useful information. One of my objects in coming to the newspaper office was to find out as much as I could about the constituency.

'Three?'

'Jonas Tedder, yourself and John Prest. He's standing as an Independent Temperance Liberal. The official Liberals were supposed to be standing down in favour of the Coalition candidate, but the temperance wing of the local Liberals didn't think Tedder was strong enough against the demon drink.'

'What are people saying about the chances?'

'At the Three Tuns they've stopped taking bets on Tedder because they think he's a certainty to win.'

'Isn't John Prest a strong candidate then?'

'He's got a voice that would carry from here to Hereford without a megaphone and a following among the chapel goers, but in a constituency that grows hops and practically swims in cider, temperance isn't the most popular cause. The farmers won't vote for him.'

'Now they have another choice.'

'Without intending to be insulting, if you get any of our farmers voting for a woman you can watch out for pigs flying.'

He wasn't being hostile, just straight-talking.

'But farmers have wives.'

'They do what their husbands tell them – in public, at any rate. It's a different matter at home.'

'It's a secret ballot.'

'You'd have trouble convincing them of that round here.'

'What about the soldiers' vote?' That was the big unknown factor in the election. Legislation had to be rushed through parliament to give the men in the trenches their chance to vote.

'They'll vote Tory like their fathers will.'

'After all that's happened to them?'

'In their place, there'd be only one thing I'd want to know, and that's when I'd be coming home.'

I couldn't disagree about that. Seeing a pile of local maps on his counter I bought a couple of them.

'Would you print posters and leaflets for me?'

'Glad to.'

We had a discussion on prices and I beat him down by fourpence per gross on the leaflets, twopence per dozen on the posters.

'When do you want these?'

'As soon as possible,' I said, and promised to get the copy to him by the end of the afternoon. By the time I left his office it was close to midday, time to go back to the snug at the King's Head and break the news to Bill. He took it so calmly that I realised he'd expected me to stay all along.

'You should leave posters and so on to your agent.'

'I haven't got an agent.'

'What about me?'

'You're in the Army. You're supposed to be back in hospital in a few days.'

'I haven't wasted the morning either. I've sent a few telegrams, even made a telephone call. The War Office is now considering whether an injured officer may be given temporary unpaid leave of absence to serve the cause of democracy.'

'Bill!'

'I will admit that I haven't told them it would be for a wild woman. Still, that shouldn't make any difference. I'm no more useless here than in slippers and dressing-gown back in your old college smoking my head off.'

I'd have hugged him, only Mrs Hincham walked into the snug to ask if we'd be taking lunch. 'Just cheese sandwiches and cider,' I said. Suddenly there were a dozen things to do – electoral address, wording for the leaflets and posters, signatures on the nomination form, a whole campaign to plan. Before everything,

Lucinda Sollers must be told that I'd accepted her proposition. This time I decided that Bill, as my provisional agent, should come with me. It would be useful to have a third opinion on her sanity.

The drive to Whitehorn Hall in the pony cart gave me a chance to look at parts of my constituency for the first time by daylight. The solid prosperity of the buildings in the square and at the centre of town gave way to small terraces of brick houses fronting on to the street, with the occasional older cottage of crumbling plaster and exposed oak timbers whose colour had weathered from brown to dull silver. The road crossed a bridge over a fast-running little river. On the other side of the bridge the good road surface changed to mud and gravel, with a raised pavement on one side and a row of sagging cottages that looked as if they managed to keep standing from habit rather than structure. A rotten animal stink rose up from a cluster of low brick buildings and wooden sheds lying a few hundred yards behind the cottages on the river bank.

'I think it must be a tannery. Ye gods, the smell. If it's like this in winter, what must it be like in summer?'

After the sagging cottages and the tannery, the town ran out altogether and we went along a muddy rutted road between hedges, with gates leading off it into small pastures or apple orchards. Great round bunches of mistletoe on the apple trees were a startling bright green against the damp dark greens and browns of the rest of the country.

Whitehorn Hall was even more odd by day than by night, with the squat and ancient tower sprouting gargoyles that looked as if they'd been added in the last few years, Elizabethan stone and narrow windows making up the main part of the house, an extension of solid Victorian brickwork at the other end. A medieval tithe barn, with bales of hay visible through narrow window slits, stood at right angles to the house just across the moat with a gate beside it that probably led to the farmyard. Lucinda herself opened the door within seconds of our ringing. She was wearing a cream-coloured satin blouse and a black skirt, but the purple was there in the form of a fringed woollen shawl. She took my hand even before we were through the door.

'I knew you would. I *knew* you would.'

Even by day and without the candles, her sitting-room had its aquarium feel, probably because the moat was just a few feet below her window. I introduced Bill and she shook his hand in her intense way, thanking him for helping. I explained to her that it had to be a quick visit because there was a lot to be done back in Duxbury and presented her with my nomination form. She signed without hesitation and added the address of the Hall in her beautiful handwriting.

'Have you spoken to Mr Rees?'

'Yes, this morning.'

'What did he tell you?'

'That he thinks the explosives were probably put in the firework deliberately . . .'

'Ah.'

'But he doesn't suspect Jonas Tedder.'

'He's a solicitor in a small town. He doesn't want to offend anyone.'

I'd expected annoyance, but she said it quite matter-of-factly. Bill spoke to her for the first time since being introduced.

'Yesterday, Miss Bray understood you to say that your husband had accused Mr Tedder of an intention to murder him. Was she right about that?'

'More than intention.'

'What exactly did he say?'

She looked at Bill then glanced up at the ceiling. 'Can you come back tonight? Both of you, tonight after dinner?'

Bill and I looked at each other. I said yes and suggested nine o'clock.

'Yes, come at nine. Where are you staying? I'll send the motor car for you.'

After that, she seemed almost in a hurry to get us to leave. We couldn't say much with young John in the pony cart and once we were back in Duxbury there was a flurry of things to do. I commandeered a table in the snug to draft my leaflets and posters and Bill took them round to the newspaper office. After that the most urgent business was getting nine other signatures on my nomination form. I knew that Moira and her husband lived and worked in a cottage not far from the forge so I got directions from Mrs Hincham and walked there with the precious form in my pocket. The forge was at the edge of the town on the main road to Hereford, through an archway in a terrace of brick cottages that was wide enough to take a farm cart. The blacksmith was hammering at a billhook on his anvil, but paused to give me directions along a footpath to a black-and-white cottage, standing on its own at the edge of the fields. In a lean-to shed beside it a man was chiselling at a block of stone. I waved to him and went on to the front door. I'd met Moira's husband once in London, a fine craftsman but shy with people he didn't know well and not talkative. Moira came to the door in an old skirt and cardigan with wood shavings all over her, annoyed at being interrupted in her work until she saw who it was.

'Nell, you are standing? I'm so glad.'

She signed the form on her work bench among the wood shavings. Then she read the signature at the head of it.

'So she really is going to support you. I was never quite sure she'd do it.'

'How did you meet her?' I hadn't expected the wives of Tory MPs to be in Moira's social circle.

'Just before the war she commissioned Morgan to carve a sundial for her. He liked her more than he expected and she paid well. That sundial fed us for a month.'

'You know what she's saying?'

'About Jonas Tedder blowing up her husband? Of course. I should think the whole town does.'

'And you told her I'd investigate?'

'I told her some of the things you've done, yes.' She seemed quite certain I'd be grateful for that.

'Do you think Tedder did it?'

'Goodness knows. I've never met him.'

'What's the gossip in town?'

'That Mrs Sollers has gone mad. Still, that doesn't stop them passing on the story.'

'You weren't at the party, of course.'

'Conscientious objectors and their wives don't get invited to victory parties.' Her husband had refused to fight and spent months in prison, until his health broke down so badly that they had to release him.

'So you've got me into this and you can't help me?'

'I'll campaign for you. Let's go and get Morgan to sign your nomination.'

She took pen and ink out to the lean-to and her husband signed while I looked at what he'd been carving. It was a polished slab of green Westmorland slate with a design of entwined poppies at the top. Under the poppies, names were marked in yellow crayon, ready for carving.

'A war memorial?'

'Not an official one. I dare say they'll put up something in due course, with a dutiful soldier on a plinth and *Pro Patria Mori*. This is ours, for the church.'

I counted the names. 'Twelve killed.'

'Yes.' She touched the first of them. 'Tom Carter. We knew him. He used to work at the forge there until he was called up. He had a friend named Simon Whittern.' Her hand moved to the last name on the list. 'They were both of them killed on the same day in the same battle last spring.' We stood for a while without saying anything, looking down at the memorial slab, then she picked up the nomination paper. 'Come on, I know at least four more people who'll sign.'

They did, but it took some time to find them. It was evening when I got back to the King's Head, with seven signatures on the form and just time to write my electoral address for the local paper before joining Bill in the snug for a working dinner. He'd already got a map spread out over a table and the list of places in the constituency I'd collected from the returning officer.

'We've got our work cut out with this lot.'

The sheer size of the constituency came as a shock, not in population but the amount of country it covered. Duxbury was the market town and accounted for just under half the total voters. Another quarter lived in or around a smaller town called Bennington, out to the west and not far from the Welsh border. When Mrs Hincham came in to collect the plates and heard us talking about it, she said Bennington was pronounced Benton and the people there had a reputation for being 'a bit of a crowsty lot'. On questioning by Bill it emerged that crowsty meant awkward-tempered and there was a local saying 'as crowsty as a Benton sow'. The remaining quarter of the electorate was scattered among dozens of villages that looked as if somebody had spilt a pepper pot over otherwise white spaces on the map. The general rule seemed to be the smaller the village the longer the name. There were Stockingtop and Perrywick, Knockley-under-Hill and Lurton-by-Lugg, Bailey cum Verret and Little Besthope, all probably pleasant places for a summer bicycling tour with honeysuckle in hedges and ducks on ponds. A logistic nightmare in mid-winter with eleven days to run an election campaign from a standing start. With pencil and paper we began to sort out a strategy. There must be public meetings in Duxbury and Bennington, plus an open-air meeting in Duxbury on market day. That was Friday, said Mrs Hincham, coming in with more cider. She put it down where she could find space and stood there while we tried to go on with our discussion.

'We can't possibly canvass all the villages, but we'll try and get posters up in all of them. Goodness know what we're going to use for transport. I'll have my bicycle sent from London and—'

'There's John and the pony cart,' said Mrs Hincham.

We stared at her.

'You're up for the election. I've heard about that and I've got just one question to ask you.'

She stood there in her white apron, as dignified as a minister at the despatch box. A great moment – first question from a voter. Would it be the peace settlement, housing, employment?

'Are you for or against the working man having his pint?'

Bill spluttered over his cider. I kept a straight face.

'I'm certainly not teetotal. I'm in favour of the working man or anybody else having a pint when he wants it.'

'In that case, I'm voting for you and so's anybody else I can speak for. We've always been Liberals in this house, but not when it means taking my livelihood. So if you want John and the pony cart, you can have them.' She meant it as a grand gesture and in our circumstances, that was exactly what it was. I stood up and shook her hand, accepted the services of young John and the pony cart but explained that I'd be paying the proper rate for them. Did she by any chance know of anywhere we could rent cheaply as our committee rooms?

'There's the old brewhouse in our yard you could have if we clear it out. You'd be starved with cold though. There's no fire.'

It didn't matter, I told her. We'd be working too hard to feel the cold. Rent was fixed, by mutual agreement, at ten shillings a week. I seized the moment and asked her if she'd sign my nomination paper, which she did with a flourish.

'How many more do you need?'

'Two would do it.'

'Shan't be long.'

'Well,' Bill said, when she'd gone out with the form, 'there goes your teetotal vote. Public house pony trap for a campaign vehicle and committee rooms in a brewhouse.'

'I never had a hope with the teetotallers anyway. This is astounding luck.'

It's an odd fact of election campaigns that, however slim your chances, there are times, just now and again, when you feel a surge of hope that against prediction, likelihood, or even sanity you might after all actually win. This was one of the times. I was almost giddy with relief at having got finance, leaflets, posters, transport, committee rooms and – please the gods – agent organised in one day. I was aware of a sudden silence in the public bar next door, then Mrs Hincham's voice and some uneasy laughter. In a few minutes she was back, flourishing the paper. The last two signatures and addresses were written with the same scratchy pen but they completed the tally of ten electors that made my candidacy legal.

'Those last two, are they really supporting me?'

'They decided to when I told them they needn't expect to go on drinking in this house if they didn't.'

Bill said when she'd gone, 'You've only been here a day and you've already got people blackmailing voters on your behalf.'

'I know. Isn't it wonderful?'

Soon after that, a motor car, driven by a young lad in a waterproof coat several sizes too big for him, arrived to take us back to Whitehorn Hall. Someone inside the house must have been watching for the headlamps coming down the drive because the housekeeper opened the door to us before we were halfway across the bridge. She seemed nervous, barely opening her mouth to say good evening then clamping her lower lip with her teeth as if she'd said too much already. She opened the door to Mrs Sollers' sitting-room then disappeared along the corridor without waiting to show us in, keeping her distance.

The room was in semi-darkness. There was a single lamp glowing under a frame of some kind with a purple shawl thrown across it. All the mirrors, even smallest panels of them, were covered by sheets. The fire had been newly heaped with coal so it made no impression on the dimness. I guessed what we were in for and felt my skin prickling with resentment. In bright light the room had been an aquarium. Now it was pond where blind things stirred flabby fins. Lucinda Sollers was standing by the fire, wearing a dark skirt and a shawl, clasping it tightly over her chest with her left hand as if she expected it to make a break for freedom.

She told us in a throaty whisper to sit down and pointed to three high-backed dining-chairs pulled up to a round table with a dark cloth over it. There was a fourth chair at the table but that was already occupied by Peter Chivas. He was wearing his velvet smoking jacket and a loose cravat, sitting with his head back, eyes closed and such an expression of conscious nobility on his face that I felt a nursery urge to slip an earthworm down the back of his neck. Behind him was an upright piano with the lid open. I looked at Bill, hoping he'd find a way to break up the charade before it started, but he was taking his seat obediently with his back to the fire and Peter on his left. I sat opposite him with my back to the door, Peter on my right, and Lucinda floated into the remaining chair, opposite Peter. While this was going on the boy sat there, apparently unaware of anybody else in the room. He was resting his hands on the table, palms down, one on top of the other. It looked deliberate and self-conscious, like everything else about him.

Lucinda said in her throaty whisper, 'He's been like this for an hour. It's a terrible strain on him. He didn't want to do it again, but I persuaded him so that you could hear for yourself.'

I'd expected her to produce some of the ragbag of a seance, letters and a pointer or even a planchette with a pencil but the table-top stayed bare and Lucinda did nothing except sit there with her hands clasped in front of her, staring at Peter. This went on for ten minutes or more. The occasional coal shifted on the fire. I was approaching the state of boredom and irritation in which every muscle of your body tugs and twitches with the desire to be elsewhere but Bill caught my eye across the table and signalled patience. Then it happened. The piano sounded, very softly, one low note. It was so soft that it was hardly a sound at all, more a slight rearrangement of the air, but Lucinda gasped and sat bolt upright, fingers twisting together.

'Yes, my dearest. Yes, we're here. We're listening.'

The piano sounded the same note three times more, slightly louder, with gaps of several seconds in between.

'Yes, yes, dearest. We understand.'

Same note: pum, pum, pum. I was watching it. The black key of the lowest sharp note dipped and rose, dipped and rose, dipped and rose. Peter's posture didn't change and he gave no sign that he was hearing it.

'What's the matter, dearest? Can't you find it? Like this.' Into the silence, she sang seven ascending notes of a scale in a husky voice. 'Doh Ray Me Fah Soh Lah Te. Like that dearest, like last time.'

Hesitantly at first, then more fluently, the piano followed her. Doh Ray Me Fah Soh Lah Te. With every note she rocked forward and back, like a mother encouraging a toddler's first attempt on a xylophone. I watched the black keys rising and falling. Then she and the piano did it again in awful duet. There were tears running down her cheeks. It was worse than I'd expected, much worse. After that there were another few minutes of silence. Peter gave a little groan and stirred in his chair.

'No, don't touch him. It would be dangerous for him. It's such a struggle. Charles was never very musical, you see. Even while he was alive he was never very musical.'

Then the piano started again, the same two notes repeated. Lah Lah. Lah Lah.

A smile came over her face. 'Yes dearest, it's me.' She explained to us, hurriedly. 'His name for me. He called me Lulu. Yes dear, we have visitors. We're all listening to you.'

Te Me. Te Me. The piano was getting into its stride now and she was as ecstatic as if it were giving out the music of the spheres.

'You see, T and M. His name.'

'Whose name?'

'His of course. My husband's.'

'Shouldn't it be C and S?'

'I called him Tumtum.' Quite unembarrassed. 'Yes, my dearest, what do you want to tell us?'

I looked at Peter's face. There were beads of sweat on his forehead and he was breathing heavily. His top hand was still clasped over the lower one as if trying to stop it escaping. The piano played a single Doh, then its lowest note, impatiently repeated several times.

'He's annoyed when there isn't a letter for what he wants to say. He always hated it when he couldn't find things. Go on, dearest. We'll understand.'

Doh pum pum Ray pum Soh Te. 'Dearest.' It was at least an easy language to learn. All you had to do was fill in the vowels. As far as I could see this exchange of domestic endearments was set to go on all night.

Then rescue came from Bill. He leaned sideways towards the piano and asked it, in a perfectly polite and ordinary voice, if Mr Sollers wanted to say anything about his untimely death. For a while that struck the thing into merciful silence, then it started again, hesitantly.

Me pum Ray Doh pum Ray.

'Murder?'

It agreed, playing the same sequence of notes twice over, more fluently.

'By whom?'

A pause, then it played a sequence of notes more loudly and firmly than before: Te pum Doh Doh pum Ray.

'T something DD something R. Do you mean Toddor?'

Pum pum, angrily.

'Taddir?'

Pum pum pum, very loudly, shaking the piano.

'Oh, don't make him angry. He means Tedder, don't you dearest? Tedder.'

Te pum Doh Doh pum Ray. Te pum Doh Doh pum Ray. The piano played it quite quickly, several times over, like a triumphant bell peal.

'Why?'

That seemed to puzzle it. There was a long gap before it offered tentatively, Me Doh.

'Mad? Tedder murdered you because he's mad?'

Me Doh, still without much confidence. Peter groaned more loudly this time and rolled his head from side to side against the chair back.

'It's too much for him. It's a terrible strain. We'll have to stop.'

The piano gave one last pum with its lowest note and that was the end of it. We stood up and the three of us moved away from the table, leaving Peter Chivas sitting there.

'Well, do you believe it now? You've heard for yourselves.' She was trembling, still crying but exultant at the same time. Bill said that it was certainly very remarkable. I couldn't trust myself to say anything. She opened the door for us, with a backward glance at Peter.

'Poor Peter. It's such a terrible burden, a gift like that.'

Bill asked if somebody should stay with him until he woke up.

'He says it's best to leave him alone for half an hour or so. I'll look in later.'

She found our hats and coats, still with that ex-ultant air, and showed us out. The motor car was standing on the gravel outside but there was no sign of the driver. That brought her back to earth and she peered round in the darkness.

'I should have told him to stay. Can you drive it?'

I said no, firmly, still disgusted with her. Bill said yes. 'It's a Wolseley, isn't it? Nice cars.'

'Take it with you. Keep it until the election. You'll need it for going round talking to people.'

As Bill couldn't be expected to go through the starting procedures with only one functional arm I had to help, mentally cursing him for the usual male confidence that any piece of machinery would instantly obey. Between us, with Lucinda watching from a distance, we managed to get the engine running and the lamps lit. Bill released the brake and I scrambled into the passenger seat. We turned in a scatter of gravel and Lucinda, white-faced, waved goodbye to us as we started up the rutted track.

'Can you just hold the wheel steady while I change gear? Steady, for goodness' sake. There are ditches both sides.'

'We'd have been better walking.'

'Nonsense. We needed a campaign vehicle.'

This went on at the tops of our voices. We couldn't hold a normal conversation until we were on the main road back to Duxbury and had somehow got into a quieter gear.

'Nell, if I ever feel the need to send you messages from beyond the grave, I promise I'll choose something more expressive than tonic sol-fa.'

'Easy to fake, though.'

'Ingenious, in its awful way. I've been thinking about it. He'd somehow have to fix wires to the bottom of the keys and drill holes in the base of the piano to lead them through. But then he's got to find a way of operating them without using his hands.'

69

'Some kind of foot levers. Did you notice there was a rug on the floor between his chair and the piano? He could run the wires under that. But it would take practice to operate.'

'He's probably had practice. It's just the sort of thing boys would do for a joke. Can't you imagine them all sniggering over it in the music room at school? Anyway, he wasn't so good at it. He was nowhere near so confident when I asked a question he wasn't expecting.'

'Just as well your legal friends couldn't hear you putting leading questions to a piano.'

'It was as much as I could do not to tip him out of the chair and make a grab for the wires or whatever he was using.'

'Lucinda wouldn't have liked that.'

'The woman must be crazy to be taken in by it.'

'Or want to believe it very much. The question is, why he's doing it. It might have started as a schoolboy trick, but this is a lot worse.'

'And he's hardly a schoolboy any more. If the war hadn't ended when it did he'd have found himself out in France in a few months' time. That's one of the things that makes me angry. A little monster like that alive when so many no older than he is . . .'

'So why?'

'Power over the poor woman. It will make it easy to get money out of her. All he'll have to do is plonk out messages from her husband.'

'He could have had the power just by pretending to be in touch with him. Why accuse Tedder?'

'If you only have seven consonants to play with your choice of names is limited.'

'But why anybody?'

'I suppose she wanted to know. Did you tell me he was away at school when it happened?'

'Yes.'

'Shrewsbury's only about forty miles away from here. The solicitor said there'd been friction between him and his uncle over money.'

Looking back on that conversation, I wondered if Mr Rees had been trying to point me towards young Chivas.

'Do you think Mrs Sollers has any suspicions?' Bill said.

'I'm quite sure not. The question is, what are we going to do about it? Even if it's no more than a matter of playing on her emotions, it's got to be stopped. I'll have to speak to Mr Rees again to-morrow.'

'Would you like me to do it?'

'Would you. There's so much to do and the nomination to get in.'

It was past eleven o'clock when we got back to Duxbury. Most of the town looked asleep, but Mrs Hincham and young John came out when they heard the motor in the yard and admired it. As we went upstairs, Mrs Hincham mentioned that another gentleman had booked in to the King's Head.

'Say what you like about elections, they're good for trade. We've never been so busy in December.'

I lay awake for a while in the dip in the middle of the soft mattress, listening to footsteps in the street outside, doors opening and closing downstairs and voices saying goodnights. I thought of Lucinda and what it must be like to want somebody so much that you were at the mercy of a few faked notes on a piano. Then I remembered what Bill had said about choosing something more expressive than tonic sol-fa and thought that if he joked about messages from beyond the grave he must be imagining some future for us on this side of it. I fell asleep at last wondering if it were some fault in me that I could never imagine wanting to call anybody Tumtum.

Chapter Six

The deadline for the delivery of nomination papers was twelve noon on Wednesday. I'd gathered that the custom in Duxbury was to do it with some ceremony, so an hour before it my procession was forming up in the yard of the King's Head. The Sollers' motor car, by daylight, was a huge and gleaming black beast of a thing with brass lamps, yellow lines picking out the wheel spokes and a yellow hood, folded back. Far too imposing for my liking but it was already drawing some admirers. Moira and Morgan were tying posters to the hood, doors and bonnet: VOTE NELL BRAY FOR A FAIR FUTURE. The King's Head trap with its plump grey pony was drawn up beside it and Mrs Hincham and a couple of her barmaids were looping it artistically with purple ribbon. I'd made an early raid on the town's two draper's shops and emptied them of all the purple ribbon they had. Also, for old time's sake, white and green to make up the suffragette colours. Mrs Hincham unearthed some dusty red, white and blue paper garlands stored since the coronation and we piled those on as well, although they clashed horribly with the purple. As I was standing back to look at it Bill arrived from his visit to Lucinda Sollers' solicitor. I took him aside and asked how he'd got on.

'He didn't know about the seances but he was worried anyway. Mrs Sollers is going to take over from her husband as a trustee of the boy's money and Rees thinks he'll do what he likes with her.'

'Anything more than that?'

'I didn't come straight out and ask if he thought Chivas might have murdered his uncle. We've no proof whatsoever.'

'Is he going to warn her about the trickery with the piano?'

'He said he'd see what he could do, but I don't think he's looking forward to it.'

The boy from the newspaper office arrived with bundles of leaflets, still damp from the press. A small crowd had collected already, neither hostile nor enthusiastic but very curious. Willing and fairly expert hands helped Bill get the car started. He caught my hand and gave it an encouraging squeeze then got into the driving seat. I settled beside him, with the nomination paper and a bundle of campaign leaflets. Mrs Hincham got in the back and Moira and one of the barmaids climbed into the pony trap, with young John driving. The rest of the King's Head staff, under the iron discipline of Mrs Hincham, raised a ragged cheer and we were off, round the corner into the square, then lurching across the cobble stones, first gear all the way because in this confined space Bill needed his good arm for steering. The ribbons fluttered in the wind, young John blew a few blasts on a hunting horn and everybody in the square and the streets leading off it stopped what they were doing and stared. There was already one motor car parked outside the town hall, as big and glossy as our own although more soberly dressed. It had blue ribbons from bonnet to windscreen and a single poster on the side VOTE TEDDER FOR DUXBURY.

As I got out of the car, the town hall door opened and two men came out. Both were wearing overcoats and bowler hats, one elderly and grey bearded, the other plump and red-faced. They had blue rosettes pinned to their coats. Behind them in the doorway was an elegant woman in a blue coat and toque hat. When he saw us the plump man blinked and looked as if he'd have liked to bolt inside again, but the older man said something to him and the three of them walked on down the steps and in our direction.

'Am I speaking to Miss Bray?'

The plump one. His face, close-up, was the healthy red of a man who spent time outdoors, but his eyes were anxious and bulging. He was almost painfully clean shaven and the hair showing below the bowler had touches of grey, although he was probably no older than mid-forties. His ears were large and stuck out. His manner was both bluff and nervous at the same time, as if out of his depth but doing his best. The fashionable woman stood a few steps beside him. Her face under the toque hat might have been beautiful, except that it seemed to be registering a distant dislike of everything including the plump man. Presumably the candidate's wife. I told him he was right and he put out a large hand gloved in new brown leather.

'I'm Jonas Tedder, standing in the Coalition interest. I gather you're . . . um, throwing your hat in the ring.' We shook hands. 'I'm sure it will be . . . um . . . a fair fight and so on. May the best, er, man win.'

'Certainly a fair fight, and may the best man or woman win.'

75

It was impossible to tell from his manner whether he knew that Mrs Sollers was my patron. I suspected he did because Duxbury seemed to be a town where news travelled fast. Sooner or later I'd have to speak to him about the other matter, but not on the steps of the town hall with a small crowd watching and the clock standing at five minutes to twelve. All the time Mrs Tedder was staring as if she hoped somebody would come and take me away. I wished them a civil good morning and went up the steps. A few minutes later I was walking down them as, officially, the Independent candidate for Duxbury and – as I learned later – one of just eighteen women standing in that first election.

By then the Conservative-Coalition party had gone but the crowd had grown, still without signs of either hostility or enthusiasm. Then from the steps, over the browns and greys of caps and overcoats, I saw a cheering and unexpected sight. Two women, one middle-aged and one younger, were wearing in their hats the purple white and green cockades of the suffragette movement. The older one raised the cry 'Vote for Nell Bray' in a voice shrill with nervousness and the younger one took it up. There was some laughter from the crowd, but young John drowned it with a blast on his hunting horn. I went through the crowd to my unexpected supporters and found they were mother and daughter from Bennington who'd heard about me and had come to town specially for the occasion. So as not to waste their enthusiasm I went and got handfuls of leaflets from the car and we started distributing them through the crowd. What struck me was how politely people took them, even saying thank you. I was used to a stormier sort of campaigning. Things were going nicely when a deep male voice spoke from behind me.

'Are you aware that you're causing an obstruction?'

I turned round. It was a big man in his sixties, ruddy faced with the air of expecting people to make way for him. He wore a black wool coat and a bowler hat a size too small for him and carried a rolled umbrella.

'No, I wasn't aware of it. If the police are concerned about it, I'm sure they'll let me know.'

'I have informed the police constable.' He pointed with his umbrella across the square and I saw an elderly constable approaching, looking sheepish.

'May I ask who you are?'

'My name is John Prest.'

He said it as if he grudged me the information. From beside me, young John said in a very audible whisper, 'He's the temperance man.'

'I am the Independent Liberal candidate.'

He didn't even spare a look for John, being too busy glaring at me.

Unexpectedly a woman's voice shouted from the edge of the crowd: 'You leave her alone, you old misery.'

It wasn't the voice of either of my Bennington supporters. This one was working class and – from the sound of her – she'd be good in a fight. I didn't have the chance to see who she was or let her know I was grateful because by then the constable had got to us.

'What's going on here, Miss?'

I told him that I was exercising my democratic right to speak to the voters.

'She hasn't got the right to create an obstruction.'

It was clear from the constable's manner that he'd had dealings with John Prest before. The man was quite possibly a magistrate. He reminded me of types who'd lectured me from the bench over the years.

'He's right, miss. If you could kindly move your vehicles on and do your campaigning elsewhere . . .'

I agreed at once. There was no point in picking quarrels with the police. The constable began to chivvy the people away and Bill set about getting the motor car started. While this was going on I looked round for the woman who'd shouted and picked her out as one of a group of three. They'd moved away far enough to satisfy the constable, but were still watching us. They were drably dressed, in grey cloth coats with broad leather belts. Two of them had soft caps, like boys', on their heads and the other had a shawl hitched well back, showing a mop of thick brown hair. This one was in her thirties, with a practical look about her that I liked. I went over to them and as I got closer was aware of a meaty, animal smell. I suppose I must have wrinkled my nose without meaning to, because the brown-haired woman laughed.

'Don't come too close until you get used to it. We can't help it.'

I put out my hand, keeping my nose carefully unwrinkled. After a pause, she put out hers. It was bare and walnut brown in colour. Even through my glove I could feel the hardness of her skin.

'Was it you who shouted?'

'I can't stand people being picked on. That's why I'm always getting in trouble.' Very much a local voice, with a lift and rhythm to it. 'We work at the tannery. That's why we smell like we do. My name's Molly Davitt. This is Tabitha Brown – we call her Tabby – and that's Annie Carter.'

Tabby was plump and cheerful looking, with red-brown frizzy hair and a squint. Annie looked no older than sixteen or seventeen. She was small, pretty and probably slim under the bulky coat, judging from her narrow bare hands and her brown-stockinged ankles. She had strands of curling dark brown hair escaping from the cloth cap, a pale face and rounded childlike cheeks. Her dark eyes though were anything but childlike. They looked into mine with the hardness of an old woman who'd stopped expecting anything good to happen. Tabby shook hands with me, Annie didn't. I asked Molly if she had a vote.

'Tabby and I have, because we're over thirty. Annie hasn't, of course. What we want to know is what happens to our jobs when the men get back? They needed us in the tannery because of all the leather that was wanted for the war for belts and so on and the men weren't here to do it. Now the men are coming back it's goodbye and thank you, and what are we supposed to do?'

I told her, truthfully, that one of the main planks in my election plaform was that the government should step in to provide jobs for all, women as well as men if they wanted them.

'I'll vote for you then, and I'll tell the other women at the tannery to do the same.'

'Would you like me to come and speak to them?'

'Why not, only it will have to be outside in the lunch break. The boss isn't bad as they go, but he's a Tory.'

I asked her if she'd like to help with the campaign and she agreed at once and said she'd call at my

Committee Room in the King's Head brewhouse after work. I offered them a lift back to the tannery in the motor car, but she said regretfully that they'd never hear the last of it from the boss. While we'd been talking, Annie had wandered away to the corner of the square, outside a rough-looking public house called the Three Tuns. On my way back to the motor car I noticed a young man coming up to talk to her. He was wearing a dirty-looking Norfolk jacket and cap, no overcoat. His right eye was covered with a black patch and the skin above it pulled tight by a slash of pink scar, shiny as enamel. War wounded. He said something to the girl. She looked alarmed, asked a question. He replied and she turned away from him. He put a hand on her elbow to stop her. Molly's voice carried loudly across the square.

'Come on, Annie. We'll be late back.'

The girl spoke a couple of words to the man over her shoulder, words that didn't please him judging by the look on his face, then pulled herself away and joined the other two tannery women. We passed them as we lurched back across the cobbles, Annie sandwiched protectively between the older two.

Back at the King's Head, Mrs Hincham had already set a man to work clearing out the old brewhouse, a brick rectangle in the corner of the yard. It was dim and musty, with lines of wooden beer casks stacked up along one side and cobwebs hanging like banners from the beams. I changed out of my best suit into my tweed walking skirt and jacket, borrowed a broom and started doing something about the cobwebs. Mrs Hincham offered a table and some chairs from the public bar as furniture and Bill helped carry them in, until I saw that his face was grey and drawn and guiltily remembered his elbow.

'For goodness' sake, you're still on the sick list. Go and rest for a while.'

'No time for that. I'll go and see if they've got the rest of your leaflets ready, then I'll try to telephone and see what's happening about my application for extended leave. After that I might drive out to White-horn Hall. There are questions to be asked there and you won't have time to do them. We need to talk to the staff about those confounded fireworks.'

I asked him what he'd made of Jonas Tedder.

'Exactly what you'd expect for a Tory in a rural area.'

'Did he strike you as a man who'd kill to be a candidate?'

'No. His wife was looking daggers at you, though.'

Moira joined me and we worked on through the afternoon. By the time it was getting dark the brew-house looked halfway respectable, with maps of the constituency pinned to beams inside, a new oil lamp casting a warm glow that was deceptive because the temperature wasn't far above freezing and posters round the outside. Molly Davitt arrived to collect a pile of leaflets and deliver the news that the tannery women were solid for me – a matter of nineteen votes. Mrs Hincham looked in while she was there and sniffed the air pointedly after she'd gone.

'You don't want to have much to do with those tannery women. They're as rough as a carter's breeches and they use language that would shrivel your ears up.'

As we swept and dusted Moira told me about the constituency and warned me that my anti-conscription activities would cause problems. Duxbury was strongly patriotic, with sons from almost every family serving with the Herefordshire Regiment or the King's Shropshire Light Infantry, and the losses had been as bad there as everywhere else. Still, there was a strong little Quaker community and I'd probably get their votes. Along with the tannery women and Mrs Hincham's obedient customers, that might take my total into dozens already.

It was nearly nine o'clock by the time we'd got the place straight. I saw Moira to her home and when I got back to the King's Head there was still no sign of Bill. Mrs Hincham had come out twice through the evening wanting to know when he'd be back for dinner, and rather than face her again I buttoned my coat up and waited in the Committee Room, making a list of things to be done by the light of the paraffin lamps. At last there was the noise of a motor and the car swept into the yard, its front lamp throwing a swathe of light across the brewhouse. Bill switched off the engine. He looked pinched with cold.

'Sorry to be such a long time. They invited me to tea up at the home farm.'

'The Sollers' home farm?'

'Yes. Nice man, the farmer. He told me something might—'

Before he could tell me what it was, Mrs Hincham appeared and ordered the two of us in for something to eat – poached eggs on toast because the pie had dried up in the oven long ago. What was worse, we couldn't talk freely about the Sollers household in the snug because a corner table was occupied by the man who'd arrived the night before.

He was a tidy, gloomy man who looked like a commercial traveller in disinfectants or cattle wormers and was sitting with a half-pint of beer and a notebook in front of him. Bill and I talked election instead and we went upstairs at about eleven o'clock, leaving the gloomy man in possession of the snug. I opened the door to my room.

'You'd better come in.'

'Are you sure?'

'Where else can we talk?'

Bill sat on the bed, almost toppling backwards into the hollow in the middle of the mattress. I took the chair by the washstand. From the street outside we could hear customers leaving the bar, calling goodnights.

'So what happened at Whitehorn Farm?'

'I went up to the house first to get Mrs Sollers' permission to speak to the people there. She gave me a free hand, but I had the impression she thought it was a waste of time.'

'She thinks anything's a waste of time unless it points directly to Jonas Tedder.'

'I went over and introduced myself to the farmer. He and his family have been there for about eight years, since Charles Sollers decided to build up a herd of Herefords. Before that he was a tenant farmer a few miles away. I told him straight out that we were investigating Sollers' death and asked if I could talk to the two lads who'd helped carry the fireworks in from Mr Sollers' car on the Thursday evening. He made no trouble about it and took me to where they were working in the barn. Ordinary farm lads they are, fourteen or fifteen years old.'

'Were they nervous of you?'

'No more than you'd expect. I told them that nobody was suggesting they'd done anything wrong, but I wanted to know what had happened. They confirmed Mrs Sollers' account. They were told they were wanted over at the Hall to unload some things from the car. They carried the boxes round to the room at the back and left them there.'

'Did they know they were fireworks?'

'Yes. The lads told their families about them and one of them has a sister who works in a shop, so she'll have passed it on. Friday was market day and both lads were in town seeing their friends. The firework party was one of the main subjects of conversation. So by Friday evening anybody in town or around it could have known about the fireworks and where they were being kept.'

'Giving a full day before the party to doctor one of them. But you'd still have to get hold of the explosive.'

'That wouldn't be a problem. I dare say some soldiers home on leave brought grenades back as souvenirs, or with all the ammunition manufacturing going on, some Amatol or whatever was bound to get into the wrong hands.'

'So what you've established is that it wouldn't necessarily have to be somebody from Whitehorn Hall or the estate. Were the lads at the party?'

'They were on duty, helping to stoke up the bonfire and so on. They couldn't add anything to what we know already, apart from one thing. As they were carrying wood over from the farmyard just before the party, one of them heard a woman talking round the back of the barn.'

'Was that so unusual? There must have been a lot of people coming and going.'

'It wasn't a voice he recognised. He said she sounded upset and was saying something like it wouldn't do.'

'What wouldn't do and who was she talking to?'

'He didn't know.'

'Miserable lack of curiosity in a lad. Why didn't he go round the barn and have a look?'

'With a bonfire and fireworks to think about, why should he be interested? He only remembered when I asked if they'd heard or seen anything unusual that evening.'

'You said the farmer told you something.'

'Yes. I'm not sure how it fits in with what happened to Sollers. It might not fit in at all and it happened weeks before.'

'Another attack?'

'Not directly.' Bill abandoned the struggle to stay upright on the bed, took off his shoes and lay back, staring up at the bulge in the plaster ceiling that matched the dip in the mattress. 'I only heard about it because the farmer invited me to join the family at tea. His wife and daughter were there and we were talking about the herd of Herefords. His daughter said something about one of the young bulls that had been killed. I don't think her father liked it, but once it had come out, he told me. It happened about six weeks ago, back end of October. One of their best young bulls had its throat cut.'

'How did it happen?'

'It was out in the field one night. In the morning they found it stone dead. It had been done quite cleanly, apparently. The farmer said it looked as if whoever did it had some experience of slaughtering cattle, or watching it at least. Then two great chunks had been cut out of its hind quarters.'

'It sounds as if somebody was hungry for a good steak.'

'That's what I suggested, but the farmer didn't think so. In this part of the world there are easier ways of getting meat. Sheer malice was what he called it.'

'Malice against Charles Sollers?'

'The farmer didn't like talking about it, but I got that impression. Significant, don't you think?'

He closed his eyes while I thought about it. Jonas Tedder creeping into his fellow Conservative's home with a cannister of high explosive was unlikely enough. Jonas Tedder butchering bulls and carving pieces from them was even less likely. True the man was a farmer, but of the gentleman variety. The same applied to young Chivas. Even if he had been home at the time, he struck me as a dandified young specimen. This was the first hint we'd had, apart from the killing itself, that the late Charles Sollers had not been universally liked.

I started to say something along those lines to Bill, then realised that he was asleep. He slept tidily, arms at his sides, like a man who'd got used to having little space. His mouth was shut. I wondered if any woman could ever get used to living with a man who slept with his mouth open, but supposed that thousands did so that it must be one of those things that didn't matter if you loved somebody. Or needed somebody enough perhaps. He looked worn out. The vitality in him had stopped me noticing while he was conscious, but now in the light of the candle I could see that the lines on his face were deeper than before the war, his neck thin and sinewy. He was in pain too. When a slight shift in position brought weight on the injured elbow he groaned softly in his sleep and moved back again. I doubted his assurance that he'd rather be here fighting an election than sitting around in a military hospital. I'd dragged him here unthinkingly because of my needs, taking for granted that it was what he wanted too. Years ago, in that other world before the war, I'd been able to help Bill when he needed it badly. It struck me that he was here now simply to repay that debt. I'd have to ask him in the morning. Meanwhile, after a whirlwind three days, it was good sitting here watching the candlelight wavering on the white walls. Bill slept on, taking deep slow breaths and I found that my breathing slipped into the same rhythm. The building was so quiet now that I could hear the gentle creaking of the oak beams, in a settling and readjusting of weight that would have been going on since the place was built three or four centuries ago. Like being in a ship on a calm sea.

Twelve o'clock struck from the town hall clock, then one. The candle burned down wafting a last smell of hot wax round the room. I suppose I dozed in the chair.

It was about two o'clock in the morning that it happened. I know that from what other people told me later, but at the time looking at my watch was the last thing on my mind. It was an explosion that rocked the building, then a terrified whinnying. It seemed to suspend time and thought, because I just sat there waiting for beams and ceiling to fall round my head. I heard Bill's voice from the darkness, in a sharp tone I hadn't heard from him before.

'Direct hit. Get out.' Then, in a different bewildered voice, 'Nell? Nell, are you there?'

Nothing was falling. I got up, fumbled my way to the window and opened the curtains. There was the red glow of fire that seemed to be coming from the yard at the side. By its light we managed to open the window. More whinnying, then a clatter of bolting hooves. The square was deserted. We still couldn't see the source of the fire but there was a strong smell of burning petroleum.

'We'd better get down there. I think . . .'

Feet running up the stairs, somebody pounding on the door.

'Miss Bray.'

Mrs Hincham's voice, sharp with alarm but not panicking.

'What's happening?'

'It's your motor car. It's on fire.'

I found my shoes and rushed out of the door, Bill just behind me, and registered the surprise on Mrs Hincham's face at finding two people where there should be one. I was dimly conscious of one of the barmaids in her nightdress looking out from a door on the other side of the landing. Mrs Hincham was wearing a coat over her nightdress. We followed her at a run downstairs, out of the side door into the yard. Where Mrs Sollers' glossy motor car had stood a few hours before was a transparent curtain of orange flame with the black skeleton of a motor car inside it and oily smoke spiralling sparks into the sky. The roaring of the fire sounded like an oncoming train and, even from the far side of the yard, the heat was scorching. Before the smoke got in my eyes and made them water I saw my new posters peeling off the walls of the brewhouse and windows jagged with broken glass.

'Better get away. The petrol tank might explode.'

Even saying that much sucked the oily smoke into my chest and I started coughing.

Bill said, 'I think the tank's already gone up. That's what we heard. Where's the fire station?'

Between coughs, Mrs Hincham managed to say that she'd sent young John running for them. He'd had to let out the pony which had been in its stall on the far side of the yard, going half-mad from fear, and it was somewhere out there in the town, God knows where. The car was well beyond saving and the only thing we could do was to try to stop the fire spreading to the brewhouse.

The two barmaids and the commercial-traveller-type I'd mentally tagged as Mr Worm Powder arrived, fully clothed, and the six of us ran with buckets and cans of water from the kitchen, throwing it as best we could into the hot canyon between the burning car and the brewhouse wall. While we were doing this the firemen arrived on their motor wagon, bell clanging loud enough to wake any of the town that might have slept through the explosion. They were elderly men mostly, war stand-ins, but they did an efficient job. A black and steaming framework of metal was all that was left of the car but the brewhouse was saved, although the brickwork along one side was blackened and scorched. By that time a small crowd had gathered. Young John returned with the news that the pony had been rounded up safely and put in somebody else's stable for the night.

'And the police have arrested somebody. I saw them with him in the square.'

They arrived in the yard soon afterwards, a sergeant and the constable who'd moved me on that morning, supporting a slumped man whose feet were still making walking movements but without much effect.

'Did any of you see him round here before it happened?' The light from a window fell on the man's face, an eye-patch and a slash of pink scar.

Mrs Hincham said disgustedly, 'It's Luke Dobbs.'

The man I'd seen trying to talk to Annie from the tannery.

'Did you see him round here?'

Nobody had, although I noticed that Mr Worm Powder was giving him a long look.

The sergeant said, 'We found him in sitting the street with his back against the Three Tuns.'

Luke Dobbs moved his head round, trying to focus, and moaned something about not doing anyone any harm. As far as I could see he was too drunk to be able to strike a match and must have been that way for hours. The sergeant manoeuvred him round so that he was facing the burnt-out motor car.

'Did you do that?'

'No 'arm . . . not doing any 'arm to anybody.'

The sergeant said they'd lock him up for the night and see if he made any more sense in the morning. They walked him away and the firemen finished dousing the yard and brewhouse, coiled up their hose and drove away. The rest of us crowded into the bar of the King's Head while the barmaids brewed pots of strong tea. The constable, looking bone weary, came back to take statements. Mrs Hincham was the main witness. Her room overlooked the yard and she'd been woken up by the light of the fire and the crackling of flames. She'd roused young John and they'd both gone down to see what was happening. By good luck, they were still in the corridor leading to the yard door when the explosion happened otherwise they'd have been killed. Even so, John had been cut by flying glass from a broken window. All Bill or I could add to that was that we'd left the car in the yard sometime between half-past nine and ten o'clock and had known nothing about the fire until Mrs Hincham called us. (She hadn't mentioned that we were both in the same bedroom at the time, though I got an odd look from the barmaid when she gave me my tea.) At last the constable put his notebook away and said we could all go to the police station to sign statements in the morning. I asked what had happened to Luke Dobbs.

'Sobering up in a cell, ma'am. Don't worry, it's home from home to him.'

Mrs Hincham said, 'I can't see Luke Dobbs doing a thing like that. He was drunken and useless before he went in the Army and got wounded and he's worse now, but there's no real harm in him.'

The constable left. As we were finishing our tea I thanked Mr Worm Powder for his help in saving our Committee Room. He was polite enough, but seemed surprised. After that we all went to our beds, separate rooms this time, although I had time for just a few words with Bill on the landing before the barmaid came up to her room.

'I don't think that pathetic drunk had anything to do with it. Could it have caught fire accidentally?'

'I doubt it. And if you're thinking of my pipe, don't worry. It's hard enough dealing with a steering wheel and gear change one-handed without smoking as well.'

'Deliberate then. The question is was it because it was the Sollers' car . . . ?'

'Or your campaign vehicle? I shouldn't have thought even you had been in town long enough to provoke arson. Though you never know.'

The barmaid came past on the way to her room. 'Good night, Miss Bray. Goodnight, Mr Musgrave. Sleep well.'

'Oh hell.'

Chapter Seven

L ucinda Sollers took it remarkably well.
'I never liked motor cars. Charles insisted.'
After a few hours' sleep and a hurried breakfast, Bill
and I had walked the mile and a half out to Whitehorn
Hall, gloomy at the prospect of reporting the loss of
around five hundred pounds' worth of her property. She
received us in her drawing-room with the curtains
drawn halfway across the windows, turning the grey
morning to an undersea dusk. She seemed wearier than
before and from the violet shadows under her eyes she
hadn't slept well either. I told her that we thought
somebody must have set light to the car deliberately
and her expression didn't change.
'Of course. Now he knows what you're doing here,
he's trying to scare you away.'
The door opened and Peter Chivas walked in.
'Lucinda, I can't find . . .'
When he saw Bill and me he stopped in mid-stride
and raised his eyebrows. Stagey, I thought. He must
have heard visitors at the front door, so why the
surprise? Even in riding breeches and Norfolk jacket
there was still an air of the dandy about him, plus a
smell of hair oil.
'They came to tell us the motor car's been burnt.'
It took a moment to register.

'How?'

Bill started explaining but Peter cut across him, appealing loudly to his aunt. 'But I was going to drive it. You said I could have it.'

This time he sounded younger than his seventeen or eighteen years, a child wailing when a favourite toy's been crushed underfoot. It jolted her out of her mermaid-like calm. Her face creased in distress, making her look older.

'We'll get you another one when you leave school. You're not old enough to drive now in any case.'

'Yes I am. I don't want another one. I wanted that one.'

If he'd stamped his foot and burst into tears I'd hardly have been surprised. Bill caught my eye and made a disgusted face. Lucinda floated over to Peter, took his arm and led him to a chair, making soothing noises. '. . . another one, promise. You shall choose it . . . in the summer, when you leave school.'

He shook her hand off and settled in a chair by the window, sulking at us. Bill changed the subject abruptly, probably trying to hide his disgust.

'Mrs Sollers, did you know anything about the attack on one of your husband's cattle a few weeks before he died?'

It caught her by surprise. 'There . . . there was something about a bull that was killed.'

'Did your husband say anything to you about it?'

'He . . . was angry. It was a good bull.'

'Did he say who he thought might have done it?'

She shook her head. 'Why are you interested in that?'

'Because it suggests somebody with malice against your husband. It might cast some light on what happened after that.'

'It had nothing to do with that.'

After a silence I said we had work to do back in the town, which was true. I hoped she might ask about the progress of the election campaign, but she stood up silently to show us out. It looked as if Peter Chivas was going to keep his seat until a glance from Bill brought him sulkily upright. Lucinda escorted us down the steps and stood watching us as we walked up the track. She looked chilled and vulnerable, on her own.

Bill said, 'Another minute and I'd have kicked him.'

'She seems terrified of offending the brat. Like an older woman with a young lover.'

'Ye gods, do you think so?'

'I don't know. You know we've both been wondering why Peter Chivas annoys us so much. I think it's sexual.' In the way he stood and looked and dressed there was the triumph of a young man discovering a new power.

'If you're right and Sollers had guessed it . . .'

'Blowing himself up deliberately in front of her? Stranger things have happened. If so, all this Tedder business is no more than a smoke screen.'

'But from what we know of Charles Sollers, does it seem likely?'

'Rich, successful, politically ambitious. I'd say he was more likely to blow young Chivas to pieces than himself.'

'Unless young Chivas got in first.'

'But he wouldn't have known the fireworks were there. He was away at school.'

'If his aunt wrote to him on Thursday, he could know by Friday morning.'

'So the two of them are in a conspiracy, are they? If that was it, would she go to so much trouble to get us to come and investigate?'

'I'd like to know more about what he was doing on the night of the party.'

Back at the King's Head, a long telegram was waiting for Bill. The good news was that he could be released, reluctantly, to act as my agent. The bad news was that he was wanted back in Oxford for various formalities. He packed hastily and I walked with him to the railway station. I said I supposed he might not be back before Saturday.

'I might make it Sunday. I've a sudden urge to see an old friend. We were at college together. He's a schoolmaster these days.'

'Can I guess where?'

'You probably can. Convenient, isn't it?'

I saw him off on the Worcester train. 'Be careful,' he said, leaning out of the window as the porter banged doors. Then again, more urgently, as the train began to move, 'Be careful.'

There were a dozen things to do at the Committee Room, starting with clearing up. Greasy smoke had got in through broken windows, spoiling some of our leaflets and there was glass to be swept up and new posters to be pasted to the blackened outside wall. While I was doing it people drifted in and out of the yard, most of them unknown to me, staring and saying what a terrible thing it was. After that, I found my way to the police station and spoke to another sergeant who didn't give the impression that the matter was being pursued with much urgency. There was no proof, after all, that the fire hadn't started by accident and in his opinion motor cars were chancy things. I asked what had happened to Luke Dobbs.

'Up before the bench this morning, for being drunk and disorderly. Fined ten shillings and given another warning.'

I spent an hour fixing up a hall for my two public meetings in Duxbury. I'd decided to hold one next Tuesday night to give people a chance to ask me questions, another on the eve of the poll on Friday. Luckily Moira knew some Baptists who were willing to hire me a hall just a short stroll from the centre of town for a pound an evening and a guarantee against breakages. I gathered the score at the last election meeting had been two cracked windows and a broken pew, which suggested Duxbury didn't always take its politics quietly. Most of my other campaign meetings would be in the open air, which was what I was used to. By the time I'd finished at the Baptist hall it was midday, with a light drizzle falling, and I remembered my promise to go and speak outside the tannery. I collected some leaflets from my Committee Room, borrowed a wooden lemonade crate from the bar and followed the smell down the street and over the bridge.

I'd struck it right – lunchtime. In spite of the drizzle about a dozen men and women were standing around outside a building of damp red brick that looked as if it had spent a hundred years or more sinking back towards mud. They wore thick leather aprons over their clothes. The men wore caps. Some of the women were bare-headed and others had men's caps or old felt hats in various faded colours pulled down tightly over their heads. Men and women mostly kept to their separate groups. They were all smoking cigarettes except for one or two eating sandwiches – quite an achievement considering a smell so thick and clotted

97

that you expected to see it hanging over the place in a yellowish cloud.

Seized with that momentary nervousness that always comes to you before speaking in public however often you've done it, I put the lemonade crate down in the mud and stood on it, took a deep breath, and started speaking. It went well enough. Of course there were some comments shouted by the men, including the inevitable question of why I didn't go and find myself a husband, but I'd learned long since that 'Are you offering?' dealt with that one. Work for everybody and better housing brought some murmurs of agreement, and there were even shouts of 'yes' from Molly and one of the other women at allowances for mothers.

Foreign policy was rockier territory and it was here that something odd happened. I was being given a rough ride by some of the men about peace terms. They were in favour of humiliating the Germans so that they wouldn't try it again. One of them even suggested that the Armistice had been declared too early and we shouldn't have stopped until there were English soldiers in every German city.

I said, 'For goodness sake, haven't enough men died already?'

As I said it there was a little stir, just on the edge of my field of vision. I looked and it came from my trio of supporters. Annie had doubled up as if in pain and Molly and Tabby were supporting her, arms round her shoulders. When I stopped speaking Molly signed to me to go on, it was all right. It obviously wasn't. As the questions and answers went on I saw Tabby leading Annie away, the thin girl leaning against the solid woman and moving in a dazed shuffle, like walking wounded. I brought the session to an end as soon as I could. Tabby was back by then, without Annie. I asked Molly what the trouble was.

'Annie'll be alright. It was just when you talked about people dying in the war. It gets her like that sometimes.'

'She lost somebody?'

'Two. Her only brother and the lad she was going to marry. They got called up together and they both died on the same day.'

The names on the memorial stone.

'Tom Carter and Simon Whittern.'

'That's right.'

She told me the story, standing there with the people around us drifting back into work, throwing cigarette butts into the mud. Annie Carter was seventeen. She and her brother Tom had been orphaned as children and were boarded out with relatives.

'They were everything to each other. Tom and Simon were best friends and it was always understood that Simon and Annie were going to marry. Tom worked at the forge and Simon at a farm. They both of them hoped they wouldn't have to go in the Army because of being essential trades, but they got called up just the same.'

'So Annie's got nobody?'

'She lodges with Mum and me and I got her the job here. She'll have to get over it like the rest. She's been worse since the peace came. I worry sometimes it's sent her not quite right. I think it's because she hears the other girls talking about brothers and sweethearts coming home, and it's sinking in with her that hers aren't going to.'

I mentioned casually that I'd seen Annie talking to Luke Dobbs the day before and her face went dark.

'I don't know why she sees him. I've warned her about it. He's no good to anyone.'

'Was he a friend of her brother or her fiancé?'

'They all used to hang about together before the war. Luke lost his eye in the same battle the other two got killed in. Her brother was killed straight out. At first Simon Whittern was only posted missing and we hoped he might have been taken prisoner, but he wasn't.'

Anger at the waste of it fuelled me as I walked round Duxbury all afternoon, delivering leaflets and talking to as many voters as I could persuade out of their houses. They were a kindly lot on the whole, which I found disconcerting after the rough and tumble of city politics. Even when they made it clear that they had no intention of voting for me they were anxious to know how I liked their town or concerned for me walking round in the wet. In three hours' work I scored two cups of tea, one superficial dog bite, three firm promises and four possibles. There was even a trade unionist down by the railway station who quizzed me on employment policy for twenty minutes and agreed to put one of my posters on his front gate. Altogether a pretty fair afternoon's canvassing. Dinner in the snug that evening was a quiet affair, with Bill away and Mr Worm Powder still in residence. That surprised me, because I'd assumed he'd be moving on to the next town. Mrs Hincham had set separate small tables for us and he stood up and gave me a civil good evening when I came in and hoped the weather would improve. His voice was not local, more home counties, and his posture stiff and upright. Ex-soldier, probably. He had his nose in a book throughout the meal, which suited me as I'd had enough conversation for one day. After the excitements of the last two nights I was mortally tired and planned to wash my smalls and go to bed early. The plates were cleared away and I was toasting my still-damp shoes at the fire when Mrs Hincham came in and said there were a lady and gentleman to see me.

'They want to speak to you in private. I've shown them into the dining-room.'

It was a barn of a room, probably intended for the likes of agricultural show dinners, now a cold expanse of stacked chairs and empty tables. At a table by the door two chairs had been unstacked. Beside one of them stood a plump man with red face and sticking-out ears, clearly ill at ease. A woman sat in the other, the russet fox fur collar of her coat drawn up close to her determined chin, slim ankles in stockings of bracken-coloured silk elegantly crossed. Jonas and Felicity Tedder. He got a chair for me, sat down and apologised for intruding, humming and hawing like a man who'd give a lot to be elsewhere. Felicity cut through it with a voice like a pruning knife.

'I'm sure Miss Bray doesn't grudge us her time. After all, it's in her interest to stop the nonsense.'

'What nonsense had you in mind?'

She didn't reply, only stared at me as if I should have known.

Jonas Tedder said, 'This . . . um . . . this unfortunate business about poor Charles Sollers.'

'What aspect of it?'

While he searched for words, she came in like Lady Macbeth demanding the daggers. 'Everybody's saying that she's paying you to put around the story that Jonas was responsible. It's a disgusting dishonourable thing to do and if you don't stop it at once we'll sue you for libel.'

'I think it would be slander, dear,' he said, diffidently. And to me, 'I'm not actually thinking of suing, so to speak. But it's got to stop. It's making the whole election look ridiculous and my wife's quite ill with the strain of it.'

To me she looked about as ill as a boxer in training. She was quite a lot younger than her husband, early thirties probably and easily the most stylish woman I'd seen in Duxbury.

'To get one thing clear, Mrs Sollers is not paying me to put round any sort of story. She's agreed to pay my election expenses and I put my policies to her in some detail. She also asked me to investigate her husband's death. I agreed to do that.'

Felicity said 'Ah' in a way that implied case proven. I went on, shifting my chair so that I could watch both their faces.

'Before I agreed, I made it clear to her that there would be no preconceptions. I didn't know then who killed her husband. I still don't know now.'

'But you're putting it about that it's Jonas.'

'I'm doing nothing of the kind. Any suspicion there might be against Mr Tedder rests on an assumption that I don't find at all convincing.'

He couldn't help puffing out a sigh of relief at that, but she pounced.

'What assumption?'

'That Mr Tedder wants to be MP for Duxbury so much that he'd kill for it.' I looked at him. 'Do you?'

She started answering for him, but to his credit he made a sign to her to be quiet.

'I don't. To be honest with you, I'd be as happy not being an MP. I've got my work and my family here and they're enough for me. I only stood against him for the nomination because people thought there should be a choice. Poor Charles would have been a much better MP than me.'

She made an impatient noise. I'd been watching her face while he was speaking and got the impression that, while he might be happy not to be an MP, she had no intention of passing up the chance of being an MP's wife.

'Would you say you and he were friends?'

He glanced at this wife. She nodded.

'Quite friendly, yes. We dined with each other occasionally, met on committees and so on.'

'So you weren't surprised to be invited to his victory party?'

'Jonas, she's digging.'

'Mrs Tedder, I've already told you I'm investigating his death. Wouldn't it be in all our interests to get this cleared up as soon as possible?'

It silenced her just long enough for him to make up mind.

'I don't care if she is digging. We've got nothing to hide. No, we weren't surprised. Everybody in the constituency association was invited.'

'Did you know the fireworks were at the house when you went to collect your wife from a meeting there the day before the party?'

His eyes widened. Felicity looked furious but kept quiet for once.

'I'm not sure. I knew there'd be fireworks and I think he'd mentioned he was driving over to Wolver-hampton to collect them. If I'd thought about it I suppose I'd have assumed they were in the house somewhere.'

'What about you, Mrs Tedder? Was there any discussion of the fireworks at the meeting about the Christmas bazaar?'

'I think Mrs Sollers may have referred to them. I can't remember.'

'I gather that you had to leave the party itself with a headache?'

She'd been resentful up to then, but that made her furious.

'Who told you that? I suppose she did.'

'It's hardly a crime to leave a party early.'

'I know what she was implying and what you're implying.'

Her husband was making calming noises at her, but she didn't take any notice.

'I'm not implying anything. The more I can find out about what happened that evening, the better chance there is of putting this to rest.'

'Miss Bray's right dear.' Quite brave of the man and he'd probably suffer for it later from the look she gave him. 'What do you want to know?'

'Everything you can tell me.'

'We got there quite early because Felicity wanted to speak to Lucinda about something to do with the bazaar. We parked the car and Felicity went to look for her while I went to see how they were getting on with making the bonfire. Charles was there on the old tennis court. He was worried that there might not be enough wood and he'd sent the farm lads to bring bits of an old gate from the farmyard.'

'Did Mr Sollers seem normal?'

104

'Very cheerful. We talked about the election a bit and what the Liberals were doing, but mainly about the bonfire party. By that time there were more people arriving and the housekeeper came out with glasses of punch. Charles lit the bonfire himself. We watched it for a bit, then Felicity came back and said she had a headache, so we thought we'd better go before the fireworks started.'

I said to Felicity, 'Did you find Lucinda Sollers?'

'What?'

'You'd gone to look for Mrs Sollers. Did you find her?'

For a moment her face stayed blank then, 'No, I couldn't find her and I had such a blinding headache I decided it could wait.'

'So you didn't see her before it happened?'

'I haven't see her at all. Jonas and I went round the day afterwards to offer our sympathies, but she was too ill to see us. She wasn't too ill to start putting rumours round about Jonas.'

'When exactly did these rumours start circulating?'

For once they waited for each other to answer, then he said, 'It must have been the first week after he died, after the meeting when I was chosen as prospective candidate.'

Felicity said, 'She still hasn't answered.'

'Answered what?'

'Whether you're going to stop what you're doing.'

'If you mean investigating, no I'm not. If you mean spreading slanders against Mr Tedder, I haven't done it and I'm not doing it now.'

The unbelieving noise she made was on the edge of being unladylike, but he had the sense to recognise a deadlock when he saw it and changed the subject.

'I heard what happened to the motor car. I'm sorry. Have you any idea how it happened?'

'None at all.'

'I ask because of something rather odd that happened to us, just after I was nominated. On its own it seemed like a senseless piece of vandalism, but now this has happened, I wonder.'

'What happened?'

'The Saturday evening after I was chosen as candidate, we had a few friends from the Conservative association in for a drink. Not a party, of course. That would have been disrespectful after what had happened to Charles but it was thought that we should mark the occasion in some way. Anyway, while we were drinking and talking in the front lounge we heard this crash of glass from the back of the house. We all rushed out and found somebody had thrown a stone through our conservatory.'

'A brick,' Felicity said. 'It ruined the orange tree.'

'Did you catch anybody?'

'No. There's quite an extensive shrubbery at the back of our house. We assumed the person responsible must be in there. But while we were searching this there was another crash, from the front of the house this time. He'd gone round to the front and broken a window in the dining-room while we were looking out the back, and got clean away.'

'Taking a bottle of brandy with him,' she said.

'Yes. He must have reached through the window and grabbed it off the table.'

'Did you tell the police?'

'Of course. They made a search but didn't find anything. There were quite a lot of drunkenness and high spirits around the time of the Armistice and they thought it was all part of that. It occurs to me now, in the light of what happened to the motor car, that it might be something more sinister.'

'Do you think it might be connected with Mr Soller's death?'

'I admit I did wonder.'

Felicity said, 'I thought it might be Lucinda.'

'Even if Mrs Sollers did throw stones through your windows, she's hardly likely to have stolen a bottle of brandy, is she?'

Felicity shrugged her shoulders, as if Lucinda were capable of anything. I was thinking that the attack, with its mixture of vandalism and theft, had more in common with the slaughter of Mr Sollers' bull back in October. I asked Jonas Tedder about that. He said he'd heard about it but hadn't associated it with the attack on him, until now.

'Do you think there's any connection?'

'If there is, I don't know what it is. If anything else happens in the campaign that seems odd to you, will you tell me about it?'

That didn't please Felicity, but he said he would. He got up, shook my hand and hoped we'd get to polling day without any more dramas. Felicity didn't shake my hand. From the look she gave me, it was still war between us.

Chapter Eight

⚘

Friday was market day. From early morning, lying in the trough of the bed while it was still dark outside, I'd been aware of carts grinding over the cobblestones and the rattle and thump of people putting up stalls. By the time I looked out at daylight the square was almost covered with green-and-white canvas awnings and early shoppers were already out with their bags. Mrs Hincham had let me know that Duxbury Liberal candidates always spoke in the square on market days. The Conservatives were too grand for that sort of thing. I owed John Prest a grudge for having me moved on by the police and I didn't intend to leave him a clear field.

At eleven o'clock, with the town more crowded than I'd seen it before, I was on my way across the square with Moira and our two Bennington suffragettes in support and young John who'd been detailed by Mrs Hincham to carry the lemonade box for me. Judging by his embarrassment at some of the remarks shouted at us by the market boys he was regretting his entry into politics. I couldn't help being distracted by the sight of all the food around us. In London wartime restrictions had made for dismal eating but Herefordshire had gone on growing what it liked. There were stalls piled with different varieties of apples that glowed like lanterns on a dull day, golden-skinned russets, yellow-and-red Worcesters and some with green-and-red stripes that I couldn't name. Even cabbages were colourful, piled up in swathes of blue-green and globes of white and red. Bright-feathered bodies of pheasants hung by the neck in limp braces, alongside hares upside-down with their heads in little tin buckets to catch the blood. Walnuts and chestnuts came in willow baskets, cheeses in great cloth-bound rounds with wedges cut out of them to show moist and crumbly insides. I'd have liked to stop and smell and touch, but it was important to get a good pitch and start attracting a crowd before the Independent Temperance Liberal arrived. I asked young John to put the lemonade box down on a broad area of pavement in front of the town hall, stationed my three supporters alongside holding posters we'd pasted on to boards and opened the meeting.

'Voters of Duxbury . . .'

I'd left my megaphone in London and had to shout. Faces turned my way from the stalls. Some of them, after that first curious glance, went back to their cabbages and potatoes but a few people drifted in my direction. I hadn't been going long and had collected a crowd of no more than a dozen or so when I heard the sound of a concertina playing a quick march. As it came closer I had to speak even louder. My audience got restive, started looking round. Between the ranks of cabbages and dead pheasants came the concertina player, two men in bowler hats who could have doubled as funeral mutes and a boy holding a placard: PREST for PEACE, PROSPERITY, PROBITY. Behind them stalked the man himself, glaring. They marched straight up to the edge of my little crowd while I tried to ignore them and went on talking about money for hospitals. The concertina stopped playing.

'That's my place.' John Prest's voice, at full roar.

I pressed on. 'Can we be content with a country where life or death depend on how much you can pay? Can we be content with infant death rates—'

'I said that's my place.'

His roar brought the whole market to a halt. People stopped buying and selling and stared in our direction. I pretended to notice him for the first time.

'Oh? Have you bought the pavement?'

Some laughter. A man's voice yelled, 'She got there first.' The crowd was growing now, thirty or forty at least. John Prest and his little group waited but when it became obvious that nothing but physical attack would move us he marched off to the opposite corner of the town hall frontage, about thirty paces away. From there I heard his voice cutting across mine.

'Voters of Duxbury . . .'

For some time we spoke in combative duet. His voice was louder, but when it came to hostile debates I'd probably had more practice than him and managed to slip in some pointed remarks when he had to pause for breath. All the time the crowd was growing and getting noisier. I don't suppose they heard much of what either of us was saying, but any pretence of sensible political discussion had been abandoned a long time ago. It was a straightforward case of him against me, almost as physical as a wrestling match. I sensed that some of the crowd were on my side in a purely sporting spirit, not because they agreed with what I was saying but because I was the outsider and the underdog. The other factor was the drinking men. Just a few buildings along from the town hall was the Three Tuns, doing good business from the market traders. Some of them came out to see what the noise was about and recognised Prest as an enemy.

'He's the one who wants to stop us having a drink.'

'The temperance man.'

'Hey, missus, you wouldn't stop a man having a drink, would you?'

Unwisely, Prest decided to reply. 'I've never made any secret about my attitude to the licensing laws. Yes, I am a temperance candidate. I—'

The Three Tuns contingent and some of the other market men started barracking him. A chant began, to the familiar tune of 'Tramp, tramp, tramp the boys are marching'.

> 'Vote, vote, vote for Nellie Bra-a-ay.
> Kick old John Prest out the door.
> If I had a lump of lead
> I would knock him on the head
> And he wouldn't go a-voting any more.'

No election campaign was complete without that chant. I'd heard it many times in campaigning for other people and it was a political coming-of-age, in its way, to hear my own name slotted into it. I knew, though, that the people chanting it so joyfully probably had not the slightest intention of voting for me and, even though Prest had richly deserved it, I couldn't help being sorry that the debate had come down to this level.

I was trying to persuade the chanters to be quiet and to get things back under some sort of control when Prest went mad. The first I knew of it was when his voice, loud enough before, roared to a different scale altogether. I stopped speaking. I couldn't help it. If a gigantic bull from Homerian myth had swayed into the market square and started bellowing fit to wake the gods, that might have been the sort of noise that Duxbury's Independent Liberal Temperance candidate made in full cry.

'Temperance candidate? Well, I'm not ashamed of that. It's better than some other things.' He was pointing at me. His bowler hat had slipped back on his head and his face had turned the colour of rare roast beef. 'It's better than being the *intemperance* candidate.'

I opened my mouth to protest, then decided to give him enough rope to hang himself. In terms of volume, I couldn't compete. The crowd had gone quiet.

'If you're thinking of voting for *Miss* Bray, ask yourself what you'll be voting for? Are you voting for the safety of your country, for the security of your families, for the sanctity of the marriage bond? Or are you voting . . .' His voice dropped. He could do it now that he had them. 'Or are you voting for something else altogether? For a woman who spent the war helping men to evade their duty. For a woman who comes here, sets up her headquarters in a public house and preaches by example the pernicious doctrine of so-called free love, who—'

Gasps from the crowd, and a little shout of protest from Moira. Time to start hitting back.

'Our loud friend over there thinks that if you haven't got policies you might as well try lies. If he's hoping . . .'

But it wasn't making much impression and the crowd were getting noisier, my supporters and his yelling at each other.

112

Moira called, vainly but bravely, 'Give her a chance to reply.'

Some lout who'd probably had enough of women raising their voices in public threw a cabbage at her. It was, to be fair, quite a small cabbage, more a collection of floppy leaves and not one of the big white cannon-balls, and it simply hit her on the shoulder and went slithering down her arm without doing any damage. She stared at it, amazed, as if it had been some kind of exotic butterfly, not being used to this kind of campaigning. That cabbage was the signal for all hell to be let loose. The men from the Three Tuns yelled with concerted rage about not doing that to ladies and started lobbing root vegetables – turnips I think – towards Prest and his party. Within seconds the air was full of flying vege-tables and shouting. My supporters, not stirring from their posts, looked up at me and I hopped off the lemonade box.

'No use saying anything now. We'll just have to wait while it burns itself out.'

The Prest camp seemed to have come to the same conclusion. He'd gone quiet and got down from his crate. Through the rain of turnips and cabbage leaves I could see his bowler hat and red face, surrounded by a knot of worried-looking supporters. They knew he'd gone too far. Men were struggling on the ground now. There was a cracking sound and a potato stall slowly collapsed, tipping its stock on to the cobbles, providing more ammunition. An errand boy slipped and went down. I saw his pale face and terrified eyes among a stampede of skirmishing boots, started push-ing people aside to get to him, went sliding on a crushed potato and ended up sprawling face down on the wet cobbles. Still face down I heard a whistle

113

shrilling, shouts of police. The noise and the fighting stopped. As I struggled to my knees I saw some of the men diving back into the Three Tuns, others going back behind their market stalls as if nothing had happened. Moira and the other two, looking shaken, came over and helped me up. A constable arrived – a different one this time – glanced at Prest then at me and sensibly decided that getting the square tidied up was more important than making inquiries. Under his eye brooms and shovels were produced, crushed vegetables chivvied into heaps. Prest, without looking in my direction, marched away among his friends, this time without the concertina music.

'Are you alright?' A man's voice behind me, with a touch of concern but mostly amusement. I turned and recognised the lively eyes and thick glasses of the editor of the *Duxbury Chronicle*.

'Quite alright, thank you, Mr Jones. But I'm sorry this has happened.'

I had that deflated guilty feeling that comes to you after anger and violence, whether it was your fault or not. Here was this peaceful little market town and if it hadn't been for the fight between Prest and me it would be getting on with its lawful Friday business undisturbed.

'Don't worry, Duxbury wouldn't think it was a proper election without a riot on market day. Part of the democratic process. But I must say Prest was out of bounds.'

'It shows he's more worried about losing votes to me than I realised.' But the editor would be wondering if there were any truth in what Prest had been saying. 'This business of helping men to evade their duty. From the end of nineteen sixteen I thought we could make an honourable peace. Once I'd decided that,

I couldn't sit quietly in London and see trainloads of men going off to kill and be killed. I never encouraged any man to desert, but I did what I could to help those who were following their own consciences. If the voters don't like that, I'm sorry, but there it is.'

'Most of them won't like it. Do you want me to print that as a statement from you?'

'Better get it out in the open, yes. I'll put it in writing and drop it in later today. As for preaching free love, that's bilious nonsense.'

True enough. I'd never believed in telling people what they should do with their personal lives, partly because I'm not always sure what I'm doing with my own. He wouldn't print that, so there was no point in saying it. It was Prest's accusation of preaching 'by example' that was meant to sting. Clearly, the barmaid at the King's Head had been gossiping. She could hardly have failed to gossip about a male and female guest rushing out of the same bedroom in the early hours of the morning, even if they were fully clothed. No point in taking space in the *Duxbury Chronicle* to explain that Bill had only been asleep and I'd been watching him. An implied lie in any case. Bill and I might not have been lovers in Duxbury, but we had been elsewhere. Whether we ever would be again, I didn't know and wasn't thinking that far ahead.

Alexander Jones went back to his office and we retrieved our posters, badly trampled in the scuffle. There was no sign of young John, and I didn't blame him. He'd never been more than a reluctant recruit. While I was looking round for him I glanced at the men on the corner by the Three Tuns and saw one I recognised. The wounded soldier, Luke Dobbs, was standing a little apart from the rest, looking scornfully at the sweeping and shovelling going on in the market square. On an impulse I went up to him. He'd never seemed to me a likely candidate for setting fire to the motor car, but he had been in the square about the time it happened and might have noticed something, even in his fuddled state. He took a step back, looking scared, and muttered something about not being political. He couldn't have been much older than early twenties, but his teeth were black stumps, his fingers stained yellow with nicotine. After a first glance at me he looked away, hiding the patched eye.

'Don't worry, I'm not going to talk politics. I'm sorry you were arrested the other night. That had nothing to do with me.'

He mumbled, 'Too many people interferin'. . .' Even sideways on, his breath reeked of beer and bad teeth.

'I wanted to ask if you saw anybody going towards the King's Head before the motor car caught fire.'

He twitched his face towards me and away in a vestigial head-shake. 'Too many people asking questions. The police and 'im and now you. Too many bloody questions.'

One of the other men overheard and said over his shoulder, 'You mind your language in front of ladies, Luke Dobbs.' Then, to me, 'Your motor car that got burnt then, was it?'

'Not mine, but Mrs Sollers had lent it to me for—'

Luke spat. Not casually but with force and accuracy right on to the toe of my shoe. Then, as the other men shouted at him, he turned and walked away down the side street without another word, leaving me standing there staring. The others were instantly apologetic on his behalf. They'd been temporarily on my side in any case because of the row with Prest and as one of them put it, spitting at a woman wasn't right, not even if you were married to her let alone a visitor. They fetched straw to wipe my shoe, assured me that nobody took any notice of Luke Dobbs, he'd gone odd since he lost his eye.

'But what was it I said that annoyed him so much?'

'Mentioning the name Sollers. He blames him for what happened to him and a friend of his.'

'What was the friend's name.'

'Simon Whittern. He and Luke used to work for old Sollers in his cow yard. He could have got them off having to go in the Army, only he wouldn't register them.'

Men registered as skilled agricultural workers were exempt from military service.

'Why wouldn't he?'

The man shrugged. 'Said he could manage with the older and younger ones and it wasn't patriotic to keep men from the service. We tell Luke there are plenty like that, only he won't listen to us, will he?'

The other men agreed that no, Luke wouldn't listen. Now the drama was over they were bored with the discussion and wanted to get back to the bar. By now Luke Dobbs was out of sight. I thanked them and walked back with the others to the Committee Room. Moira must have thought from my silence that I was worrying about what John Prest had said because she assured me that nobody would take any notice of him. I was sure she was wrong about that, but it wasn't what was worrying me.

Chapter Nine

I'd already arranged to take the afternoon train back to London, a necessary trip because I'd arrived in Duxbury with clothes for only two days, more than half-convinced that I wouldn't be staying. So far I'd managed by rinsing my smalls in the washbasin and hanging them over the brass bedrail to dry, but my best suit was already getting campaign-stained and the battle of the market place hadn't improved it. With two public meetings in the coming week I had to look respectable. Also, I wanted my battered old megaphone for the next confrontation with John Prest. Before I went to catch the train I made a point of telling Mrs Hincham, in the presence of the talkative barmaid, that I'd be back on Sunday. I wasn't going to let Prest think he'd chased me out of town.

I got back, hauling two suitcases, as it was getting dark on Sunday afternoon and left one of them at the station to be collected later. Bill arrived just in time for dinner but we couldn't talk about anything that mattered because Mr Worm Powder was still in residence. I could tell Bill was as puzzled as I was to find him still there because he gave him a long look when they said good evening. After the meal, when Bill and I had moved over to the cold Committee

Room and lit the oil lamp, he said, 'That man's in the Army.'

'Mr Worm Powder?'

'His name's Wilby. I asked Mrs Hincham.'

'There is something military about him. I'd assumed he was an ex-NCO.'

'I think he's still serving and on leave.'

'A funny way to spend your leave, on your own with a notebook in a public house.'

But we had more immediate things to talk about. Bill, as my agent, had to know what had happened on market day but I did my best to play down the free love part of the attack. He was furious, though.

'I'll go and see the man first thing tomorrow.'

'No! It would make things worse. Besides, what could you say to him?'

'That he's a filthy-minded scoundrel and if he tries to blacken a lady's reputation in public he must take the consequences.'

'A lady's reputation! Oh my dear, nobody's going to be fighting duels over mine.'

I was surprised, touched even, that he was so annoyed. Still it wouldn't help my cause to have them quarrelling, so I changed the subject to the thing that was worrying me most. Two days' thinking about it hadn't improved it.

'Luke Dobbs hated Sollers, with very good reason. And look at all the things that have happened. He was a cattleman so he could have slaughtered that bull. He's a drunkard so he might have stolen that brandy from Tedder's house. He wasn't far away when someone set fire to the motor car.'

'But you said yourself that he looked too drunk to light a match that night.'

119

'He might have been acting. Better to get fined ten bob for being drunk than a life sentence for arson – or something even worse.'

'Such as blowing up Sollers?'

'He had the motive, and from what we found out about the fireworks, almost anybody had the opportunity.'

'What are you going to do then? Tell Lucinda Sollers? Tell the police?'

'No, not while it's only a suspicion.'

'It may have occurred to the police in any case. Luke Dobbs is known to them and if he's been going around talking about Sollers, they'll know.'

'He said the police had been asking him questions, but I assumed that was just about the motor car. There was another "him" who'd been asking him questions as well – or perhaps that was just Luke being fuddled.'

'If Sollers was murdered, that wasn't the crime of a fuddled or unintelligent man. It would take cool planning.'

'Are you thinking of anybody in particular?'

He didn't answer directly. 'I called on my schoolmaster friend in Shrewsbury.'

'Well?'

'He assured me that the school's celebrations on victory Saturday were conducted with all the order and decorum that parents have a right to expect and there's no possibility whatsoever that any of the boys could have played truant.'

My stab of disappointment told me how much my instinctive dislike of young Peter Chivas had warped my judgement.

'At least, that was what he said when I first raised the subject. A couple of hours later, when we were sitting over a couple of mugs of beer a safe distance from the school, I got the real picture.'

'Which was?'

'Nothing terrible. Nothing you wouldn't expect at a boys' school on a celebration day. Discipline a bit lax, boys wandering into the town and not coming back till late, beer drinking in the studies and so on. When I put it to my friend – mentioning no names – that it was just in the realms of possibility that a senior boy might disappear all day or even all night without anyone knowing, he didn't disagree too strenuously. Of course, there'd be a roll-call at some point, but it's easy enough to answer for another person at a roll-call.'

'So he might have been here?'

'He might. On my way back, I made a few inquiries at Duxbury station, again mentioning no names. I got into conversation with the station master and introduced the subject of the Saturday night after the Armistice. As you'd expect, there were more people travelling than usual and they had a couple of men off sick with flu. So they wouldn't necessarily have noticed every passenger travelling between here and Shrewsbury.'

'I'd like to have a talk with Peter Chivas without Lucinda there.'

Bill took something out of his coat pocket clumsily, his hand gloved against the cold in the brewhouse. 'I've made another arrangement. I hope you approve.' He handed me a copy of a telegram form, dated from Shrewsbury the previous day, addressed to Mrs Lucinda Sollers, Whitehorn Hall. PLEASE COME TO KING'S HEAD WITH MR CHIVAS NINE PM MONDAY STOP BRAY.

'Can you manage the campaign without me tomor-

121

row, Nell? For her own sake, we have to shake her faith in that young man.'

I had an idea that I wasn't going to like it, but he'd earned the right to try things his way. When I left the King's Head after an early breakfast for a day of canvassing in Bennington he was deep in conversation with Mrs Hincham.

A full day of canvassing with Moira and her friends yielded eleven firm promises, four probables and thirteen possibles. If you think that's not much to show for a day's work, then you've never canvassed as an independent radical in a farming area. We were invited to stay for high tea by one of the Quaker families and stayed talking afterwards longer than I'd intended. It was after seven when we left and I had to keep the pony to a brisk trot to get back to Duxbury in time for whatever Bill was planning. I was trusted now with the driving of the trap. After the events of market day, young John had retired from active politics. I dropped Moira off by the forge, saw the pony settled to his supper and was hoping to get upstairs unobserved to wash and change when I was accosted in the passage from the back door by Mr Worm Powder of all people. He wished me a civil good evening and asked whether I'd had a good day. I hope I made some suitably polite reply but I was conscious that straw from the stables was clinging to the bottom of my skirt and my cheeks were glowing from the cold outside.

'I understand that you had some trouble on Friday with the notorious Mr Dobbs.'

He was still entirely civil, but there was something I didn't like about his tone. I said, not taking too much care to be polite, that it was the kind of thing that happened in elections.

'What exactly was the man saying to you?' There was an eagerness in his voice and the way he was standing that made it more than a casual question.

'Nothing of any consequence. Now, if you'll excuse me . . .' I sidestepped past him and escaped upstairs, fuming. I was still annoyed when I came down, washed and changed, to look for Bill. The snug was empty and Mrs Hincham told me that Mr Musgrave was in the big dining-room.

'He's been in there most of the day. Are you planning a sing-song?'

Cursing under my breath, I opened the door of the dining-room. It was as cavernous and empty as when I'd last seen it, apart from one corner where Bill was bent down, adjusting a rug. One of the round restaurant tables had been drawn up close to a paraffin stove that was producing more smell than warmth. There was a green baize cloth over the table and four chairs round it. A few yards from the table an old upright piano stood against the wall with its lid open. It took me a while to make all this out because only one of the electric globes on the wall had been switched on and that one had a table napkin draped over it.

'Bill, it's not a good idea.'

He straightened up and I noticed that his shoes were unlaced. 'It's the one thing I can think of that might convince her. It's more difficult than I expected. You have to give Chivas some credit for dexterity if nothing else. It wasn't a job for one hand, so I had to borrow young John. Luckily he was able to get hold of some bits of a Meccano set. I'm pretty sure that's how Chivas did it.'

He sat down in the chair nearest the piano and put his hands ostentatiously on the table, as Peter Chivas had done. There was some scrabbling at floor level.

'You have to slip your shoes off or you can't feel the levers with your toes. I'm afraid I'll have to stay sitting when our guests arrive. I suggest Mrs Sollers on my left, you on my right and Chivas opposite where I can see his face.'

I might have argued more, but I heard Mrs Hincham's voice and several sets of footsteps in the corridor.

'Will you go and bring them in, Nell?'

I went reluctantly. They were still in their outdoor coats and hats. Lucinda was tense and impatient, Peter Chivas affecting a world-weary air. As I opened the door he stood back to let her go first into the dining-room. When she saw what was inside she stopped dead on the threshold.

'Oh.'

At least Bill wasn't feigning a mediumistic trance. In his normal voice he asked her to come in. She hesitated for a moment and then walked slowly towards the table.

'What's happened? Why did . . . ?'

Chivas, who couldn't see past me into the room, sounded rattled. I signed to him to go in. He took a step, jibbed, looked as if he wanted to bolt.

'What is this?' His voice went high, jumping back a few years to when it was unbroken.

'An experiment,' Bill said. 'Would you please sit down?'

Peter glanced back at me, then at Lucinda. I think it

was still in his mind to bolt but that would have meant leaving her with us. 'Lucinda, don't have anything to do with them.'

She hesitated for a moment, but the lure of the open piano was too strong. 'It can't do any harm.'

'It won't work anywhere else, Lucinda. It will only work where he lived.'

'In that case,' Bill said, 'Mrs Sollers is right. Nothing will happen and this can't do any harm.'

He gestured to the chair on his left, inviting her to come and sit down. She went to it like somebody walking under water. Full of misgiving, I sat on his right while Peter stayed just inside the doorway, glaring at us.

'Of course, if Mr Chivas prefers not to take part . . .'

'Peter, please do it for us.'

She stretched out her black-gloved hand to him. There was pleading in the voice, but a touch of authority too, perhaps a reminder that she held the purse strings. Whether it was that or a reluctance to leave the game in Bill's hands he sat down, sulky and glaring, and planted his wide-brimmed hat on the green baize in front of him. Bill waited until he was well settled, then suggested we should sit quietly for a while and see what happened. The ordinary evening sounds of the public house seeped into the room, but seemed to come from a long way off, less loud than our breathing or Chivas' fingers drumming impatiently on the table.

'Peter dear, be quiet.'

He sighed, propped his elbow on the table and his chin in his hand.

Pum, pum, pum.

When the first low note sounded from the piano, the look he gave Bill was so furious that even in the circumstances I found it hard not to laugh. Bill's technique was less smooth than Chivas'. From where I was sitting I could see his leg moving. Chivas started to get to his feet, then stopped. I could understand his problem. He knew exactly what Bill was doing and could have exposed it by getting down on the floor and grabbing the lines that led under the rug to the foot levers. But to do that would have exposed his own act. Still, for a second I thought that was what he intended to do and would have respected him for taking a last stab at honesty. I think Bill had hoped as well that he might do that and the rest of the charade wouldn't be necessary. But after that Chivas sank down on the chair again and I gave him up as a lost cause. Lucinda had hardly noticed, staring raptly at the piano. I hated that part of it.

'Dearest? Is it you, dearest? We're listening.'

And, just as she'd done at home, she sang her way huskily up the scale. Haltingly, the piano echoed her, stumbling over a couple of notes. I decided that if Bill made it play Tumtum I'd get up and leave. There were limits.

Pum pum pum.

Silence all round and puzzlement on her face. Chivas was pretending not to take an interest, but his fingers were clenched tight against his jaw bone.

'Is it a message for me, dearest?'

Pum.

Bill managed to make it soft and unemphatic. With more practice he might have a career as a fraudulent medium.

'Not for me. For somebody else?'

126

Pum, more strongly.

'For Peter?'

Pum pum pum, fast and emphatic.

'What is it that you want to say to Peter?'

There was quite a long pause and Bill's thigh moved so perceptibly that even Lucinda might have noticed if her eyes weren't still on the piano. At last he got it to utter.

Fah pum Lah pum.

'F and L. Yes we understand.'

I'd been watching Lucinda but a thump on the table drew my attention back to Chivas. No pose of indifference now. The thump had been his hand hitting the table, leaving his unsupported jaw dropping. The piano laboured on, producing notes as slow and heavy as drops of treacle.

Fah pum Lah Soh pum Te pum.

'F,L,S,T. F something L S something Te something. Peter dear, does it mean anything to you?'

No answer, except another, louder thump and a hat dislodged rolling on to the floor. Peter Chivas had keeled over, eyes closed, head on the table, arm hanging down.

Later, when they'd gone, Bill and I debated whether his faint was real. I thought it was, on the grounds that a young man as vain as Peter Chivas would have kept his mouth closed and managed not to dribble on the green baize. Bill said he was cunning enough for anything and had a lot to lose. At the time though there were other worries. Lucinda, distraught, knelt on the floor beside him and kept begging him to talk to her. Bill hastily wedged his feet back into his shoes and went to the bar for brandy. I opened a window or two and loosened Peter's collar. Bill arrived back with Mrs Hincham and the brandy and Chivas spluttered and allowed himself to be brought round. The first thing he focused on was Bill bending over him with the glass. Like the fainting fit, the sweep of the arm that knocked the brandy all over Bill might or might not have been deliberate. The glare he gave him certainly was. Still, he said nothing as we got him to the Whitehorn Hall governess cart, waiting patiently with its driver in the yard. We bundled Chivas and his resentment into a travelling blanket and Bill insisted on going to see them safely home. I went to wait upstairs with my door ajar. It was close to midnight when I heard Bill coming upstairs and whispered to him to come into my room. He was still pleased with himself.

'Chivas pretended to be asleep all the way home. Exactly what I'd have done in his place.'

'What about her?'

'Very solicitous for him, shaken. I didn't leave until I'd seen her into the housekeeper's hands.'

'Did you have to do it that way? We knew it was bogus, but as far as she's concerned, it's the link with her husband.'

'Which the boy was exploiting quite ruthlessly. Would you want that for anyone?'

'No, but you might have let her down gently.'

'Nell, I am letting her down gently. If she wants to think it was her husband talking tonight, there's nothing to stop her. She'll let go of this link of hers when she's ready to. All I've done is to make it easier and safer. Look, if she's even an halfway intelligent woman, and I think she might be underneath it all, she'd have had her doubts sooner or later. The thing was to make that boy realise the game's up and he can't go on exploiting her.'

'That seems to have been successful at any rate.'

'It certainly was. I must admit, I'm pleased by my ingenuity. I'd have liked to say "Liar" or "Lies" but it wouldn't have worked with the letters we had to play with. Still, "Falsity" did very well.'

I stared at him. 'Was that what it was?'

'Of course.' He strummed with his fingers on the bed rail. 'Fah space Lah Soh space Te space. Falsity.' Then, seeing the look on my face, 'Well what in the world did you think I meant?'

Chapter Ten

The following morning, a Tuesday, with the election only four days away, Bill and I planned the day's campaigning over breakfast in the snug. The big event was my first indoor meeting at Duxbury in the evening. We settled that Bill would stay in town, put up more posters and check the hall while I took the pony cart and toured some of the villages between Duxbury and Bennington. While we were making our plans Mr Worm Powder, or Wilby, ate toast and marmalade and read his newspaper at a separate table. He finished before we did, wished us a good day and went out. Until then, the oddity of his question about Luke Dobbs the day before had gone out of my head. I told Bill about it and was surprised how seriously he took it.

'There's something wrong about that man, Nell. I don't think he's on leave at all. I think he's working.'

'What at?'

'Has it occurred to you that he might just be keeping an eye on you?'

'Because I was against conscription? But the war's over. None of that matters any more.'

'To the military mind, no war's over until they're getting ready for the next one. It will still matter a lot to some people. You must have made enemies.'

'Of course I did.' I could think of one in Wales in particular. 'But why go to the trouble of keeping me under observation in an election campaign I haven't a hope of winning?'

'It doesn't sound as if it makes sense, I agree. But then I've spent the last three years in the Army, so I don't expect things to make sense. Another thing, didn't it strike you that our Independent Liberal was surprisingly well informed about your anti-conscription career?'

'But he could have found that out from anywhere. I didn't make a secret of it.'

'I suppose they might even be interested in what I'm doing. I'm still a serving officer even if I am on the sick list.'

'If it's so bad that they've put a spy on us, you'd better go. I don't want to get you into trouble.'

'And blight my distinguished military career? Nell, I only have one ambition in the Army and that's to get out of it as soon as possible.'

I harnessed the pony and drove northwards out of town, over the river bridge and past the tannery. It was a breezy morning with the wintery brown grass of the pastureland still wet from overnight showers but the sun had come out and robins were shouting from bare hedges. The pony trotted along steadily, snorting occasionally at cattle over gates. Now and then, when I saw a ruined barn or a usefully placed tree I'd loop the reins over the cart rail, get out and put up a poster. By lunchtime we'd covered six villages and hamlets and were about ten miles from home. I'd brought sandwiches and a flask of tea with me, along with a net of hay for the pony, and we picnicked on a grass verge near a bridge over a stream with a line of pollarded willows along the bank. There were about two hours of daylight left and I looked at the map as I ate the last sandwich, working out how we could use them best. The answer seemed to be to take a loop south-westwards via Long Swinton, Little Swinton and King's Swinton then strike the main road back to Duxbury.

As we got nearer the Swintons it was obvious that the Independent Liberals had been there before me. Most of the best sites were flaunting their bright pink posters, PREST for PEACE, PROSPERITY, PROBITY. In rougher campaigns I'd have simply stuck mine over the top, but I was minding my manners in this one so we trotted past them and I tried not to get depressed. I delivered some leaflets in Long Swinton and got into an argument with a man of the squire variety, tied a poster to an oak tree beside the duck pond in Little Swinton and spent precious time discussing health insurance with a deaf old woman who, it turned out, didn't approve of all this voting. By the time we'd got that settled to our mutual dissatisfaction the sun was a red disc behind a copse of black trees and it was a race to get to King's Swinton before dusk. We struck a good patch of road and were going along it at a spanking trot when we saw the other cart.

It was facing us, a tradesman's delivery wagonette with no driver on the box, slewed diagonally across the road. Between the shafts a dark bay cob with a white blaze stood head-down, cropping the tough grass on the roadside verge. We slowed to a walk and halted a few yards away. The cob raised his head and snorted at us. I called 'hello'. I wasn't worried at first. Even my short time in Duxbury had taught me that local road manners were casual and horses used to waiting. For all I knew, the owner of the wagonette might be chatting with somebody in a field over the hedge. I called again and got no answer. Annoyed to be held up when time was short I knotted the reins and got down. The grass verge was wide and I thought if I could get the cob to move a few steps on to it there'd be room for us to drive past and no harm done. I went up to him and stroked his neck, put my hand on the rein – and heard a groan from the back of the wagonette. I dropped the rein and ran round, to be faced with another of those bright pink posters, PREST for PEACE, PROSPERITY, PROBITY. It was tied to the back rail of the wagonette. A lot of rolled-up posters were on a bench inside. Because of their bright colour they caught my eye a split second before the thing on the floor. Dark-trousered legs were uptilted towards the driver's box as if he'd fallen backwards, head wedged sideways on under a bench with only one large pale ear and an expanse of wet hair visible, upturned bowler hat on the floor beside him. There was a smell over everything, familiar but wrong for where we were. As I clambered in, taking care not to tread on him, the wagonette rocked and he groaned again. When I knelt I felt the sticky wetness of the floor even through the fabric of my skirt.

'I'll have to try to move you.'

Not easy. Before I could move his head from under the bench I had to open the door and get his legs sticking out to unwedge the rest of him. No sign of breakages there, at least. Once that was done, there was room to roll him over. I took off my coat and made a pillow for him, and he winced as his head came down on it. His ruddy face was grey, his eyes bleary and not focusing.

'Hit me. Hit me from behind.'

John Prest's voice was no more than a croak. The smell of rough country cider was over everything. It had soaked into his hair, his shirt, his jacket, slopped over the floor and benches. He was just about conscious enough to help me shift his legs back inside, so that I could get him flat on the floor of the wagonette. Looking for something to cover him, I found an old blanket stuffed under one of the benches. When I picked it up a heavy object clunked down on the road. It was a stoneware jar that would have held half a gallon of cider, quite empty. I put it back under the bench and considered what to do next. The sun was below the horizon, the temperature was dropping and there was no sign of any other human being. A signpost at a crossroads a few dozen yards away told me that we were two miles from King's Swinton, seven miles from Duxbury in the other direction. I thought about it for a while, then went back to my cart and persuaded the pony to draw it up on the verge and unharnessed him.

By the time I got back to the wagonette, Prest was unconscious again, or asleep. I took the cob by the bridle and managed to get him and the cart turned round, facing back to the crossroads. I collected my own pony and hitched him to the back left-hand side of Prest's wagonette, then got on the box and picked up the reins. The cob proved mercifully easy to drive. I'd decided to make for Duxbury because Prest needed medical help and I'd no idea what we'd find at King's Swinton. We turned left at the crossroads, went at a slow walk along what felt like an endless road between hedges, then right on the main road to Duxbury. I kept glancing down at Prest. He was snoring, mouth open, his head rocking from the motion of the wagonette. Occasionally he gave a little moan between the snores. It was dark by the time we were on the main road. I hadn't thought to light the lamps before we started and wasn't going to risk disturbing the arrangement by getting down, so just had to hope that anybody coming the other way saw us in time. An oncoming motor car swerved past us with a few inches to spare, tooting, but that was all.

We got safely to Duxbury, attracting some curious looks as we went up the High Street and turned into the yard of the King's Head. Young John was sweeping the yard and nearly dropped the broom when he saw me driving a strange horse and vehicle with his pony hitched on behind. Before he had a chance to see what was in the back I sent him running for Mrs Hincham. Bill must have been in the Committee Room because he appeared all of a sudden. He saw the back of the wagonette with the Liberal poster still on it, then his eyes travelled on to the pony and finally to me and his jaw dropped.

'For God's sake, Nell, you haven't captured the thing, have you?'

'Worse than that.'

I opened the door and let him see inside. The only light came from the lamp in the window of the Committee Room, but it was still enough to identify Duxbury's temperance candidate. The cider smell came billowing out.

'Nell, I don't believe it. You've gone and got him drunk. You can't just . . .'

135

I didn't know whether to be hurt or flattered that he thought I was capable of such low electioneering tactics.

'Drunk or not, he's had a terrible bang on the back of the head. I found him. He needs a doctor, but it's not fair to the man to let him be seen like this.' Mrs Hincham came out. Her face when she found her enemy insensible and cider-soaked on her premises was like Boadicea's counting Roman heads.

'The wicked old hypocrite.'

I tried to tell her that I wasn't sure what had happened, but she wasn't listening. The three of us got him inside and on to a sofa in her parlour and she sent young John running for a doctor. In the warm, Prest started coming round.

'. . . from behind . . . hid in the back and hit me.'

Bill said, 'His agent had better know about this. I'll go to his Committee Room.'

The agent and the doctor arrived in a dead heat. While the doctor was examining Prest we had a tense conversation outside the door in whispers. The Independent Liberal agent was a small grey-haired man, struck almost incoherent by what had happened. I gave him my account of finding Prest and bringing him home and he was still asking questions when the doctor came out.

'He's had a nasty knock on the back of the head. He should stay here tonight and take things very quietly for a day or two. I'll send—'

The door behind him crashed open and there was Prest filling the doorway, supporting himself with one hand against the frame. There was a bandage round his head and his eyes, although wild, were focusing. 'I'm not staying here. I've been brought to this place against my will.' He staggered a step or two and transferred his hand to his agent's shoulder. 'Take me home.'

The small man almost buckled under the weight, but they began to shuffle together towards the outside door. As he passed me, Prest glared into my face from a few inches away.

'You'll be hearing from us.'

From his tone, it wouldn't be a note saying thank you. The doctor tried to protest, but when it was obvious that Prest was determined he said he'd drive him home in the wagonette and all three of them went together. Mrs Hincham went back to the bar, and young John took the pony and said he'd ride out and recover the trap in the morning. That left Bill and me alone in the yard.

'It could have happened the way he said. Somebody might have knocked him out then poured cider all over him.'

'Who? If it wasn't us, then the only people who might want to do it would be the Tories. Is this supposed to be the wretched Tedder as well?'

'Hardly. Prest's no great threat to Tedder as far as the election's concerned, certainly not enough to risk sabotage.'

'A practical joke, then?'

'If it had been that wouldn't they have left him somewhere more obvious, like the town square? It could have been hours before anybody found him on that road, or even all night.'

'In which case he'd probably have died from exposure.'

We looked at each other and I knew we were thinking the same thing – that everybody standing for election in Duxbury had now been attacked. Charles Sollers was dead, John Prest might have been dead by morning and our campaign vehicle had been destroyed in a way that might have killed anybody who went too close. In comparison with that, the attack on the Tedders' conservatory was small beer, but looked like part of the pattern.

'It's as if somebody here hates anybody involved in politics.'

Bill said, 'A lot of people do.'

'Not murderously. One thing—'

I was going to say that if you followed this line, it weakened the case against Peter Chivas, but Bill looked at his watch and grabbed my arm.

'You're supposed to be addressing your meeting in forty minutes. You look as if you've been mucking out a stable and you smell like a cider press.'

Thirty-five minutes later, scrubbed, brushed and dressed in my best green suit, with rakish hat to match, I was walking into the Baptist hall with Bill at my side. The first person we saw, waiting in the little lobby, was the newspaper editor, Alexander Jones.

'What's this about Prest?'

Bill and I had decided on our line. I explained that I'd found Mr Prest while out canvassing. He'd clearly had an accident and I'd brought him home.

'According to his account, somebody hid under a blanket at the back of his wagonette and knocked him out with something, probably a flagon of cider, then poured cider all over him. As a matter of fact, he blames you.'

He was smiling, so I smiled too.

'I have an alibi.' A bad-tempered squire and a deaf old woman.

'Not you personally. He thinks you paid somebody to do it.'

'My election expenses don't run to bravos.'

Bill said, sharply, 'Anybody making those kind of allegations will find himself in serious trouble. It would be entirely against Miss Bray's character and principles.'

You'd never have guessed that an hour ago he'd suspected me himself. There was a low rumble of many voices coming from the other side of the door, the sound of feet shuffling and chairs scraping.

'It sounds as if you have a full house, Miss Bray.' Alexander Jones seemed quite unworried by Bill's severity. 'By the way, there was a man asking for you in the newspaper office this afternoon. He didn't know the town. When we told him you were having your meeting this evening he wanted directions to the hall.'

I thought of Mr Worm Powder.

'Military sort of man with sleek brown hair?'

'No, artistic-looking type, quite tall, untidy hair. Good luck.'

He slipped into the main hall. We followed and found Moira waiting inside the door. Although nervous of public speaking, she'd gamely agreed to introduce me. Bill would take the chair. As we settled ourselves on the platform I was pleased to see that the hall was packed and that Molly Davitt from the tannery was in the front row, with Annie on one side of her and Tabby on the other. She gave me a great grin and a thumbs-up sign. No sign of Lucinda Sollers, which was just as well. Bill glanced at Moira and me to see that we were ready, gave me an encouraging smile and stood up.

'Ladies and gentlemen, it's good to see so many of you here tonight . . .'

Not a bad meeting on the whole. Duxbury was showing its good political manners, with no hint of flying turnips. Although I knew very well that most of the people there wouldn't vote for me and had come to see the woman candidate in much the same spirit as they'd come to see a giraffe, they were prepared to give me a fair hearing. We allowed plenty of time for questions at the end, and though they were slow in coming at first, people grew in confidence and they soon flew thick and fast. Molly Davitt got to her feet and asked about jobs, voice harsh from nervousness. I could sense a rustle in the audience that one of the tannery women should have the nerve to stand up and talk in public, but it was a milestone of a kind. Compulsory schooling up to the age of fifteen wasn't popular and a farmer wanted to know where they'd get lads to work the land if they were all in school. The League of Nations made only slight progress. An old character from the middle of the hall made quite a speech saying that it might be alright as long as it didn't include the Germans (pause) or the French because you couldn't trust them (pause) or too many Americans (applause and laughter). Where we struck trouble, predictably, was on the subject of my activities in the war. Prest's outburst on market day had done its work and a few people in the audience seemed even to have convinced themselves that I'd been on the side of the Germans. I tried to meet it head on, explaining several times over that my stand had been against compulsory military service and the unnecessary prolonging of the fighting. However hard I tried, I could feel the meeting slipping away from me. There was a low muttering from parts of the audience, some timid hissing. I glanced at Bill and saw he was looking anxious. Then support came unexpectedly from the back of the room.

'As an officer who served in France . . .'

The muttering stopped. Heads turned to look at the tall man who'd stood up. It wasn't a local voice. He was in his mid-forties, but his hair was already mostly grey. A face full of intelligence, brown and lined. I knew with a shock who'd been asking for me at the newspaper office.

'As an officer who served in France, I'd like to say that quite a lot of the officers and men I met out there would have agreed with Miss Bray that the war should have ended sooner. It went on because of the criminal vanity of most politicians and some generals. Some people were brave enough to say so at the time, and Duxbury is fortunate to have the chance of electing one of them as its representative in parliament.'

That silenced everybody. It wasn't that they agreed with him and Duxbury had certainly given very little sign that it considered itself fortunate in having me. But there was something about the emphatic way he spoke and unexpectedness of the intervention, because nobody in Duxbury was likely to have set eyes on him before that evening, that made people drop their eyes and fidget, like a noisy classroom when a schoolteacher walks in. Even Bill was caught by surprise, but he recovered quickly, catching my eye in the silence and giving a questioning look. I nodded

141

and Bill got to his feet and rounded off the proceedings, thanking the gentleman who'd just spoken and all the other questioners, reminding them to vote Bray on Saturday.

As we came off the platform, most of the audience were walking out, quiet as from church. A few stayed to congratulate me and shake hands, even to offer help in the campaign, most of them friends of Moira or Molly. While this was going on the officer who'd served in France waited by the door and people kept glancing over their shoulders at him, wondering where he came from. I could see Bill was wondering too. When the caretaker arrived to switch off the lights and lock up and my group filed out, I made sure that Bill and I were the last to go and paused by the man at the door. I said, knowing that it almost certainly was not a good idea but seeing no alternative, 'Bill, I'd like you to meet David Ellward.'

Chapter Eleven

⊗

'Tell him to go away.'

Wednesday morning. In my Committee Room, with three days to go to the election, I was on the verge of quarrelling with my agent. Upstairs, in his own room at the King's Head, David Ellward was getting ready to fling himself into canvassing. The discovery the night before that the new arrival had booked into the same public house as we had was somewhere near the last straw for Bill. When they'd met again at breakfast he'd been barely polite.

'We haven't got so many helpers that I can drive them away,' I said. 'Besides, why should I? He's given up his leave to come and work for me.'

David had explained the night before, when the three of us were walking back to the King's Head from the Baptist hall, with Bill saying nothing and missing nothing. He was on leave because the training camp where he'd been posted was being run down. He'd seen my name on the list of people nominated in *The Times* and got free of other commitments as soon as he could to come and help.

'If he really wants to be helpful, he'll see he's an embarrassment and go. And if Wilby really is something to do with military intelligence, the last thing you need is another Army officer here. He'll think you're planning a mutiny.'

'I've no intention of letting Mr Worm Powder or anybody from Army intelligence dictate how I run my campaign. Besides, it would hurt David's feelings and he's had a bad time.'

'So has everybody else.'

I'd last seen David Ellward more than a year ago, at a hospital in Wales for the mental casualties of the war. He'd tried to walk away from it all and was lucky to have been sent to the hospital instead of being shot as a deserter. I'd explained that to Bill, and now I tried to be fair to him and not think that it was the reason for his resentment of David.

'I tried to help him. He's here because he sees it as returning a favour.' Which made both of them, I supposed.

'It won't help. Surely you can see that?'

'Why won't it?'

Bill heaved a sigh and started walking up and down the cold stone floor of the old brewhouse, talking at me as if I were one of his hostile witnesses.

'Nell, may I just remind you of some of our problems? The Conservative candidate thinks you're in a plot to slander him. The Liberal thinks you had him coshed and pickled in cider. Half the town has doubts about your patriotism and probably more than half is convinced that you and I are living openly together as lovers. Would you say that's a fair summary so far?'

'So far, yes.'

'Thank you. Wouldn't you say that in the circumstances the last thing you need is the appearance of another . . . man from your past?'

'Were you going to say "another lover"?'

Late the night before, when I'd been explaining David to Bill, I'd told him that a long time ago – years before the war and before I even knew of Bill's existence – David and I had been lovers. It had been for one short summer – almost as short as the one Bill and I had had together – and since then David had married somebody else and parted from her. When we'd met again in Wales it wasn't in circumstances that encouraged the revival of a long-dead love affair.

'No, but that's what Duxbury will say. If the news of the mysterious stranger riding to your rescue isn't round the town already, it soon will be.'

'He did *not* ride to my rescue. I'd have managed perfectly well without David.'

'That's not what he thinks.'

'I don't care what he thinks. He's come here to help and I'm very grateful. You said yourself that we couldn't get round all the villages before Saturday.'

'He can't take the pony cart. You'll need that.'

'He'll walk. He's a great walker.'

The brewhouse door scraped open and in came David. By daylight he looked better than when I'd last seen him at the hospital. He was still thin and vibrating almost visibly with impatience and nervous energy, but he'd been like that even before the war. His dark eyes were less sunken but still restless, not staying on anything for long. He was wearing a new-looking brown woollen overcoat, a brown felt hat, tweed breeches and walking boots and he carried an empty haversack.

'Ready for orders, ma'am, sir.'

He looked from me to Bill and back. I'd explained David to Bill but had seen no reason to explain Bill to

David, beyond that he was both friend and agent. Somebody as sensitive to his surroundings as David must have sensed Bill's hostility, but he didn't react to it. I showed him the map and suggested that he might take some leaflets and posters to King's Swinton, the village I'd been hoping to get to before I had to rescue Prest. He took a long look at the map, tucked leaflets and some rolled up posters into his haversack and went swinging out as if a twenty-mile round walk on a grey December day was exactly what he'd planned to do with his leave. Bill watched him go and heaved another sigh.

'At least it gets him out of town.'

Bill was supposed to stay in the Committee Room, to deal with any inquiries and catch up with the correspondence. A surprising number of letters were arriving already and were piled on a table waiting for answers. I picked up one of them at random, straggling capitals in mauve indelible pencil on rough lined paper. WHORE AND TRAITOR GET BACK WHERE YOU COME FROM. WE DONT WANT YOU. No signature, of course.

'At least he can spell whore. Are there many like this?'

'Not many. Most of them are quite sane.'

Bill was ill at ease. I wondered if he'd have shown me the letter if I hadn't happened to pick it up. It struck me again that I'd been wrong to pull him into this so lightly, because he hadn't had time to grow the extra skin that years of political campaigning give you.

'Don't let them worry you. You always get a few of those.'

He'd been sitting down sorting through the post in an abstracted way. Now he put down his handful of letters.

'I think I'd better come with you today.'

'Why? We agreed you'd be more use here.'

'It's not just the white knight charging in who's concerned about you. Haven't I got a right to worry as well?'

'Bill, you surely don't think—'

But he went on as if I hadn't spoken. It wasn't often that Bill got wound up and angry, but when he did he was unstoppable.

'You know what's happening here – what we talked about last night. So when I see letters like this I can't just dismiss them as from some crank. I look at them and wonder if the person who wrote them had anything to do with what happened – and if so what he's planning next. Then I'm supposed to be happy at the idea of you wandering round the countryside on your own?'

'It's not wandering. If I'm not allowed out on my own, I can hardly put myself up as their prospective MP.'

'That's all very well as a gesture, but we've had one man killed, another injured and the person or people who did it are still out there.'

'If anybody's in danger today it's David Ellward. We've sent him out to King's Swinton and that's where the latest attack happened.'

'Ellward can look after himself. It's you I'm worried about.'

I won in the end. Bill was far from happy but stayed where an agent should be, in the Committee Room. I left him bent over the piles of letters with a guilty feeling that he was giving a lot and getting very little. After the election I'd try to be more generous, except in mid-campaign it's always difficult to believe in the existence of a world on the other side of polling day, just as people who've been at sea for a long time don't quite believe in the possibility of land. I spent the morning in Duxbury, canvassing and calling on people who'd shown interest at the meeting the night before.

Around lunchtime I was at a house on the far side of the river and as I walked back it struck me that the tannery workers would be taking their break. In spite of the cold, they were there in the muddy yard outside the red brick barn, standing in little groups. Somebody had tied one of my posters to the wooden fence round the yard but it had been ripped away, with only a ragged corner left. Molly was with a group of other women but came over when she saw me looking at it.

'I tried, but the manager came out and tore it down.'

'Please don't get into trouble for me. I don't want you to lose your job.'

She took a long pull on her cigarette. 'Not much odds. I'll be losing it anyway when the boys come back. You don't know anybody with three hundred pounds to spare, do you?'

'Nobody who'd part with it. Why?'

'Me and some of the other women have got this idea of setting up on our own, making belts and bags, like this.'

Her brown coat was secured round her with a broad leather belt like a man's. She undid the buckle, opened the coat and showed me a finer belt round her waist, green leather embossed with a pattern of ivy leaves.

'We got one of the old men to teach us. We reckon if we had enough to rent a workshop and buy some leather and second-hand tools we could make a go of it.'

She unbuckled the belt and handed it over. It was beautiful work and supple as a live snake.

'Keep it, if you like. For good luck.'

I tried to protest, but she took it out of my hands and stuffed it into my bag.

'You're trying to do something for us, we know that.'

I noticed Annie standing on the other side of the yard with some of the younger women, and asked how she was. Molly made a disgusted face.

'She's driving me mad. She stays out all hours – Mum and I never know when she's coming back – and she's seeing that Luke Dobbs. He's no good for her. I've told her that, but she takes no more notice of me than a stone on the path.'

I said that perhaps she spent time with Luke because he'd been her brother's and fiancé's friend.

'Then why's she just taken up with him now? He's been back here since the summer and she didn't take any notice of him. It's only these last few weeks.'

'Since the Armistice?'

'Yes. I don't know why, but it seems to have done something to her. And another thing.' She glanced round to see that nobody could hear us and lowered her voice. 'She's stealing money, and I'm sure it's to give Luke Dobbs for drink. Until these last few weeks she was that honest, you could leave a five-pound note on a table and she wouldn't even look at it. But there was some money my mum left out for the funeral club man that I know she must have taken and the girls here have been missing bits of change out of their pockets. Nobody's accused her yet, but they will if this goes on. I'm being driven out of my mind over it.'

149

We both looked across the yard at Annie. One of the girls in her group must have made a joke because the rest were laughing, but she wasn't.

Molly said, 'Would you have a talk to her?'

'Why should she listen to an outsider like me if she won't to you?'

'It might shake her up a bit.'

'I should think she's had more than enough shaking. By the way, did her fiancé Simon Whittern used to work for Mr Sollers?'

'That's right. Cattle man.'

'Somebody told me that Mr Sollers could have kept Simon and Luke out of the Army if he'd signed them up as essential agricultural workers.'

'Yes, but that's true of half the men round here. Only the unlucky ones had to go.'

'Did Annie resent that?'

'If so she's never said anything.'

The others had started trailing back into work. Molly said she'd better go while she still had a job, took a long drag on her cigarette and followed them, promising to be at my eve-of-poll meeting on Friday.

I missed seeing Bill at lunchtime because I had to drive the pony trap over to Bennington in a hurry, where I was booked to address a meeting of women voters at the house of my suffragette supporters. A few wanted to talk about policies but touchingly a lot of them, especially the older ones, wanted guidance on this business of voting. Were people looking at you when you did it? Did you have to say anything out loud? One of them even asked if you were expected to tip the polling clerk. I stayed for a cup of tea and by the time I turned the pony for home the sun was setting in the clouds over the Black

Mountains to the west, making a barrier of purple and gold between England and Wales. We got lost for a while among winding roads and crossroads without signposts but found our way to the main road back to Duxbury by dusk. About three miles out of town I saw a tall figure, striding along ahead of us, drew alongside him and reined in the trap.

'Unless you insist on walking back to town.'

David Ellward sketched me a mock salute and stepped in, swinging his empty haversack from his shoulder.

'Should I report that King's Swinton is solid for Bray?'

'Not if you want me to believe you. Did you have a good day?'

'A very invigorating one as it happens. I'd no idea country canvassing could be so lively.'

I couldn't see his face, because I was concentrating on the road and he was on the bench behind me, but the tone of his voice told me that he'd been up to something.

'You haven't been fighting, have you?'

'It didn't come to that, although I almost hoped it might. Did you know they'd set a spy on us?'

I dropped a rein and grabbed for it. 'What happened?'

'I'd been walking around King's Swinton for an hour or so spreading the good word, then this man appeared on a bicycle – soft cap, waterproof rolled up on the handlebars, map, binoculars round his neck – for all the world like someone taking a cycling holiday, except who in his right senses would do it in the middle of December? He pulled up beside me, said good morning and did I happen to know the way to World's End Farm. He didn't recognise me but I recognised him. He was standing talking to the landlady when I came down to breakfast.'

I asked, over my shoulder, what he looked like.

'Superior commercial traveller, slicked down hair. You must have noticed him.'

'Mr Worm Powder.'

'I beg your pardon?'

'That's what I call him. His name's Wilby. Bill thinks he's a spy as well.'

A prickly little silence, then, 'It's obvious enough. Anyway, I think I spoilt his day for him. As it happens, I did know where World's End Farm was, not far away from King's Swinton. I'd already been there on your behalf and got chased off by an old harridan in a man's overcoat with two snappy sheepdogs. I shouldn't count on her vote.'

'If he had a map, why did he ask you for directions?'

'Two possibilities. One that he can't read a map very well, two that he wanted to get into conversation with me.'

'What did you tell him?'

'I was frank and candid as always – told him I was from Cambridge University studying small hibernatory mammals.'

'With a haversack full of election posters?'

'Then I pointed to the most distant farmhouse I could see, at the top of a hill, and assured him it was World's End Farm. Since he'd asked me for directions he had to pedal off to it, though I could see he had his suspicions. That was the last I saw of him for a couple of hours, then later on I saw his bicycle parked against a tree on a muddy track that leads down to the real World's End Farm, so he must have found his way there in spite of my help. No sign of the man himself, until I saw a fresh lot of footprints and tracked them through a gate and along a hedge. Where do you think I found him?'

'Couldn't guess,' I said, hoping the answer wasn't dead in a ditch.

'Halfway up an oak tree, scanning the countryside through binoculars.'

'For you?'

'I suppose so. When I shouted hello to him he damn nearly fell out of his tree. I said to let me know if he found any hibernating dormice up there and he gave me a sickly sort of smile. I did a circuit of a few fields to keep him guessing then got back to the road near where he'd left his bicycle. It seemed a pity to leave it there so I rode it a few miles nearer home for him, propped it against a gate and tied one of your posters to it to cheer him up when he found it. Good day's work, don't you think?'

I didn't. All he'd managed to do was to give our spy – if he was that – a personal grudge to fuel his work and added bicycle theft to my list of campaign sins. I said nothing, pretending to concentrate on the driving although the pony knew the way home on its own. Over my shoulder I was aware of the scrape and flare of a match as he lit a cigarette and a smell of sharp, cheap tobacco, soldiers' taste.

'What are you doing here, Nell?'

'Fighting an election.'

I'd decided, for the time being at least, not to tell him about Sollers' death. To talk about my detective activities could open up too many memories from when we'd last met and I knew that his pretence of light-heartedness was as thin as burned skin.

'Why in this place? Did your agent choose it?'

'I chose it. Bill Musgrave got leave to work with me.'

'Ah, yes, our happy warrior. I suppose he'd be in favour of shooting attempted deserters like me.'

In civilian life, David too had been a barrister. I shouldn't have risen to the bait, but I did.

'He's not a happy warrior. He'd probably have been trying to save your life.'

'Very decent of him. Known him long?'

'Five years.' Four of them war and absence.

'What are you going to do when this is over, Nell?'

'Earn a living. Will you go back to law?'

'No.' Very emphatic. 'Couldn't take it seriously. I'd sit there in court laughing at the judge and the whole bloody charade.'

'What will you do then?'

'I don't know. Maybe go to Italy and learn to make violins. Is this Musgrave fellow musical?'

'He likes Richard Strauss and plays the piano very badly.' Even when he wasn't trying to do it with his feet. David, on the other hand, played the piano better than anybody I knew.

'I've got some money saved up. Funny thing, the Army. They thought I was crazy and shut me up in a hospital, but they went on paying me. We could live for a long time in Italy on that.'

I pretended to ignore the 'we'.

'A hut in the olive groves smelling of herbs and violin varnish, bread and wine and mushrooms in the autumn, a path down to the sea.'

'Last time it was going to be a cottage in the Welsh hills and goats' cheese.' I suppose he'd got me off balance after all, because I hadn't intended to say it.

There was a hurt silence in the back of the cart then three words. '*Après la guerre.*' Then more silence for the rest of the journey.

Chapter Twelve

A t breakfast, Bill was still moaning to me about what David had done. 'It was a schoolboy trick. Whatever the man is, there was no point in annoying him unnecessarily.'

David Ellward wasn't there. I'd got up early and found from Mrs Hincham that he'd left even earlier, while it was still dark, after no more than a cup of tea and a slice of bread and butter. He'd been in stock-inged feet when she saw him, with walking boots and haversack waiting by the door, so we assumed he'd gone out to deliver more leaflets. The atmosphere over dinner the night before had been strained. Even before he heard the story of Mr Worm Powder and his bicycle, Bill hadn't been pleased to see David driving back in the pony cart with me and David made things worse by going into one of his sociable acts, talking almost non-stop about music and travelling and the idiocies of Army life, pausing now and then for my response but never for Bill's. In the face of this, Bill retreated into an act of his own, the no-nonsense Northern circuit barrister. If he'd wanted to he could have capped most of David's travel and Army stories with at least as good ones of his own, but he'd declined the game and sat there tearing bread to pieces and staring at Mrs Hincham's unremarkable

hunting prints on the wall as if they were maps of a
better world with no David Ellwards in it.

At least this morning it was down to business again,
with the eve-of-poll meeting to organise. The form was
that the candidates should have these at different times,
so that the seriously politically inclined could go to them
all. The Conservatives, traditionally, had the Corn
Exchange at seven o'clock, the Liberals the Methodist
hall at eight. That left us, as the newcomers, with the
Baptist hall at nine. We'd sent in an advertisement for
the *Duxbury Chronicle* and Bill was just reminding me
that we must look in at the newspaper office before
midday to check the proof when young John came in
with a letter for me, delivered by hand. Mrs Sollers'
mauve stationery. I read it and passed it to Bill.

Dear Miss Bray,
I should be grateful if you and Mr Musgrave would
kindly come and see me as soon as possible.
                    Yours sincerely,
                    Lucinda Sollers

More of a command than an invitation.

'We'd better go this morning and get it out of the
way. I suppose it's about young Chivas.'

Bill agreed reluctantly and said he'd been hoping
for a word with Mr Worm Powder, who hadn't
appeared for breakfast yet.

'Whatever for?'

'Somebody's got to apologise, and Ellward's clearly
not going to do it.'

'Apologise!'

'Yes. Let's assume that the man is what we think he
is. If so, we've nothing to gain by going out of our way

to annoy him. He's been given a stupid job to do, but that's not his fault.'

'Only doing his duty?'

'Yes. We don't have to like the man, but there are only two more days of this to go and I'd like to get through it without any more dramas.'

I had to admit it was reasonable but couldn't trust myself to be polite to the man, so I said he could wait for him in the snug while I went up to get my hat and coat. When I came down again Mrs Hincham was clearing away our breakfast things and Mr Worm Powder still hadn't appeared. It was odd, she said, because he was usually as regular as clockwork, but she supposed he'd come back late because he wasn't in for dinner the night before.

Mrs Sollers was waiting just inside her front door, in a dark dress and paisley shawl. The skin of her face seemed to be dragged taut by the violet pouches under her eyes and she looked even more strained than the last time I'd seen her. Once she'd got us settled in the drawing-room she sat with her great dark eyes on us as if she expected to communicate by telepathy about why she wanted us there so urgently. When she did at last manage to get words out they came as a surprise.

'It's about the meetings tomorrow night.'

I wished she hadn't remembered them. As my nominator and sponsor, Lucinda was entitled to a place on my platform, even the right to speak if she wanted it. But the last thing I needed in an already turbulent campaign were public accusations against Jonas Tedder. Bill, with the same thing in mind, said she didn't have to impose that strain on herself.

157

'I think I have to be there – to set things right.'

Bill rolled his eyes to the ceiling, past caring whether he offended her or not. I hoped we could at least confine her to a non-speaking role.

'You don't have to make a speech.'

'Oh no, I shan't. Felicity says it will be quite enough to be there on the platform with them.'

'Felicity! Felicity Tedder?'

She nodded. 'I went to see Mrs Tedder yesterday evening. We agreed that it was only right for me to show public support of Jonas. Charles would have wanted it.'

It wasn't often that Bill and I ran out of words simultaneously, but it happened this time. Bill recovered first.

'So two days before the polls open, you're transferring your support to one of Miss Bray's opponents?'

She ignored him and appealed to me. 'Oh no, I shan't say a word against you. Some of your ideas are really very good, mothers and hospitals and peace and that sort of thing. But I want to be fair to them as well, you see.'

I said, 'Do I take it from this that you no longer suspect Jonas Tedder of killing your husband?'

She hung her head and said, almost inaudibly, 'No. No I don't.'

'What's changed your mind?'

'I've been thinking about it. It . . . must have been an accident.'

'And that's what you told Felicity Tedder?'

'Yes.'

'What did she say?'

'She was . . . glad, I think.'

158

Of all the words not being said there were two beating around in my head like a moth in a lampshade. Peter Chivas, Peter Chivas, Peter Chivas.

'And how is young Mr Chivas this morning?' Bill said, scooping up the moth and letting it fly.

'He's . . . out riding his new motor bicycle.'

'When did he get that?'

'Yesterday. He wanted it so much. Mr Rees thinks I'm wrong, but . . .' Her voice trailed away.

'Peter's recovered from Monday night, then?' Bill made no effort to hide his contempt and it was that she answered, rather than his question.

'He really does have a gift. I know you don't believe it, but he always has even as a small boy. He says his mother and father used to come through to him when he was in his bedroom, just after they were killed.'

'How?'

'Tappings. He had a governess then. She was scared and gave in her notice.' A sad small boy, both parents dead, creating them again out of bedroom creakings. Or a small boy, already manipulating adults, getting rid of an annoying governess. Perhaps both.

I said, 'Who first suggested that you might try to make contact with Charles, you or Peter?'

'I did. He didn't want to at first. It was my fault. I shouldn't have pressed him.'

It was the nearest she came, probably the nearest she could ever come, to admitting that she knew now about the fakery. She turned her face to me, so full of distress and appeal for understanding that I had to give something to her.

'Mrs Sollers, I accept what you're saying. I'm grateful to you for giving me a chance to stand here and I don't think I'm wasting your money.'

In this election, perhaps I was, but there'd be other elections and other women who might find things a little easier than if it hadn't happened at all. No point in saying that to her. All she wanted was understanding and, judging by her tremulous smile, she thought she'd got that from me. She rubbed her hands over her eyes, offered coffee and went to find the housekeeper.

Bill said, 'I'm surprised you didn't strangle her.'

'Why? It's not going to make much difference, her appearing on Tedder's platform. He'd have won anyway. There's even a sort of justice in it. He's had to live with her calling him a murderer. The question is, what made her change her mind?'

Lucinda came back, still tremulous. We might have lifted some of the load from her, but it was obvious that things were still far from right. When the coffee arrived her hand shook as she poured and dark drops spattered on the tray cloth. I waited until the job was done before asking a question that had been nagging at me.

'Do you know a man named Luke Dobbs? Local man, wounded in the head and invalided out of the Army.'

'A little. He worked with the cattle.'

'And there was another man named Simon Whittern. He was killed.'

She nodded.

'Luke Dobbs seems to think your husband could have saved them from having to go into the Army. Do you remember any discussion about that at the time?'

'No. I left all the things about the farm to Charles. But he was a very patriotic man. I remember him saying it was an employer's duty to see that his men went to fight.'

160

'After Simon Whittern was posted as missing and Luke Dobbs was wounded, did Mr Sollers receive any threatening letters, or anything else that might have been a threat?'

She shook her head. 'I didn't go through his mail. I don't think so.'

'He never said anything about it?'

'No.' Then, urgently, as if she'd only just understood the drift of my questions, 'Anyway, I don't want to think about all that. I don't need to. It was an accident.'

We finished our coffee and went. We were driving back up the track when we heard a roaring sound coming towards us. I just had time to get the pony and trap into a gateway when a motor bicycle came skittering past, going far too fast and bouncing almost out of control on the rutted track. I only got a glimpse of the rider because even the usually quiet pony found it too much for his nerves and was showing signs of wanting to clamber over the gate and take us and the trap with him. There was a flash of dark hair under a cap, eyes that were either angry or terrified, a mouth wide open yelling something inaudible above the noise of the engine. When it had gone past and the pony was back under control Bill said, 'He hasn't wasted any time.'

'She thinks he did it?'

'She knows he lied to her. She's not letting herself think any further than that.'

'We can't leave it like this.'

'You could, if you wanted to. Take the campaign expenses and forget it.'

I manoeuvred the pony and trap out of the gateway and back on to the track. The motorcycle tyres had slashed a wavering trail in the red mud.

'But can I leave it? If the police satisfy themselves that the explosive couldn't have been in the firework when it left the factory, they'll have to go on asking questions.'

'Their job, not yours.'

And yet I had the feeling he was just putting a case, waiting to see what I'd say.

'Meanwhile,' I said, 'she's at the mercy of a young man who's certainly a cheat and may be a murderer.'

'She'll probably be safe enough – as long as she gives him what he wants. She'd pretend it never happened, let the ivy grow over it.' The wheels rolled on up the track, squishing in the mud. 'That's assuming he did it.'

Still waiting. He was good at that.

'I wonder why it was Felicity Tedder she went to see rather than Jonas.'

'Easier to talk to a woman, I suppose. I'd like to have heard what was said.'

'Why go at all? Why the public climb-down?'

'Perhaps the Tedders insisted.' In the end, even Bill's patience gave out and he put the question direct. 'Well, did he do it?'

'I don't know. Two days ago I'd have been almost sure, but . . .' Annie Carter, staying out all hours, behaving oddly since the Armistice. Luke Dobbs, glaring out of his damaged eye. A bull in a field, dead and mangled.

'But?'

'Now I only hope he did.'

'Hope he *did*?'

'Because the alternatives are worse.' Because Peter Chivas was clever, horribly so. The police might suspect him, but they'd never find proof. And

162

Lucinda would be safe, probably, as long as she let the ivy grow.

When we got back to the road he took the reins from me – the elbow no problem now the pony was its usual quiet self – and drove while I talked. At the end of it, he said, over his shoulder, 'Dobbs, then?'

'He blamed Sollers for Simon dying.'

'Enough to risk his neck for? Though I admit I've thought all along it would be a soldier's crime.'

'If so, I don't want anything else to do with it. Why should I help the police hang somebody who's probably suffered more than Sollers ever did in his life?'

'We've got there, then? Do nothing. Forget it.'

'You disapprove?' I wished I could see his face.

'Not my business to approve or disapprove. I'm your election agent, not your conscience.'

'You're a lot more than that.'

He looked round at me. 'Am I? Am I really?' Then turned back to the driving again.

On the outskirts of the town, it was a relief to both of us to find we had an election panic, with the church clock striking twelve and the advertisement due to go to press within seconds. Bill stirred up the pony to a trot, zig-zagged up the main street past tradesman's carts and into the square. We found a boy to hold the trap and ran into the *Duxbury Chronicle* office where the editor, Alexander Jones, was waiting. He told us the the under-the-counter bookmaker at the Three Tuns still had Tedder as a certainty. While I was trying to get him to reveal my starting price (around two thousand to one, at a guess) the lad who seemed to combine the jobs of messenger, printer's devil and apprentice reporter came out to the front office with a wet page proof. Alexander Jones apologised to us and spread it over the counter to check, explaining that the presses were waiting. Out of habit, I read it upside-down and noticed a paragraph about Luke Dobbs' appearance in court on the drunk and disorderly charge. I mentioned it when Alexander Jones had finished checking.

'I heard about your argument with him. Waste of time trying to canvass Luke Dobbs. If they want him to vote they'll have to put beer pumps on the ballot box. He was lucky to get off with a fine. This was the second time in a month. He drank such a skinful the Thursday the war ended that they had to keep him in prison over the weekend until he was sober enough to stand up in front of the magistrates on the Monday. Naturally, they weren't going to be hard on a wounded ex-soldier having a patriotic drink or two so they let him off with a warning. The trouble is, he doesn't seem to have stopped since.'

He mistook the impression on my face. 'I shouldn't worry about Luke Dobbs too much. He was a bit of a wild lad even before they took him into the Army.'

Bill and I walked slowly back to the pony cart.

'What's wrong?'

'Charles Sollers didn't bring those fireworks home until Thursday evening. By that time, Dobbs must have been well on the way to being drunk and he was in prison till Monday morning. Sollers was dead by then.'

'So that looks like Dobbs out of it.'

Leaving at least one possibility I didn't want to think about. I tried to shake it off.

'We've got an election to fight. Where next?'

I'd managed to get out of the editor the fact that the man at the Three Tuns was offering attractive odds against my getting more than a thousand votes and I'd given his assistant ten shillings to put on for me. We threw ourselves into it that afternoon, travelling mile after mile of country roads in the pony cart or on foot, knocking on doors in the town until well after dark, when the drizzle was coming down and smells of stews or sizzling bacon came in warm gusts out of doorways. It was nine o'clock by the time we were back in the snug at the King's Head, too tired to do more than pick at sandwiches and sip whisky and water, and I still had my speech for the eve-of-poll meeting to write.

David arrived soon after we got back and even he admitted to tiredness. He'd covered more than thirty miles on foot around villages in the south of the constituency and used up the last of his stock of leaflets. He ate a sandwich then stretched his stock-inged feet to the fire and lay back in the chair, his fingers moving a little, and I guessed that he was playing through a piece of music in his mind. He did that when he wanted to make himself calm. Bill seemed to have accepted that David was with us until polling day and called a truce, although neither of them said much to the other.

We were still all three of us in the snug, David with his eyes closed, Bill checking the list of people who'd promised to vote for us and I making some notes for the speech when we heard Mrs Hincham's voice in the corridor and the heavy tread of official feet. She showed in a weary-looking police constable in a waterproof cape, the same man who'd moved me on in the square. He gave a longing look at the applewood fire and the glasses of whisky and water, but stuck to his duty.

'Miss Bray, I've brought your bicycle back.'

'My bicycle?' As far as I knew, it was in Hampstead.

'A lad found it leaning on a gate with your poster tied to it. He said it had been there all day and he was worried in case there'd been an accident.'

David hadn't stirred when the constable came in, but now his eyes were open.

Bill said, 'Where did he find it?'

'Just off the main road, on the turning for King's Swinton.'

'Where is it now?'

'Out in the yard here. I rode it over.'

Bill and I stood up, but David stayed where he was until Bill said sharply that he'd better come and look at it too. The constable, Mrs Hincham and the three of us filed out into the yard where the bicycle was propped against the wall in the light from the door. My poster was still tied to the crossbar, creased and damp.

'Yes, it's the one.' David seemed unconcerned, talking to the constable in an officer to other ranks tone of voice.

'Yours, sir?'

'No, not mine. It belongs to a man who's staying here.' He appealed to Mrs Hincham, 'What's his name?'

'Mr Wilby.'

'What's this poster doing on it, then?'

David said, as if it were the most natural thing in the world, 'I met him out King's Swinton way yesterday and borrowed his bicycle. I left it in the gateway where I thought he'd be bound to find it.'

'Did he know you were borrowing it, sir?'

166

'No, but he was up a tree at the time, so I didn't think he'd need it for a while.'

The constable stared, not knowing what to make of him. I thought it was time to take a hand and suggested that since the owner of the bike was staying at the King's Head we should simply go up to his room and let him know it had found its way back.

'Mr Wilby isn't in yet,' Mrs Hincham said. There was the beginning of anxiety in her voice.

'When did he go out?'

'I don't know. He hadn't come down to breakfast this morning by the time I had to go out. I'll go and ask one of the girls.'

We stepped back into the warmth of the passage-way while she disappeared into the kitchens. She was back in a few minutes, looking worried.

'The girls say he never came down to breakfast at all. We don't know what time he got in last night, because I leave the side door open for the guests.'

'So when was the last time anybody saw him?' Bill's question came so sharply that we all turned to look at him, the constable included.

Mrs Hincham said, 'Breakfast time yesterday, then he went out.'

'And you saw him yesterday, sir, near King's Swinton?'

'That's right.' David was still trying to sound relaxed about it, but not succeeding.

'Up a tree, you say?'

'Up a tree with binoculars.'

'About what time was that, sir?'

'It must have been between two and three o'clock in the afternoon.'

'And nobody's seen him since?'

The constable looked from face to face and got headshakes all round. Mrs Hincham suggested, not hopefully, that he might have come in by the side door and gone straight to his room. We filed upstairs, heads turning in the bar and the noise level dropping at the sight of the police constable, to the second floor. Mrs Hincham knocked on the door at the end of the passage.

'Mr Wilby.'

After knocking again she turned the door handle and went in, the constable behind her and the rest of us watching from the landing. The small room was empty. There was a pair of slippers lined up neatly under the bed beside the bedpan, an empty case on the floor, a jacket hanging in the wardrobe. No hat, no outdoor shoes, no overcoat.

'He's not come back,' she said.

Chapter Thirteen

The last day of campaigning was a Friday the thirteenth, as it happened, and if I didn't worry about the missing Mr Wilby as much as I should have, that's because the end of the election goes by in a blur, with only the odd event standing out clearly. A married friend once told me that she had no real memory of the days leading up to the wedding ceremony until she found herself in front of the clergyman with a congregation waiting on the edge of its pews to hear her answer the question. I wasn't in quite such a bad state. For instance, I remember the market square that morning. With only twelve days to go to Christmas there were great bunches of holly and mistletoe hanging from the vegetable stalls. Good county for mistletoe, someone told me, because of all the apple orchards. By then I'd have come up with a policy on mistletoe if somebody wanted one.

If the market crowds were hoping for a second clash between me and John Prest they were disappointed. The police had let us know that they had a lot on their hands and one market day riot was the ration for this election. So the two agents, who got on better than Prest and I did, had arranged things so that we spoke at different times. The glare Prest gave me as he left and my party arrived showed he still blamed me for the cider incident. There were things I wanted to ask him about that, but it would have to wait until after polling day. Then, when the light faded and the market carts had rolled back to the remote villages, it was time for the eve-of-poll rallies. Bill, David and I watched from an upstairs window as the cavalcade of Conservative motor cars came up the High Street and turned right for the Corn Exchange. There were half a dozen of them, driving slowly bumper to bumper, with headlights blazing and hoods down, the bonnets and backs of the cars covered with Tedder election posters and looped with blue ribbons. People lined the pavements to watch, and there were a few cheers. Jonas Tedder stood uneasily upright beside the driver of the second car, raising his bowler hat up and down to the cheers like a clockwork figure that will soon need winding up. Two women sat in the rear seats, illuminated by the headlamps of the car following. One of them was Felicity Tedder, thinly gracious in dark blue with fur collar and cuffs, distributing almost regal handwaves like halfpennies to deserving beggars. The other didn't wave. Her face was pale under her purple toque hat, gloved hands clasped in the lap of her coat.

'Is that the widow?' David said.

I glanced at him and knew that he'd heard or had guessed a lot, including the answer to the question, why Duxbury? An hour later we got up from dinner to see the Liberal procession go past. This was a livelier affair, with a small brass and accordion band in front, a motor car containing John Prest, smiling for once, and a train of followers on foot carrying wax torches. Insults were flying between them and some of the crowd, then the window of the public bar opened, and

Mrs Hincham's regulars chanted in unison something about not taking the beer from the lips of the working man. Prest ignored them but the two constables escorting the march looked anxious and tried to hurry it along. I guessed that the demands of election duty were one of the reasons why the search for Mr Wilby hadn't been very energetic so far. At various points during the day when we saw Mrs Hincham or the usual constable we'd ask, 'Any sign of him?' and get a shake of the head. But, after all, it was no more than a case of a grown man gone missing. Mrs Hincham said, hopefully, he might just have been called home but I don't think she believed it.

Then there was our march, down the High Street in the opposite direction from the other two, to the Baptist hall. David Ellward went in front, playing Ethel Smyth's 'March of the Women' on a mouth organ. He'd asked me to hum it through to him just once, then he had it in his head. Earlier in the day, Bill had suggested that David should stay away from the eve-of-poll meeting on the grounds that people would gossip, but David said they were gossiping anyway and in a place like Duxbury they had to do something to pass the long winter evenings. The most Bill could extract from him was a promise not to speak or ask questions. We had no motor cars for our procession, just the pony cart, almost invisible under its posters and ribbons, with young John driving and Mrs Hincham sitting in the back to make sure he didn't bolt. Young John, that is. The pony was much less nervous.

There'd been a suggestion that I should sit in the pony cart, but I decided to walk with the rest. Molly Davitt was there, in Sunday best and smelling of violet soap, along with Tabby and several other women from the tannery. I looked for Annie Carter, but couldn't see her. The rest of the procession was made up of Moira, Morgan and their friends, the two Bennington suffragettes and some of the Quakers, obviously unused to parades but managing bravely, plus as many of Mrs Hincham's regulars as could be persuaded away from their pints and into the night air, reasonably steady on their feet considering it was now late in the evening. Instead of the Conservatives' headlamps or the Liberals' wax flares we had candles, ordinary white ones from the King's Head store-room, commandeered hastily just before we set off and distributed among the marchers. The effect of the music, jaunty but with a mournful undertone as with all music played on the mouth organ, the clatter of the pony's hooves and the beat of two dozen marching feet, the flicker of the candle flames reflected in shop windows might not have matched the size or ostentation of the two main parties, but as we went down the High Street I felt a surge of that unreasoning happiness that comes in childhood and, if you're lucky, now and again in your adult life when you know you're exactly where you want to be, doing exactly what you want to do. When I looked at Molly Davitt's face in the light of the candle she was carrying I could see she felt that too, and I knew that however the vote turned out, coming to Duxbury hadn't been a waste of time. Even the people watching from the pavement had caught something of the mood, or it might just have been that two processions so far and the pubs doing good trade had put them in a party spirit. We got some cheers, the way that some people will cheer anything that moves. Reassuringly, because I'd been missing them, we got a few boos and hisses as well. Somebody, obviously one of the Prest camp, tried to start up the chant of 'Nell Bray *In*temperance candidate' but, as I could have told him, it's a difficult thing for a crowd to chant. Molly and her friends did better. 'Peace and jobs. Peace and jobs' echoed back from the houses and shop fronts and I saw the surprise on the faces of men in the crowd who weren't used to women shouting things, at least not in that way. There were a few flies in the ointment. One was the expression in Bill's eyes every time he looked towards David. The other the memory of the worry in Mrs Hincham's voice as she took her place in the pony cart.

'He's not come back yet. That's three dinners he's missed.'

'Peace and jobs. Peace and jobs and free beer.' (That from the public bar contingent, not official policy.)

Then there was the absence of Annie Carter, and Molly's reply when I asked about her. 'God knows where she is. When I told her we were all coming she just looked at me as if I wasn't there. I think her mind's going, that's the truth.'

'Peace and jobs. Peace and jobs.'

Round the corner and along the road to the Baptist hall. It was a rough meeting, but a good one. No political subtleties, just the same messages hammered home and the reminder that, above all, tomorrow at the ballot box it was their turn and – looking at Molly and her friends – our turn at last. Enough hecklers to make life interesting, only a small outbreak of fighting, soon quelled. Then, suddenly, it was all over. Molly and friends had turned down the street towards the bridge and the houses by the tannery, the

Bennington delegation had gone to find the wagonette that was taking them home, and Bill, David, Mrs Hincham and I were bowling back to the King's Head in the pony cart. The shop windows were dark, the streets almost deserted with only a few torn posters, a muddy blue ribbon and some candle stubs to show where the processions had been. The end of the campaign, Duxbury 1918, and I knew that however many elections there might be and whatever the results of them, there'd never be another one like this.

Too wound up to sleep, not wanting anybody's company, I said goodnight to the rest of them in the yard and walked across the square to the town hall. In a few hours it would be one of the polling stations. There were lights on, a motor car drawn up outside, empty black ballot boxes being carried up the steps. A few dozen yards away the Three Tuns was into drinking-up time and still doing good business, with a hum of voices coming out of it. I walked round the square a few times, enjoying the cold of the air after the warm hall. I was near the Three Tuns when the door opened and a man came out. The light through the engraved glass panel of the door was bright enough to show the eyepatch and the bright scar pulling at the corner of his eye. Luke Dobbs. Then, from down the side street, light and hurried footsteps. She must have been waiting there in the shadows near the newspaper office. Annie Carter. She said something to him and hung her head. He said a few words in reply and from the chopping up and down movement of his head, it didn't look as if the words were kind. Then she ran back down the street and he slouched across the square, passing within a few yards of me but not looking at me. I watched him go then went down the side street. As I'd guessed, she hadn't run far. She was a dark shape hunched in the doorway of the greengrocer's shop, hands to her face.

'Annie?'

She gasped, drew back against the door. There wasn't enough light to see the look on her face but I didn't need to.

'It's Molly's friend, Nell. Are you alright?'

Obviously, far from alright, but she gulped something that might have been a yes.

'Was he bothering you?'

'No . . . no 'e weren't doing anything wrong.'

Except scaring her half to death. I offered to see her home to the tannery cottages and after thinking about it for a while she came out of the doorway as reluctantly as a winkle from its rock, sniffing and wiping the sleeve of her coat over her face. We walked across the empty square and down the High Street. No point in asking her any more questions if she didn't want to talk. We'd got all the way down to the river bridge before she said a word and then it was in such a low voice that I almost missed it.

'The one that were staying where you're staying, 'as he gone away?'

'Which one?'

'The one as were asking all the questions.' She'd stopped and was hanging on to the stone parapet of the bridge, her white face turned up at me.

'Mr Wilby? Nobody knows what's happened to him.'

'Is 'e coming back?'

'We don't know. Was he asking you questions?'

She let go of the parapet and started walking fast,

but with little unsteady steps. I could easily have caught up with her, but she wanted to get away from me and I let her go. She crossed the bridge, stumbled up a few steps to the raised pavement and the front door of Molly's house where she lodged. The latch clicked and she disappeared inside. I walked slowly back through the deserted town. Back at the King's Head there was no sound from Bill's room next door. Sometime in the early hours I heard floorboards creaking in one of the rooms on the next floor up and, half asleep, felt a surge of relief that Wilby had come back after all. Then I remembered that David's room was upstairs as well and imagined him sleepless and pacing.

Election days are odd, flat times for the candidates and their teams. You've done all you can, and now everything has to be handed over to the voters. You keep yourself busy with the ritual called Getting out the Vote, which means chasing up the people who've promised to vote for you and making sure they get to the polling booth. The pony trap, covered with our posters, went shuttling to and from the town hall, picking up my supporters and quite probably other people's who just fancied the ride. There was one thing in particular that made that day odd for all of us – perhaps the oddest general election there'll ever be – which was that we'd all have to wait two weeks before the votes were counted. In camps and hospitals, in France, Flanders, all over what had been the war zone, military men and a few women had been issued with their ballot papers. The process of getting them back to Britain would take until the far side of Christmas, and we'd know the results on 28 December.

I spent the morning walking round Duxbury, talking to people and thanking supporters, but kept being drawn back to the square to watch voters going up the steps to the polling station, trying to guess which way they'd vote. Elderly man in dark coat and bowler hat, marching on irksome but necessary duty. Tory. Man in Norfolk jacket and cap, pleased with himself, turning on the steps as if inviting applause. Probably Liberal. Woman in her forties, neatly dressed, determined but apprehensive as if expecting somebody to turn her back at the door. God knows. The women's vote was unpredictable. I knew I couldn't assume they'd be voting for me. On many doorsteps I'd had to stand biting my tongue when a woman said she didn't know anything about politics, she'd have to ask her husband. In the early afternoon, when work at the tannery had finished for the weekend, Molly and Tabby went in to vote and came down the steps looking like women who'd robbed a bank and got away with it. We celebrated with hugs and handshakes, getting some sidelong looks for being so demonstrative in public. But the excitement on Molly's face faded when I told her about Annie and Luke Dobbs.

'So that's where she was last night. She wasn't in at work this morning either, so that's a half day's pay she's lost.'

She sighed and changed the subject, saying she supposed I'd be going away now it was all over. Although it shouldn't have, that came as a jolt. For ten days the universe had been Duxbury constituency and I'd almost forgotten that any other life existed.

'I'll have to go to London on Monday, but I'll be back here for the result.'

And then? So much unfinished business, but perhaps not my business. We shook hands, I wished them a happy Christmas and watched them walk away across the square. Under my coat I was wearing the green leather belt Molly had given me. I wondered if I could find anybody among my London friends who might have three hundred pounds to invest in a good cause and doubted it.

In the afternoon we'd promised to drive a couple of our voters in from Long Swinton. Bill decided he'd have to stay in and do our campaign accounts – in a sad muddle because I'd been carrying my notes of money expended around in my coat pocket for days and they weren't much better than waste paper. David insisted on coming with me. When we'd got our voters delivered back to their cottage he suggested that we might make a detour by way of King's Swinton on the way home and I realised why he'd been so anxious to join me. He took over the reins and stopped just outside the village.

'It was here I met him on his bicycle and he asked the way to World's End Farm. That's back that way.' He pointed over his shoulder. 'I directed him that way.' He pointed in the opposite direction, to where a sagging thatched roof was just visible behind a copse of bare trees on a hill. We drove on and turned right at a signpost for Duxbury. A mile along the road he turned in at a farm track.

'That's where his bicycle was, parked against the big ash tree.'

He swung out of the trap and knotted the reins loosely round the rail, so that the pony could eat the grass on the verge. I got out and we walked down the track, through a gateway and along a hedge.

'You can still see the footmarks,' David said. He pressed his boot down in the mud alongside a similar print, more blurred. 'That's mine, so the other one must be his.' Smaller than David's with a different nail pattern.

We walked a few hundred yards. 'And that's the tree where I found him.'

An old oak on a bank, roots spread like the legs of a tarantula, trunk knobbled with woody growths sprouting tufts of bare twigs.

'He was up in the fork there with his binoculars. Easy enough to climb.'

He climbed and gave me a hand to follow. We stood wedged in the fork of the tree, one side of me pressing against him, the other against the ribbed bark. All round us were fields of pasture and wet red plough-land, divided by bare hawthorn hedges with the occasional bright flare of hollybush. Over the hedges we could see the church spire and a few roofs of King's Swinton. Nearer to us, about four hundred yards off, was a disused barn with splayed wooden walls and faded thatch sliding off the roof beams.

'Nothing much to watch here.'

'You could see the crossroads, traffic coming and going.'

'But why would he want to?'

We slid down, looked around the base of the tree and walked slowly back towards the pony trap.

'Do you notice something about these footprints?' David said.

'Yes. Yours go in both directions. So far I haven't seen any of his going back.'

'No.'

We got to the cart and drove on. Near the main road he stopped again, without getting out.

'That's where I left his bicycle, in that gateway. He couldn't have missed finding it if he'd done the obvious thing and walked back towards Duxbury.'

We drove on, slowly.

'Nell, I swear to you on anything you like that I didn't do anything to the man apart from taking his bicycle.'

'Why should you?'

'Because I was angry when I found he was spying on us, so I broke his neck and left him dead in a ditch.'

'But you didn't?'

'I didn't. After all that's happened, would I be likely to get murderously angry about something as stupid as that? If anything, I thought it was funny. That was why I took his bike.'

'I believe you.'

'He doesn't.'

'Meaning Bill?'

He urged the pony into the fastest trot it had managed in ten days and kept it up all the way back to Duxbury. Even so the light was going and Bill came out of the Committee Room looking anxious.

'You took a long time.'

'We made a detour,' David said.

Inside the King's Head, with the electric light on, Bill brushed at the green dust on the right sleeve of my coat.

'Lichen,' I said, 'from a tree.'

David's left sleeve was smudged with the same green dust. Bill had noticed and David had noticed he'd noticed. I felt tired of it all and said I was going upstairs to change my shoes. Bill followed me to the landing and caught me before I could get inside my room.

'What's been going on?'

'We were up an oak tree together.'

We were speaking in low voices because there were the usual comings and goings as they got ready for the evening trade down below.

'I suppose I can guess which oak tree. It's sheer stupidity, the way things have been going on here.'

'Do you mean the gossip or all the other things?'

'I was thinking of the other things. A man dead, another man missing, people attacked. Then you go gallivanting round the countryside climbing trees.'

'I wasn't on my own.'

'No.' He put a lot into one syllable.

'Are you implying David Ellward is some kind of threat to me? He wanted to tell me that he had nothing to do with Wilby disappearing. I never thought he had.'

Silence.

'Don't tell me you did? Because he had a bad time last year and broke down, you think he's capable of anything?'

'No. I don't think that. But I do think it's a pity he ever came here. I've never made any secret of that.'

'No, you haven't.'

'Nell, please don't let's quarrel. You're tired. We're all tired.'

I was too, and he looked worn out, probably from an afternoon of figures. What I said next, I meant as a peace offering, which in my experience is often a road to disaster.

'I'm sorry he's annoyed you. After all, if you'd met under other circumstances, you and David have so much in common.'

He looked at me for what felt like a long time. From downstairs, glasses rattled and a woman's laughter came from the kitchen.

'Perhaps we have too much, as you say, in common.'

I gaped as the force of it hit me, then bolted into my room and slammed the door in his face. It was either that or slap it. By the time the polls closed at eight o'clock that night my electoral agent and I were speaking to each other with the strained politeness of two enemies who'd met at a party.

On the Sunday we finished the accounts together, sitting on opposite sides of the largest table in the snug. After that I wrote thank-you letters to all the people who'd worked for me. David went out for a walk all day. On Monday Bill and I, very formal, called on Mr Rees with the accounts and went to the town hall to settle a few matters with the returning officer. He shook our hands and said he'd see us on the 28th. Then, feeling as flat as an ice floe, there was nothing for it but to take the early afternoon train to Worcester and the connection for Paddington. Bill, David and I travelled together because there was no reason not to. Bill was heading for Oxford, David for London then on to his training camp near the south coast where he said he'd be sorting forms and twiddling his thumbs till the Army saw fit to release him. I was going home to Hampstead, with a host of highly necessary things to do, although at the moment I couldn't think what they were. The Malverns were the colour of slate in the rain, the rich ploughland of the Vale of Evesham as sodden as cardboard in a gutter. As the train slowed down for Oxford, Bill got his bag down from the rack.

'Well tried, Nell. Have a good rest and Happy Christmas.'

Then he put the bag down and shook my hand. I watched him walking away down the long Oxford platform, left elbow held out a little awkwardly to balance the bag, like a penguin's wing. By the time the train pulled out he was nowhere in sight. David gave a sigh of relief, stretched his legs and lay back against the seat. 'I'm glad that's over.'

Bill or the election? I didn't ask. At Paddington he insisted on seeing me to a cab and I was too down to resist. As we walked across the platform he said, 'I'll write when the Army lets me go. Remember the olive groves.'

'I don't think I want the olive groves.' I did, very much, although not the way he meant. He came to a sudden stop and looked at me, his face changing.

'Oh, God, have I blundered?'

'Quite probably. No, not you. Thank you anyway.'

Not the most coherent speech I'd made in the past couple of weeks. From the taxi I saw him striding away into the mixed crowd of civilian and khaki. At least he hadn't said Happy Christmas.

Chapter Fourteen

F irst Christmas of the peace. First Christmas of the Vote. It should have been the celebration of a lifetime, only it didn't work that way. Partly it was the flatness after the election campaign but mostly there were too many friends away. There was a letter waiting from Bobbie, still driving ambulances and in no hurry to come home, a card from Simon Frater hoping (in Latin verse) to be home by spring when the vine buds were uncurling, but adding (in Latin prose to give more mental exercise to the censor) that the way the Army was dragging its feet on demobilisation, it might be any spring these next ten years. Rose, writing from Manchester, was optimistic about Jimmy's campaign. In his constituency the soldiers' vote would be solidly for him. By the new year he'd be Mr James Kendal, Labour MP.

On the morning after Boxing Day I was on the train westwards, travelling alone over countryside in deep hibernation with hardly a person or animal out in the fields. It was the trough of the year, with the shortest day over but no sign yet of the upward swing that would bring the sun back. I'd written ahead to Mrs Hincham to reserve a room and walked from the station with my bag. After a welcome and a promise of a cup of tea her first words were, 'He hasn't come back.'

'Are the police still looking for him?'

'They've looked everywhere they can think of. A man came to take away his clothes from the room.'

'Policeman or a relative?'

'I don't know. Not anyone from round here.'

I drank the tea in the snug. There was holly with berries wrinkled from heat on the mantelpiece, a great bunch of mistletoe hanging from a beam. Over everything, the feeling of a celebration past. Up in my room, I unpacked the few clothes I'd brought with me, including best suit, hat, silk stockings and shoes for the announcement of the result the next day. Then I made a list of things to do. See returning officer to check arrangements for the count. See and thank Lucinda Sollers for her support – with no sarcasm. See Molly Davitt and discuss her plans for the leather workshop. Number one was easy and I went across the square and did it straight away. As for the other two, I was moving as reluctantly as the Army was about releasing its reluctant soldiers, and I knew it was because they both represented unfinished business. I still didn't know who'd killed Charles Sollers and even though she was a backslider to the Tories I resented leaving Lucinda at the mercy of a sinister and manipulative boy. As for Molly, my inquiries over the past ten days had found nobody prepared to invest in a project for redundant female tannery workers. In the matter of Wilby all I could do there was wait, with a feeling that there was worse to come. In the end, I decided to put all of them off until after the result, spent the evening writing letters in the snug and went upstairs before ten o'clock.

I sat for a while still fully dressed, half-reading and half-dozing, dimly aware of comings and goings downstairs, but it was an inn after all. Then a knock on my door brought me wide awake. I called 'Come in', thinking it was Mrs Hincham.

'Nell, are you in bed?'

Bill's voice. I dropped the book, ran to the door. He was still wearing his overcoat, with hat and bag on the floor at his feet. He looked dreadful, hair falling into his eyes, face bones too prominent as if he hadn't slept or eaten. He hesitated and I suppose I said 'come in' again. Anyway, he came in and I closed the door. No fuss about my reputation this time, either because the election campaign was over or because he was past caring.

'Shouldn't you be back in hospital?'

'I'm still on leave. I reported back, but they weren't expecting me until after the twenty-eighth. As far as they're concerned, it's not over until the result's announced.'

'But why come back? There's nothing to do here.'

I didn't realise how ungracious that sounded until I saw his face.

'Isn't there? Are you sure?'

I didn't answer, still recovering from the surprise of seeing him. He looked at me for a while then asked if I'd had a good Christmas.

'Did you?'

'I went up to Manchester. Saw Roswal and so on.'

'Is he well?'

'Very.'

'Pleased to see you?'

'Yes. You haven't answered my question.'

'What?'

'Did you have a good Christmas?'

It dawned on me that he might think I'd spent Christmas with David Ellward. I wanted to yell at him that I hadn't, but perhaps he wasn't thinking that at all. A quiet Christmas, I said. He was standing there just inside the door as if he wanted to say something but couldn't.

'Oh, for goodness' sake, sit down. And no, of course it's not all over. It's just that I didn't expect you back, that's all.'

He sat down and undid his overcoat. His collar was crushed and his tie all over the place.

'I did something else besides going to Manchester. I got in touch with some of my Army contacts and had a talk with a man on the Provost Marshal's staff.'

'Wilby. You were asking them about Wilby?'

'Yes. There're bound to be more questions asked. They don't let one of their own go missing without finding him.'

'He really is one of theirs, then?'

'Yes. Sergeant Stephen Wilby of the Royal Military Police. He's attached to a unit that traces deserters. As far as they know he had nothing to do with you or me or the election – or your friend Ellward, come to that.'

'As far as they know?'

'That's the funny thing. Sergeant Wilby is not involved in any official investigation at present. He's on sick leave. Has been for weeks.'

'Do you believe that?'

'Yes.'

'Deserters. It can't have been Luke Dobbs. He's wounded and invalided out. Anyway, he's been walking round in broad daylight and Wilby spoke to him.'

'If Dobbs had been a deserter, it would have come out when the police arrested him for being drunk. Anyway, it shouldn't have been anything to do with Sergeant Wilby at present.'

'So what did he think he was doing, climbing trees, looking through binoculars?'

'I don't know, but I gathered from something my source said that Wilby's illness was of a nervous nature. Strain from overwork.'

'That might explain why he was behaving eccentrically, but not why he turned up here of all places. Or why he's gone and left all his things.'

Bill looked worried. In spite of everything, I wanted to tell him how glad I was to see him back, but there was a coldness about him that stopped me. Perhaps he was only doing what he saw as his duty as my agent. He stood up.

'Midday tomorrow then?'

'Yes, that's when the count starts. The returning officer says they hope to have the result out before three.'

We said goodnight to each other and he went.

The returning officer managed it, with time to spare. It was half past two on Saturday afternoon when we three candidates formed up alongside him on the steps of the town hall, Tedder on his right, John Prest on his left, me on the far left. Below us in the square a crowd of around a hundred people raised wind-reddened faces and told each other to shush. The three agents clustered on the side of the steps along with Alexander Jones from the local paper and Mrs Jonas Tedder MP, which I'm sure was how she thought of herself and what, in a minute or so, she would officially be. All of us who'd been in the count knew the result already. I don't think I've ever seen a woman so pleased with herself. She stood very straight in her grey kid shoes, her closed lips conveying a beatific little smile out over the heads of the crowd to the grey sky.

'As returning officer for the constituency of Duxbury, I certify that the number of votes cast for each candidate was as follows. Jonas Albert Tedder, eight thousand nine hundred and sixty-five.' Some thin cheers from the crowd and a scattering of applause. Tedder was smiling now, but signed to his supporters to be quiet and hear the rest out. 'John Wilberforce Prest, four thousand eight hundred and three.' Mingled cheers and groans. Prest managed a smile like a gash from a sharp knife. 'Eleanor Rebecca Bray, two thousand and forty-two.' A cheer, unmistakeably from the tannery women, a few token boos from the back of the crowd. I was smiling, more successfully than Prest I hoped, and with a reason. As we'd come out on the steps I'd asked Alexander Jones to point out to me the man who'd been keeping the book at the Three Tuns. When we got to my part of the result I was watching the man's face and saw his jaw drop and his hand go involuntarily to his pocket. He'd be paying out to anybody who'd bet on my chances of getting a thousand or more, including me. I hoped there'd be a lot of them. But apart from that little satisfaction, I felt giddy with relief. From a cold start in a constituency I didn't know, the total was more than I'd expected and more than respectable.

Jonas Tedder made a speech, thanking everybody. John Prest made a speech blaming everybody in the Liberal Party who hadn't supported him. I made a speech saying it was a good start and I looked forward to the day that Duxbury would be returning a woman to Westminster. After that, it was a kind of slow country dance of handshakes, candidates with returning officer, candidates with each other, agents with agents. Somewhere in the chain dance I found myself

189

shaking hands with Bill and wished we could have missed that out. Like his Happy Christmas to me, it was too little after all that had happened, but anything else might be too much. I issued invitations to all my supporters to a celebration party that evening at the King's Head. My winnings from the bookmaker at the Three Tuns would finance it easily. We walked back across the square as the crowd drifted away. I thought of the same scene repeated seven hundred times all over the country and wondered how Christabel had done, and the other women, and Jimmy Kendal.

Bill said, 'Now it's over, the Army will be wanting me back.'

My heart plunged. Goodness knows when I'd see him again, if at all. 'I suppose they will. Do you have to go tomorrow?'

'Monday will do. I don't think I can face the Sunday train service.'

'I suppose I'll be going back on Monday too. I've got to see Lucinda first.'

'What are you going to say to her?'

'Goodness knows.' I'd have to think about it, but not now. My little surge of triumph was ebbing away fast enough without that.

'I've been thinking about Wilby,' Bill said. 'David Ellward said he asked for directions to a particular farm.'

'World's End.'

'And Ellward misdirected him.' From the tone of his voice, no truce in sight there. 'I wondered why Wilby wanted to go there in the first place. This morning I had a look at the electoral roll.'

'David said he tried to canvass it, but an old woman drove him off.'

'There are two people on the roll at World's End Farm. Frederick Dobbs and Florence Dobbs.'

'Dobbs! But Dobbs can't be the man he was looking for.'

'And yet the last thing anybody knows about Wilby is that he was up a tree near World's End Farm.'

'Near an old barn. There was something in the old barn, or he thought there was. Can we get out there and have a look?'

'It'll be dark in an hour and you've got your party to organise. First thing tomorrow. If there's anything there, it'll keep till then.'

When I found Mrs Hincham and raised the subject of the party she was untypically embarrassed. The Tories, sure of victory, had booked the big dining-room for their celebration weeks ago. We could have the room at the back if I thought it wouldn't cause bad feeling. I reassured her that there'd be no unseemly scrapping on her premises and booked the back room, along with a cask of cider and as much as she could manage in the way of cold meat and pies. After that conversation with Bill I didn't feel like celebrating, but the supporters had a right to expect it.

The party went well too. Tannery women, Quakers, suffragettes and people I'd scarcely met before but who liked parties better than election campaigning drank cider, ate pies and even started singing. Molly and her friends knew a ballad about a maid and a man who went to mow that widened the eyes of the more respectable Bennington party and even made Bill blink. No sign of Annie, but then I hadn't expected that.

191

The Conservatives' party started later than ours and in lulls in the talking and singing we could hear motor cars arriving, confident footsteps and congratulatory voices along the passage. Somebody I needed to see would be going to that party and I knew that if I intended to do my duty by Lucinda I should get the thing over with, spoil the evening for that other person as well as for me. Stubbornly, I wanted to cling on to my evening and what was left of our celebration.

I did nothing about it until the effects of the cider sent me along the passageway to the lavatories at the back of the King's Head. Sitting in the cubicle I heard another woman come in, quick little steps, door opening, then an exclamation of annoyance, probably at finding the cubicle occupied. Even from that one little sound I knew who it would be. When I opened the cubicle and walked out there she was, standing under the dim electric light bulb by the wash-basin in blue silk dress and velvet jacket, hair elaborately curled and piled. If I'd been a cockroach she couldn't have been more alarmed or disgusted.

'Good evening, Mrs Tedder. I hope you're enjoying the party.'

'Thenk yew.' The words were like pebbles and she looked as if she'd like to sprinkle me with insecticide. She shot into the cubicle and bolted the door, while I washed my hands and thought damn, damn, damn. The fates were determined not to let me put it off until tomorrow. She came out after a long time. She must have known I was still there because she'd have been listening for the door opening and closing and her face was set and hostile. I moved aside to let her wash her hands.

192

'Was it your idea to meet Peter Chivas in the barn?'

She spun round, hands dripping down her blue silk. 'What did you say?'

I repeated it.

'I don't know what you mean.'

'The night Charles Sollers was killed. You and Peter Chivas met in the barn before the party.' I unhooked the hand towel and passed it to her. She dried her hands without taking her eyes off my face and kept hold of the towel. 'You were telling him that something wouldn't do. Can I guess what?'

She started shaking, first a quivering of the jaw, then the whole upper body. 'Did he tell you that?'

'Peter Chivas? No. He fainted at the mention of your name.'

'Oh God.'

Not really a lie. Four notes on a piano Fah Lah Soh Te. Felicity. She was almost twisting the towel in half.

'I didn't encourage him. I never encouraged him. He wrote . . . from school. I was helping him, that's all. There was no harm in it.'

'He had a schoolboy passion for you, you mean?'

I was deliberately putting it bluntly and saw the fear in her eyes give way to annoyance. Good. I preferred battling to bullying.

'That's a vulgar thing to say. I met Peter at one of Lucinda's parties during the summer holidays and found him entertaining company. He asked my permission to write to me when he went back to school.'

'And he did and you replied?'

'I don't know what you're implying, but there was nothing in my letters to Peter that I couldn't happily have shown to my husband.'

'And in his to you?' Her eyes fell. 'Not, of course, that you're responsible for what a seventeen-year-old boy chooses to write to you.'

'No, I am not.'

But I could imagine the rush for the post in the mornings, the letters with the Shrewsbury postmark carried off for reading in private. Last summer, Peter's uncle was the prospective MP, Felicity Tedder the wife of a small landowner with no prospect of anything except a lifetime of Duxbury society. The admiration of a seventeen-year-old boy, especially one as self-assured as young Peter, would be nice to have, even if she couldn't wear it in public.

'How often did you write to each other?'

She was still trembling but I sensed that, after the first shock, her brain was moving again. She thought about it for a while.

'You know blackmail's a crime? I could have you arrested for doing this.'

'I can promise you, this is not blackmail.'

'What is it then?'

'I told you when we first met. I'm investigating a murder.'

'I thought Lucinda had finished with that nonsense. She told me she accepts it was an accident.'

'I wonder why. Do you really think it was an accident?' No answer. 'Even if Lucinda has finished with it, that doesn't mean it will go away. There's still the rest of the inquest to come, remember.'

She'd forgotten that, I could tell from the alarm in her eyes. 'If Lucinda tells the coroner—'

'The police might not be so easily satisfied as Lucinda. If they heard about two people having a secret meeting at the farm just before Charles Sollers died, they'd want to know more.'

'That had nothing to do with it.'

'In that case, what's the harm in telling me about it?'

'Because you'll spread it around, make me and Jonas a laughing stock.'

Spoil their triumphant entry to Westminster was what she meant. She'd just been handed the biggest present of her life and I was going to break it.

'I've no intention of spreading anything around. I'm not interested in what went on between you and Peter Chivas . . .'

'Nothing did.'

'. . . except as part of the picture of what happened that night. Isn't it better to tell me and have done with it?'

She untwisted the towel and dried her hands again, finger by finger, working carefully round her rings. They must have been dry long since but she was giving herself time to think. 'What do you want to know?'

'I asked you how often you and Peter wrote to each other when he was away at school. I promise you there's a good reason for wanting to know.'

'Every week.'

'Did you tell him there was going to be a party at his uncle's?'

'I may have mentioned it.'

'Can you remember what exactly you said?'

'I think I said I supposed Charles and Lucinda would be planning something for Saturday night and we'd have to go to it.'

'Did you mention fireworks?'

'Possibly. I can't remember.'

'When did you send this letter?'

'I always wrote to him on Thursdays.'

'So he'd have got it at school on the Friday morning before the party?'

'He must have. He wrote back to me by return. I got his letter on Saturday morning.'

'Saying what?'

'Asking me to meet him in the big barn before the party.'

'Did he say why?'

'He . . . he said he didn't want to spend the evening playing silly games with schoolboys. He wanted to be where I was and he didn't mind if he got in trouble at school.'

'What was your reaction to that?'

'I was horrified.' That sounded quite genuine. 'The school might have expelled him, his uncle would be furious and . . . everything.'

The letters, the flirtation between a schoolboy and a married woman more than ten years his senior would have been out in the open. More of a silliness than a drama, I'd have thought, but then I wasn't a Conservative's wife in Duxbury.

'So what did you do?'

'There wasn't time to write and tell him not to come. He said he'd be on his way by the time I got the letter. I . . . I told Jonas we had to be at the party early because I wanted to talk to Lucinda. I met Peter in the barn and told him that he'd compromised me, he must go straight back to school before anybody saw him and not write to me again.'

'He accepted that?'

'He was . . . emotional. He's sensitive and I think . . .' She paused, then it came out quickly. 'I think he was scared of what he'd done. It had been

. . . an adventure getting away from school but then when he'd done it . . . he's very young, after all.'

I wasn't sure whether that was meant to be a defence of him or of herself, but something about it rang true. In their game he'd been an amusing sophisticated young man and it had suited them both to play it that way. In the barn Felicity, already on edge, found she had a scared schoolboy on her hands.

'Who got there first, you or Peter?'

'I did. I had to wait for a long time. I thought he wasn't coming after all. It was horrible waiting. There were rats in the barn and I couldn't go outside because there were boys in the yard dragging wood for the bonfire.'

'And when he did arrive, you say he was scared?'

'Very scared.' I'd been right. There was a touch of contempt in her voice. 'He was shaking. He could hardly talk at first. I thought he was worried about what would happen if we were caught. He said . . . oh, it was so stupid.'

'What was stupid?'

'He said it wasn't his uncle he was worried about, it was something else. He told me . . .' She glared at me, hardly able to bring the words out. 'He said he'd just seen a ghost.'

Chapter Fifteen

'Whose ghost?' Bill said.

It was just after half past six on Sunday morning, with a cold wind blowing in our faces and more than an hour to go till daylight. We were walking northwards along the main road out of Duxbury, having decided against harnessing up the pony in the dark. There'd have been too much explaining to do and we were both good walkers. As we went, I told him about the conversation with Felicity.

'She didn't ask him that. She thought it was all nonsense and just a dramatic excuse for being scared because he was playing truant.'

'Has it occurred to her that he might have had a much more serious reason for being dead scared?'

'That he'd already stuffed that firework and knew he was within half an hour or so of killing his uncle? If it has, she's hiding it very well.'

Bill and I had met on the landing in walking clothes and carrying our boots, then let ourselves out of the side door and into the yard. My stomach felt hollow, not just from hunger, my head was still muzzy from last night's cider and I'd have given pounds for a cup of coffee. We'd worked out from the map that it was about eight miles from the town to the oak tree where

Wilby was last seen and it would be daylight by the time we got to it. We had the main road to ourselves, not even a farm cart, only the dark shape of a fox dashing across from hedge to hedge.

'It's strong circumstantial evidence against him,' Bill said. 'He knew from Felicity Tedder about the party and probably about the fireworks. He was on the estate that evening. He arrived late for their meeting. He was scared.'

'Yes, but there are gaps. For one thing, he probably wouldn't have known where the fireworks were being kept. They weren't stored in that back room until Thursday evening, and Felicity's letter was on the way to him by then. If he didn't get it until Friday morning, he'd only have a day to get his hands on explosives and a metal container.'

'In a boys' school? No problem at all.'

'You want him to be guilty.'

'Don't you?'

I thought yes, if it had to be him or Annie, but didn't say so. I still hadn't told Bill about that conversation in the shop doorway. I wasn't sure why not.

Bill said, 'And there's more of a motive now. If the creature had convinced himself that he was a romantic hero, why let a guardian holding the purse strings stand in his way? Perhaps he was going to carry Mrs Tedder off on a motor cycle like the Young Lochinvar.'

'She wouldn't have gone.'

'He didn't know that. Then there was the sheer wickedness of trying to blame her husband for the murder. Uncle disposed of, husband out of the way. All very neat.'

'If you're mad.'

'That young man is well on the way to it. I suppose most boys of that age have fantasies, but he can't tell the difference between them and reality.'

I wondered if Bill at seventeen had fantasies and if so, what they'd been. At one time I might have asked. We turned left at the signpost for King's Swinton, past the gateway where David had left Wilby's bicycle. It was still dark to the west, the way we were walking, but to the east the sky was taking on a stretched, transparent look with bare hedges and trees in silhouette. It was almost light by the time we got to the track to World's End Farm, and there was still no sign of anybody. We turned off the track and followed the route David and I had taken alongside the hedge to the oak tree on the bank. Its bark was black and damp. On the other side of it the field sloped downwards to the abandoned barn. Any path had been overgrown a long time ago. Now there was only rough tussocky grass and dead docks and thistles alongside a choked ditch. We slowed to a crawl.

'Can't tell if anybody's been down here,' Bill said.

We scrambled up and over the bank, crossed the ditch on the other side and followed it towards the barn. It was back end on to us and as we got nearer wide gaps between the warped timbers showed beams fallen slantwise inside. We stumbled our way over a heap of fallen thatch overgrown with brambles, moved round the corner and down the other side. A cock pheasant flew up with a noise like a policeman's rattle and went clattering off to a copse. Bill showed signs of wanting to go first, but I stayed in front as we went round a corner, to the end of the barn where the door should be. There was a door, but it was hanging open at an angle on one rusty hinge,

200

pulled down so low by brambles and warping that the top of it was almost touching the ground. Over it I could see some rusty farm machinery, more leaning beams.

'Nell, let me . . .'

I stepped over the threshold, sniffing a musty smell of old straw. But something sharper too – the smell of ash. It was still quite dark inside. I moved forward cautiously and Bill came alongside me.

'What's that?'

A rustle in his pocket and a match striking. I knelt down and felt something damp and coarse-woven.

'Only a pile of sacks and an old coat, I think.'

The ash smell was sharper. I was kneeling in the remains of a small fire. The ashes were cold and damp, but they hadn't got to the solid impacted stage.

'Someone made a fire here, not so long ago. Days maybe.'

Bill struck another match and kept striking. The sacks and an old brown coat were arranged in a nest near the fire. There were some things scattered round. A corned beef tin, crudely hacked open, the stub of a candle, an empty bottle. Bill picked it up and sniffed.

'Brandy.'

'The person who smashed Tedder's conservatory took a bottle of brandy.'

'There's a smell in here.'

While we were looking the daylight had been coming in through the gaps in the walls and roof. The match flames were paler, then we didn't need them any more to see the circle of black and grey ash, the damp nest of sacks, the rusty harrow and broken-down cart. We searched tentatively at first then behind things, moving musty straw bales and bits of wood. The far corner had been used as a lavatory. That, and a rabbit with most of the meat hacked away but head and legs still clinging to the stiff skin, accounted for the smell. Nothing else. We went outside. Bill puffed out a sigh of relief and lit his pipe.

'No Wilby.'

'But somebody's been there. And whoever it was is connected to a least one of the things that happened.'

'Luke Dobbs?'

'It's odd, though. He wouldn't need to sleep and cook out here. He goes around quite openly in town and has money to buy drink.'

'Whoever it was, he was what Wilby was watching.'

I felt boneless from relief at not finding what I expected to find. When Bill, through clouds of pipe smoke, suggested that we should take a short cut by following the hedge round back to the road I agreed with him. The sun was up by then, gleaming on wet tree trunks. A holly tree covered in berries flared against the grey sky and the few brown leaves on the hedges stirred in gusts of wind from the northwest, giving a feeling of rain to come. In the next field we struck a track that made the going easier and it was almost possible to believe that we were walking for the fun of it. Bill said we'd be back in time to get a late breakfast. Then we'd better look up trains for Monday, I said. We walked on in silence for half the length of a field.

'Nell, that other night, I said something stupid. I didn't mean it the way it came out.'

'It doesn't matter.'

The track was just about wide enough to walk side by side. As he put his pipe back into his pocket, his gloved hand brushed against mine.

'Have you thought what you're going to do when all this is over?'

'Go back to London. See if I can do something for Molly and the tannery women.'

'I was thinking longer term than that. I mean, what are you going to *do*?'

I wished he hadn't asked that. Back at home between the end of the campaign and Christmas, with the days at their shortest and the sap at its lowest, it had struck me that I had no idea what I was going to do. All my adult life, from university onwards, had been about getting the Vote. Then there'd been the war and the need to fight conscription and quite suddenly there they were both over at once and there I was without money, career or plans for the future. Of course, there was everything still to do, enough fighting against poverty and injustice and warmongering to last several lifetimes. But at that low point it seemed to me that none of it would ever have the same blazing certainty again. I said I supposed I'd have to earn a living.

'How?'

'Perhaps journalism if I can. Translation work if I can't. There should be more of it now the war's over.'

'Drudging for a pittance for little magazines.'

I was surprised at the anger in his voice, until the next question explained it.

'And what's David Ellward going to do after the war?'

'Who knows, with him? Lotus eating in Italy seems to be the present plan.'

On an impulse, probably still from the relief of not finding Wilby in the barn, I gave him the explanation I wasn't sure he deserved, even though I'd spent some of Christmas weighing that very question.

'He asked me to go with him – or half-asked me, the way he does. I said no – or rather, said something he knew was no.'

'Why did you do that?'

'I suppose lotuses aren't my meat.'

I'd intended to say more than that, but couldn't find the right words. Odd how they'd taken to deserting me. Election fatigue, perhaps. The words that came out were nothing to do with anything. I happened to glance over the hedge into the next field.

'What a very realistic scarecrow.'

'Oh damn the scarecrow. What I want . . .' Then, 'Stay here, Nell. I said stay here.'

Then he was pushing through a gap in the hedge like a badger. I followed, and a crow took off sluggishly from the scarecrow's head and went away into the sky like a rag flung upwards against the wind. A scarecrow that didn't scare crows. A scarecrow in a field in December when no crops were growing. We ran across the plough, Bill a few steps ahead, I gaining on him.

He got to it, turned, shouted to me not to come. I looked and thought no wonder the crow had been reluctant to fly, it had been eating. But the hair under the battered hat was still terribly sleek from the damp, as if combed that morning and the laces of the shoes dangling against the plough were tied in neat double bows, loops precisely equal. I noticed that before I turned away and was sick on the ground.

Chapter Sixteen

⊗

W e got back to the road somehow, muddy and wordless. Still without saying anything we marched several miles in the direction of Duxbury before we were overtaken and offered a lift by a farmer and his wife, driving their gig to chapel. They asked no questions about our clothes covered with mud and burrs or what two strangers were doing out walking at that time of the year. As we drove we talked about the weather, the peace and sheep and Bill's voice and my own sounded as if they were coming from other people in another world. Outside the Methodist chapel we thanked them, got down, and headed up the High Street towards the police station.

Bill said, 'Anything they want to know, we tell them.'

'Of course.'

'I mean it, Nell.'

'But what is there to tell? He's dead. We found him.'

'Searching the barn, Sollers, the rest of it.'

'All that they want. If they can make sense of it, that's more than I can.'

There was a middle-aged constable on duty in the outer office, fingers covered with coal dust from making up the fire in a narrow grate. The quiet of the station showed that Duxbury didn't expect things to happen on Sunday mornings. He looked surprised at the state of us, then recognised me from election meetings and the surprise changed to wariness.

Bill said, 'We've come to report finding a body.'

The constable looked at us round-eyed for a moment then walked off into an inner room. There was a sound of running water and in half a minute he was back with us, clean fingered and ready to cope.

'Where would that be, sir?'

There was a map pinned to the wall behind the counter. We showed him, as best we could, explained about the scarecrow. He wrote it all down, occasionally giving us a sidelong glance to make sure it wasn't some joke against him.

'His name's Wilby,' Bill said. 'He was a member of the Royal Military Police.'

'The gentleman who'd been staying at the King's Head?'

'That's the one.'

That went down as well in his painstaking and unhurried handwriting, then he asked us to excuse him, went back through to an inner room and shut the door. We heard him ask for a telephone number. After that he dropped his voice and we couldn't make out what was being said, but it was obviously enough to spoil the Sunday leave of every police officer in Duxbury. Within half an hour the station was crammed with several constables, a sergeant and an inspector who arrived by motor car. Inspector Wall. I knew him by sight from the election, a thin man with iron-grey hair and a moustache the shape and colour of a mackerel's tail. He had a weary air as if he wished he could have retired before all this happened. Bill and I were sitting in the outer office as he came in. He glanced at us, said good morning, and went through to the inner room. Five minutes later we were called in to his office and found him standing by his desk with two constables in attendance, looking down at a map.

'It will be necessary for you to show us where you found him. I suggest Captain Musgrave comes with us in the motor car and Miss Bray waits here.'

I said I was either going with them or back to the King's Head and they could send for me when they wanted me. Goodness knows, I didn't want to see again what the weather and the crows had done to Wilby, but I wasn't going to let them shut me out. In the end six of us squeezed into the motor car, Inspector Wall, a sergeant, two constables, Bill and me. By then there were more people around in the town and we attracted attention going up the High Street. We left the car parked on a grass verge by the main road in the charge of one of the constables and went in a file across the fields, Bill leading the way and Inspector Wall following him. The inspector's shoes and the bottom of his trousers clotted up with red mud and he made heavy going. When we came within sight of the scarecrow three or four crows took off and the inspector stopped suddenly. The sergeant, moving up from behind me for a better view, stumbled against my shoulder.

'Poor bugger. What sort of savage would do that to a man?'

Expecting it this time, I saw things I hadn't noticed before. The slash from ear to ear had cut through the front of the windpipe. It had been a sharp knife and a long, considered cut, like a slaughterman's on a passive victim. Or a tannery worker's on a spread hide. The collar had been pulled open but the stud on the back must be holding because the points of the collar drooped, limp in the damp, on either side of the gashed throat. The top button of the shirt had been pulled away and the knot of the tie dragged down. Perhaps the person with the knife had held on to it with one hand and cut with the other.

I said, 'Whoever it was probably knocked him unconscious then cut his throat.'

The look the inspector gave me showed I was trespassing twice over, first by being there at all, then by having an opinion. I decided not to antagonise him any further by pointing out that the waistcoat and the tidily buttoned jacket were only blood-spattered, not blood-soaked as they would have been if Wilby had been standing up when the cut was made. He walked round the body several times, then commandeered the constable's overcoat to cover its head and shoulders. The sergeant said something about looking for footprints. Routine, but a waste of time. Bill and I, then the five of us had trampled the ground. Squalls of wind and rain over the past few days would have blotted out anything earlier. Still, the inspector seized on it. The sergeant and the coatless constable were to stay on guard and look for footprints or anything else that might be useful while the inspector went back to report and send detective officers, a photographer and transport for the body. He seemed in a hurry to move off, but Bill and I walked him up the field and over the bank to a point where he could see the sagging roof of the old barn.

'There's been somebody living rough in there quite recently,' Bill said. 'Miss Bray and I had a look earlier this morning before we found Wilby.'

I could sense that the inspector was being wary with Bill, because he was Captain William Musgrave, officer and a barrister, so I was the one who got the suspicious look.

I said, 'There's an empty brandy bottle in there. You might ask Mr Tedder if it looks like the one stolen from his house back in November.'

Two looks this time, resentment from the inspector and warning from Bill, but I never expected to be popular with police officers.

'We shall investigate of course,' the inspector said and sighed. I guessed that he was a sick man, holding on and doing his duty, who'd needed a Sunday morning by his fireside. He took a long look at the barn and the country round it, probably trying to place it on the map.

'What's the farm over there?'

'World's End,' I said.

'Ah.'

He'd got his bearings, and it was more than a matter of geography. The name had associations for him and he was suddenly even more anxious than he had been to get back to Duxbury. We went back across the fields, keeping to the far side of the hedge so as not to add any more footprints to the trampled area, and got back to the main road and the car. The inspector drove, with Bill in the front beside him and the constable and me in the back. As we got to the town he said something to Bill that I couldn't hear above the noise of the engine and drew up just over the bridge. Bill got down and opened the door for me and we watched as the car drove away.

'What's all this about?'

'Inspector Wall's decided he wants to keep it quiet for as long as he can. We're to go back to the King's Head, not talk about it, and they'll send for us to make formal statements later this afternoon.'

'In this town you can't keep anything quiet. I'll bet half the population knows already.'

As we walked up the street we were getting curious looks from people going home from church and chapel to Sunday lunch. Quite a lot of them knew us from the campaign, said good morning and looked curiously at our mud-caked boots. Goodness knows what they thought we'd been doing. We hoped to go in quietly through to the back door and up to our rooms to change, but Mrs Hincham was standing just inside the door of the kitchen and heard us.

'Thank the Lord you're back. When you didn't come down to breakfast I thought you two had gone missing as well.'

She obviously expected some explanation, but all we could do was apologise and ask for a pot of tea in the snug when we'd changed. When I came down in dry skirt and shoes Bill and the tea were already there. He poured.

'Mrs Hincham's not pleased with us. She knows something's up.'

'I don't blame her. I suppose once the inspector decides to let the news out, she'll have to give a statement to the police as well. She might have been one of the last people to see him alive.'

We were talking in low voices, aware of people in the bar next door.

Bill said, 'Of course that depends when he was killed. As far as we know, the last anybody saw of him was on the eleventh of December. That's eighteen days ago.'

'I'd say soon after he disappeared. After all, in a place like this there'd have been some sightings of him in eighteen days if he were still alive.'

'Unless it was Wilby living in the old barn.'

'But he was keeping a watch on the barn. Wouldn't that mean there was somebody else living there and he knew about it?'

'We have David Ellward's word that he was watching the barn, and as far as anybody knows Ellward was the last to see him alive. You realise the police will have to question him again?'

'Of course.'

The last time the police had talked to David it was simply a case of a man who'd missed a meal or two and an abandoned bicycle. But the constable should have made his report about it and even if he hadn't, he'd remember it now.

Bill said, 'I wish that man had never come here.'

'For heaven's sake, you don't really think that David killed Wilby?'

'No, if I'm honest I don't think that. I think he's self-absorbed and self-dramatising, but I don't think he's a murderer. But he has made things worse by interfering and you can't be surprised if I resent that.'

We drank tea in silence for a while. He'd changed his trousers but not his jacket and there were still burrs clinging to his sleeve. Normally I'd have told him or picked them off for him but now I felt too miserable to bother. The inspector's attitude had reminded me that he was Captain Musgrave and there was a distance between us. For a few minutes in the field, before we'd noticed the scarecrow, I'd thought that things might be coming right again.

211

Then we'd found poor Wilby and the distance had increased if anything. In the end I broke the silence.

'When we were going to the police station, you said we should tell them anything they wanted to know, including about Sollers.'

'Yes.'

'That assumes that Sollers' killing and this one are linked.'

'Do we think they are?'

'That depends on whether all the other things are linked. That's why I want to know about the brandy bottle.'

'The inspector didn't like you trying to do his job for him.'

'Somebody's got to. If the police here had made a proper job of investigating Sollers' death things might have been different. Instead of that, the official attitude seems to have been to hope it would all go away, or at least go somewhere else. First it was an accident, then when that wouldn't stand up they were obviously hoping that the explosive was put in where the fireworks came from. When somebody set fire to our car, first they arrested the town drunk then they seemed to think it might have set itself on fire. As for the attack on Prest, I wouldn't be surprised if they still think it was something to do with me.'

'So we accept that there is a link?'

'Look, you pointed out yourself that the common thread is attacks on everybody standing for election – Sollers is blown up, Tedder's house attacked, our motor car burnt and Prest knocked unconscious. That's not coincidence.'

'Perhaps Duxbury has a remarkably low level of tolerance for politicians.'

'If that brandy bottle is the one that was taken when somebody put a brick through Tedder's conservatory, that links whoever was living in the barn to at least one of the attacks.'

'And the barn is near a farm owned by a Mr and Mrs Dobbs. It clearly meant something to the inspector this morning. So we can probably take it that they are related to Luke Dobbs.'

'That doesn't mean it had to be Luke Dobbs living in the barn.'

'Nell, if your theory's right, it would be hard to think of anybody with more reason to have a grudge against politicians than the wretched Dobbs. He's seen two of his friends killed, lost an eye, taken to the bottle, been put in a prison cell for being drunk. A clear candidate, wouldn't you say?'

'Yes.'

Bill looked sideways at me. 'Only there's one little problem, isn't there? According to that same theory, the murder of Charles Sollers is part of the sequence. Only we know that Dobbs was in a police cell at the time when somebody was putting explosive in that firework.'

'Yes.' I didn't like the way this was going.

'So the logic of that would be that the Sollers business is, after all, quite distinct from the rest. Or that Luke Dobbs has an accomplice who acted for him when he was locked up.'

'It would have to be a very quick-thinking accomplice.'

'It certainly would. So if we abandon that theory . . .' I hoped he hadn't sensed my relief. '. . . we come back to a quite separate operator and motive. In other words, we come back to young Chivas. He was there when he wasn't supposed to be, he had a motive, he was scared.'

'In which case, we have two murderers, not one,' I said. 'Or are you suggesting that Peter Chivas killed Wilby as well?'

'I wouldn't put anything past that young man, but I don't know what his motive would be. It can't be that Wilby knew something about Sollers' murder, because as far as we know Wilby wasn't around at the time.'

'As far as we know, but there's a lot we don't know about Sergeant Wilby, unless your military police friends have told you something you're not passing on to me.'

'I've told you everything I know, Nell. I do wonder, though, whether there's something you're not telling me.'

Annie Carter's pale face in the shop doorway. Her whisper *'Is 'e coming back?'* If I told Bill about that, he might think it was his duty to tell the police. At one time I'd have risked it and I was tempted to even now, but I didn't know where I stood with him. I was sitting there with Bill's eyes on me when there were quick steps in the corridor and Mrs Hincham came in, face flushed and eyes resentful.

'I wish you'd told me you'd found him.'

'Have the police made it public?'

'I don't know what the police are doing. I heard it from somebody who was there when they brought him in. He said his throat was slit from ear to ear and they'd crucified him against a tree. Is that true?'

'Not quite.'

'He's been murdered, though?'

'Yes.'

'And they've arrested Luke Dobbs for it.'

'What!' We both spoke at once.

'You didn't know that, then? One of young John's friends was outside the house where he lodges when the police got there. They banged on the door and he came down half-dressed, as if he'd still been in bed at that hour. The police went inside, then they came out with him with his hat and coat on and took him round to the station.'

'When did this happen?'

'About an hour ago.'

Young John's voice called from the passage outside, 'Mum. Mum, the police are here.'

Mrs Hincham went outside and came back within seconds.

'It's just one of them. He says they want the two of you down at the police station to give your statements. They've sent the motor car for you.'

Bill and I looked at each other and got up slowly.

'Whatever they want to know, Nell.' He was trying to look a warning at me. I looked straight back at him. No promises.

In a small room at the police station we dictated our statements of finding the body separately to a police officer and signed them. That was the straightforward part. After that we were told that Inspector Wall would like to talk to us, starting with me. Either it was ladies first, or he wanted to get it over. His office was small and bleak, with the electric light reflecting off the brown linoleum on the floor and his highly polished desktop. He stood up when I came in, gave me a chair in front of the desk and settled back behind it. A constable sat taking notes at a small table in the corner.

'What puzzles me, Miss Bray, is how you and Captain Musgrave came to be there at all.'

I explained that we'd been concerned about Mr Wilby, and that we knew that he'd been watching the barn.

'Was Sergeant Wilby a friend of yours?'

'Not at all. He'd been staying at the King's Head, that's all. He was helpful the night the car was burned.'

'And yet one of your, er, supporters, stole his bicycle.'

'Stole is putting it too strongly. As he saw it, he was playing a joke.'

The inspector grimaced but said nothing about that. 'Did you speak to him – at mealtimes and so on?'

'Only to say good morning. Apart from one time when he asked me about an incident during my election campaign.'

'What was that?'

'A man spat at me. Mr Wilby seemed interested.'

'What was the man's name?'

'Luke Dobbs.'

The inspector glanced over at the constable and settled back in his chair, as if that pleased him.

'Did he say anything about why he was interested in Luke Dobbs?'

'No.'

'I'm still puzzled, Miss Bray. You say Sergeant Wilby wasn't a friend of yours and you didn't even speak to him very much, and yet more than two weeks after he disappeared, you and Captain Musgrave get up at the crack of dawn and hike out to a barn in the middle of nowhere on the off chance that he might be there.'

I said nothing. It was up to Bill, if he wanted, to explain the inquiries he'd made among his Army friends.

The inspector persisted. 'Why were you so interested?'

'It seemed to be part of a pattern of things that have been happening round here.'

'Such as?'

'Charles Sollers' death, the vandalism at Jonas Tedder's home back in November, the attack on the Liberal candidate, the burning of our campaign car.' And Annie's behaviour. But I didn't say that.

'Are you implying that all those events are connected with the death of Sergeant Wilby?'

'Have you shown Mr Tedder that brandy bottle?'

'Is this a change of subject?'

'No.'

He sighed. 'In fact, Mr Tedder has identified it. Apparently he was accustomed to mark the level in pencil on the label to make sure the housemaid wasn't having a tipple.'

'So it looks as if there was a link between whoever was living in the old barn and the person who threw a brick through the Tedders' conservatory.'

'You mentioned Mr Sollers' death. Have you any reason at all for linking it with the death of Sergeant Wilby?'

'As far as evidence is concerned, no. Logically, it seems to fit with the other chain of attacks on public figures.'

'You're still a long way from proving that there is a chain. All we can say with any confidence is that a bottle stolen from Mr Tedder's house in November was found in a barn near where Sergeant Wilby's body was found a month later. Or have you anything to add to that?'

217

'No.'

I hoped that might be the end of it, but he took another tack.

'I see that Mr Sollers' widow signed your nomination papers.'

'Yes.'

'So she's a friend of yours?'

'Not exactly.' I guessed that he knew how things stood, so there was no point in playing games with him. 'Mrs Sollers asked me to find out what I could about her husband's death.'

'Are you some form of private detective?'

'I don't claim to be. She simply thought I might be able to help.'

'And have you found out anything?'

'I don't know who killed him, if that's what you mean. Do you?'

A little wince from him, but he must have known that his force's efforts hadn't been over-energetic.

'The inquest was adjourned. We still don't know if it was accidental death.'

I didn't say anything to that. At least nobody could think that Wilby had died accidentally. That ended the proceedings as far as I was concerned. He thanked me, unconvincingly, for my help and asked me to let the police know if I were thinking of leaving Duxbury or staying anywhere other than the King's Head. They might want to speak to me again. I wondered whether to ask him if they'd charged Luke Dobbs but decided he probably wouldn't tell me.

I waited half an hour in the outer office while Bill had his session with the inspector. I couldn't tell anything from his face when he came out. A constable brought us our coats and hats and we were just putting them on when we heard a door opening down a corridor and an argument coming towards us.

'. . . no right to say where I can go and where I can't . . . 'aven't got no right to lock me up again . . .' Luke Dobbs came into view, with a grim-looking constable chivvying him along from behind.

'We're not locking you up, Dobbs. We're letting you go for now. Only don't think you can go off anywhere without us knowing about it because you can't.'

He caught the eye of the other constable and raised his eyes towards the ceiling. By then Luke Dobbs had recognised me.

' 's it 'er bin making trouble again? Sodding busybodies, blaming me for everything. There's people walking round this town done a lot worse than I've done. Sodding . . .'

'Watch your language, Dobbs.'

One constable opened the door while the other took him by the collar and practically flung him down the steps.

'Better wait till he's out of the way, ma'am.'

I knew I'd get nowhere trying to question Luke Dobbs so we waited. By the time we went out he'd vanished into the dusk and drizzle. I said to Bill that I was surprised they'd let him go so soon.

'Inspector Wall told me they were going to. There's really no evidence against him, except that his aunt and uncle own World's End Farm. If there were any sign of a motive for murdering Wilby it might be different. They've questioned him without getting very far and taken his fingerprints to see if they match up with anything in the barn. They know where to put their hands on Dobbs any time they want him. If I were in the inspector's place, I think I'd have done the same – let him loose and have him followed.'

'You and the inspector seem to get on very well.'

'Oh, he's a decent enough man. Just a bit tired, that's all.'

Bill was feeling in his pocket for his pipe. I decided not to ask him if he'd heard Dobbs ranting about the people in town who'd done worse or if it was only his guess that the inspector would have Dobbs followed. I wished they were keeping him locked up, but if I'd said that to Bill he'd have asked why and I couldn't tell him.

Chapter Seventeen

❧

Early on Monday morning a note arrived from Lucinda Sollers. She must have sent one of her staff to deliver it before first light because it was there waiting for me when I came down to breakfast. '*What's happening? Is it true what people are saying? Please come and see me urgently.*' I showed it to Bill when he came down, looking like a man who hadn't slept well.

'Are you going?'

'Not yet. There's nothing I can tell her. Anyway, there's something else I want to do this morning.'

'If it's about Wilby, for goodness' sake leave it to the police.'

'Not directly. I want to talk to John Prest.'

Bill said he'd come with me, but I persuaded him that one of us had better stay at the King's Head in case the inspector wanted us. The truth was that I wanted to tackle Prest on my own. He kept an ironmonger's shop at the bottom of the High Street, a narrow little place with a palisade of bins and brooms outside and a display of pokers, hammers and tins of grate blacking in the window as austere as the man himself. Scrubbing brushes hung on a string down one side of the door like a gallows of hedgehogs. I pushed the door open, a bell tinged and a boy at a long wooden counter looked up and gave me an apprehensive good morning. He was weighing out tacks from a wooden box into small brown paper parcels. When I asked to speak to Mr Prest he bolted into the back without speaking. Soon afterwards Prest himself came out, stooping to get through the low doorway between the back and the front of the shop. You'd have thought he'd simply have it made higher, but perhaps that would have been pandering to the weaknesses of the flesh. He was wearing a navy blue pinstriped suit and a dutiful expression that changed to annoyance when he saw who it was.

I said, 'Don't worry, I haven't come to ask for an apology, although you do owe me one.'

'I owe you no apologies.'

He moved behind the counter and took on the boy's task of weighing out tin tacks. There was an ounce weight on the balance pan. When the scoop on the other side of the scales dipped he took tacks out of it one at a time until the balance was exact. Then he tipped the ounce of tacks on to the top one of a pile of brown paper squares, folded the corners and tucked them in like one of the Fates parcelling up destinies.

'You certainly owe me some thanks. I went to quite a lot of trouble to bring you home.' Another handful of tacks pattered into the scoop. 'I hope you're not still pretending that I had something to do with the attack on you. That kind of thing's all very well for electioneering, but the election's over now. Could we please talk about it like two adults with a problem on our hands?'

'I have no problems that I want to discuss with you.'

'I think everybody in this town has a problem. A man's been murdered and it happened not far away from where you were attacked. I suppose that has occurred to you?'

'I gave the police a full account at the time. I shall naturally answer any other questions they need to put to me.'

So the police hadn't been back to him since Wilby's body was found. Not surprising. They would have more immediate things on their hands.

'I've never heard a full account of it, and I'm the one who found you, after all. You might have been dead if you'd stayed there all night.'

'Somebody would have found me.' But I sensed, for once, a faltering. The man had some sense of justice.

'Would you please satisfy my curiosity by telling me what happened? I swear to you that I had nothing to do with it whatsoever, and I need to know.'

'What business is it of yours?'

'I found Mr Wilby's body. A friend of mine was probably one of the last people to see him alive. It's my business whether I like it or not.'

'I'm at a loss to see how I can help you.'

'I've told you, by telling me everything you can remember about what happened. I take it you were canvassing the Swinton villages that day?'

He nodded, not much of a nod, but it meant the scales had dipped on my side and he acknowledged a debt to pay.

'I visited Little Swinton in the morning and then went on to King's Swinton.'

'Were you there long?'

'Yes. I have a considerable number of supporters there. I believe in calling on all of them individually.'

'So a lot of people would have known you were in the area?'

'I've always understood that to be one of the purposes of canvassing.' The smugness of it made me feel as scratchy as one of his scrubbing brushes, but I kept my temper.

'Yes, I do understand the purposes of canvassing. The point I'm trying to make is that everybody would know you were a candidate and if somebody in or around King's Swinton wanted to make an attack on you, he'd have been able to plan it between the time you arrived and when you left.'

He considered. 'Yes, I'd say that's the case.'

'Did you call at World's End Farm?'

'No. I knew old Mr Dobbs from previous elections. He's a lost cause.'

'Were you near World's End Farm?'

'I called at a row of cottages about half a mile away.'

'Did you leave your wagonette unattended?'

'Naturally, several times. If people invite me in for a conversation and a cup of tea, I always accept.'

'Could anybody have got into the back without your knowing about it?'

'It stands to reason, quite easily.' He was more animated now. Of course he'd have done a lot of thinking about it. 'I kept my posters in the back, but towards the end of the afternoon I'd put them up in most places, so I wouldn't have gone to the back at all. Anybody could have got in and concealed himself under the old blanket I keep in there.'

'And you think that's what happened?'

'I'm quite sure that's what happened and so are the police. I'd finished my calls and I was driving home. About two miles out from King's Swinton I heard something moving around in the cart behind me. I turned round, and that's when it happened.'

'Somebody hit you with a stone cider jar.'

'I was not aware of the nature of the weapon.' The cider jar still rankled.

'Did you see this person before you were hit?'

'A glance over my shoulder, no more. He had wild eyes and mud smeared all over his face.'

'Pardon me?' I'd heard him the first time, but there was one thing that had to be clear beyond doubt.

He repeated, annoyed. 'Wild eyes and mud, that's all.'

Perfectly clear.

'This mud . . . ?'

'Smeared – like a child or a savage. Not just dirty, deliberately plastered over his face.'

'As a disguise perhaps?'

'Or mad. The police think it was a madman.'

I wondered. In Prest's well-ordered world, anybody who attacked him would have to be mad by definition.

'Did you recognise him?'

'No, how could I? It was no more than a glance, hardly that even, before he hit me.'

I thanked him. I'd got what I wanted and was ready to go, but now he wanted to keep me there. Re-living the attack had softened his shell a little. It wouldn't take long to harden again but now there was a trace of fear in his eyes and he'd stopped parcelling out the tacks.

'Do you know . . . do the police think it was the same person who attacked me and murdered the poor man they found yesterday?'

I said, quite truthfully, that I'd no idea what the police thought about it.

'If it was, it could have been . . .' He didn't have to say it. He was imagining himself staked out in a field with his throat cut, or whatever even worse horrors Duxbury gossip had invented. It might have been the

225

time to press for my thank you from him if I'd really wanted it, but I didn't. I left him staring into space, hands nervously rearranging his little paper parcels.

I went back to tell Bill about it.

'Eyes. He said it twice. Even though he just got a glance, he'd have noticed if the man had only one eye.'

'So it wasn't Luke Dobbs.'

'And if Luke Dobbs wasn't the one who attacked Prest, then he probably wasn't the one who stole the brandy from Tedder's house. And if he wasn't the one who stole the brandy, he probably wasn't the lurker in the barn.'

'That's two or three unproven connections.'

'At this stage we're not talking proof, we're talking probabilities. Have you heard anything more from the police?'

'Not a word. Mrs Hincham has though. A constable came to reserve a room here tonight for Wilby's brother-in-law. He's on his way from Croydon to make a formal identification of the body.'

'I'll need a lot of convincing that Wilby's killing and the attack on Prest aren't connected. Apart from the King's Swinton connection, there's something baroque about both of them. The mind that made poor Wilby a scarecrow is the same mind that would think of battering a temperance man with a cider jar.'

'Or killing Sollers with a firework?'

'Yes. And it's got a face now.'

'Not much of a description. A pair of wild eyes and a mud-smeared face. That could be almost any man – except Luke Dobbs.'

Bill said man, just as Prest had said man. Would Prest have had time to realise it if the mud-smeared

226

face had been a woman's? Probably being knocked unconscious by a woman would be more than his mind could compass. On the other hand, he was a tall man and cider jars were heavy things.

I couldn't settle and decided to go out again. It was coming up for midday, break time at the tannery. Almost against my will I found myself walking down the High Street and over the river bridge to where the dead animal smell hung in the damp air. There were only a few people outside, Molly among them. She came towards me unsmiling for once, looking tense and tired.

'They say you found him.'

'Yes.'

'Was it as bad as they're saying?'

'Bad enough.'

'They've let Dobbs go.'

'I know.'

'Did he do it?'

'I don't know.'

'He came straight round from the police station to our house. I wouldn't let him in, but Annie came down and talked to him.'

'Do you know what they said?'

'No, but she came in with a face like a frosted turnip and went straight up to bed.'

'Is she here at work today?'

'No. I went in to wake her up this morning, but she *said* she had the flu.'

'Do you think she has?'

'God knows. She looked bad enough. I don't know how long we can go on like this. I feel sorry for the girl and I can't just throw her out, but there's my mum to think of. When are they going to get all this cleared up?'

'I don't know.'

'The girls are all getting spooked about it. Around Christmas, nobody would go anywhere after dark. When I heard yesterday they'd picked up Luke Dobbs I thought that would be an end of it.'

'Do you mind if I come and see Annie tonight?'

'I wish you would. I'll be home just after five o'clock. You could come then and we'll both try to talk some sense into her.'

I was knocking on Molly's front door at a quarter past five. She opened it, still in working clothes, wiping her hands on a piece of towel.

'Come in. She's not up yet.'

The front door opened straight into the living-room. It was comfortable, with two sagging armchairs and bright rag rugs on a linoleum floor, lit by a brass oil lamp on the table, but the air had the used-up feel of a place where a fire has been burning all day, and a trace of the tannery smell had seeped in. Molly apologised.

'We have to keep it warm because of Mum.'

A woman with a sharp brown face and white hair sat in an armchair so close to the fire that her slippers were almost touching the grate. Her eyes were milky with cataracts and when Molly introduced me her hand found its way into mine by touch rather than sight.

Molly said, 'Mum says there hasn't been a sound out of her all day. Perhaps it really is the flu.'

She offered me tea, but I wanted to see Annie and get it over. I followed her out of the living-room to a cold cube of scullery, with a scrubbed pine table, a boiler for the washing and a mangle with big wooden rollers and cast-iron handle that occupied half the room.

'Mum used to take in washing, but she can't do it any more. That's why we got a lodger.'

228

A steep wooden staircase with a right-angled bend led straight up from the scullery to a landing with just about enough room for Molly and me to stand side by side. She opened a door on the left. 'This is my room. You have to go through it to get to hers.'

The ceiling slanted down so steeply that there wouldn't have been room to stand upright by the window on the far side. There was no light in the room and I could just see outlines of a narrow bed and a washstand.

'You wait here. I'll go in and make sure she's decent.'

Molly crossed the room and knocked on the inner door. 'Annie. Annie, are you awake? There's somebody to see you.'

No answer. Molly knocked again, then opened the door and walked in.

'Come on, Annie. You can't be that bad.'

I decided not to wait and followed Molly into the far room. It was hardly more than a cupboard with a bed along one side of it. All I could see was a dark hump under the covers. When there was still no reaction from it, Molly made an impatient noise and stretched out a hand.

'It's no use . . .' Then her voice changed. 'She's not here. There's nothing here.'

I joined her at the bedside, groping among the covers. There was a bolster doubled over, a rough blanket folded in half. Matches rattled in a box and the light of a candle spread round the small room. Nothing there except bed and bedclothes.

'Can you see if she's taken her things with her.'

'She didn't have much in any case. Her good coat's gone. She hangs it on that hook on the door.'

'What about shoes?'

Molly put the candle holder on the floor and looked under the bed.

'Same thing, her good shoes gone.'

'Could she have got downstairs and out of the back door without your mother knowing?'

'Easy.'

'What about somebody coming up? Would your mother have noticed if somebody had come in from outside and taken her away?'

Molly, still kneeling by the bed, stared up at me.

'You thinking of who I think you are?'

'Not anybody, yet. Just trying to understand.'

'I think she'd have noticed. Mum's used to Annie moving about, but if anybody else came in I think she'd have known.'

'So she went of her own accord and left the bolster so it would have looked as if she were still in bed. What time did you leave the house this morning?'

'Just before half past seven.'

'So she left some time after that, possibly not long after while it was still dark. You're sure she said nothing to you after she spoke to Luke Dobbs last night?'

'Nothing that mattered. I said she was a fool to speak to him. She didn't say anything to that, just that she felt ill and was going up to bed. You think she's gone away with him?'

'If so, she won't have gone far.' The police were watching Luke Dobbs. They wouldn't let him leave town, in company or alone.

'Do you think we ought to go to the police?'

I could tell from Molly's voice that she didn't want to. I agreed. 'What could they do? She's a grown-up person with a right to go where she wants.'

'We'll go and talk to Dobbs. If he's still around, he'll be at the Three Tuns any time now.'

'No, you stay here and get word to me at the King's Head if she comes back.' (I didn't think she would.) 'Bill and I will go and talk to Dobbs.'

We shut the door on Annie's room and went back downstairs. Molly put the candleholder on the table in the scullery and said in a low voice, 'I won't tell Mum yet. It would only worry her.'

'Yes.'

'Do you think she's in any danger – after the others?'

I didn't answer that. 'If we find out anything, I'll let you know.'

She let me out of the front door. I walked quickly through the town and found Bill in the saloon bar of the King's Head, talking to a man I didn't recognise. He came out to the corridor when he saw my face.

'What's up now?'

'Annie Carter's missing. She was talking to Luke Dobbs after they let him go yesterday.'

He got his coat and hat and we walked across the square to the Three Tuns. I waited outside while he went in. Five minutes later he came out.

'Dobbs is in the public bar, drinking beer and bad-mouthing the police. He was there at lunchtime too so he's well pickled by now.'

'Do you think the police are still watching him?'

'I'm sure they are. I recognised one of the constables in plain clothes drinking in a corner of the bar. Dobbs knew he was there, hence the bad-mouthing.'

'Did you speak to Dobbs?'

'I went up to him and said I was looking for Miss Annie Carter and did he know where I might find her. He said something I won't repeat, but the gist of it was that he doesn't know and he doesn't care. What do we do now?'

'I don't know. Wait, I suppose.'

As we walked slowly back to the King's Head, I asked who he'd been drinking with when I arrived.

'A man from the military police. He's as puzzled as the rest of them. He confirms that Wilby was supposed to be on sick leave staying with his married sister in Croydon and had no known connection with Duxbury or anywhere near it.'

'What about Wilby's brother-in-law? Is he here yet?'

'He wasn't on the train the police expected. They think he must have missed a connection and he'll be on the next one.'

He arrived, apprehensive and travel-weary, as we'd finished dinner and were going upstairs to our rooms, a plump man in his forties, with pale skin and crinkly red hair. The sergeant who delivered him into the care of Mrs Hincham said he should try to get a good night's rest and they'd come and collect him at half past eight in the morning. Wilby's brother-in-law was doubled up with coughing by then from the transition into warmth from the cold moist air outside and could only nod at the sergeant over his handkerchief. The sergeant didn't need to say where they'd be taking him at half past eight in the morning. The knowledge of it subdued the whole house and even the voices in the public bar dropped as young John carried his bag upstairs.

Chapter Eighteen

✍

In the morning, the last day of the old year, I waited in my room with the door open so as not to miss the police bringing Wilby's brother-in-law back. At intervals through the night I'd heard him coughing in the room above mine – the one that used to be Wilby's – and guessed he hadn't slept much. I didn't want to add to the man's burdens but I had to speak to him and once he'd identified the body he'd probably take the first train home to Croydon. As it happened, somebody else arrived first. Soon after nine o'clock I heard a familiar voice in the passage downstairs demanding to speak to Miss Bray. Lucinda Sollers. I went down and found her confronting Mrs Hincham. She was dressed dramatically as ever, in a black cloak and hat, but her face looked bare and gaunt. At other times, even at her most desperate, she'd been conscious of the effect she was making. Now she didn't care.

'Didn't you get my note? Why didn't you come and see me?'

I caught Mrs Hincham's eye and guided Lucinda into the snug. She looked out of place there and stood like an angular bird not knowing where to perch. I sat down at a table and she folded herself into the chair opposite without taking her eyes off my face.

I said, 'I didn't come because I didn't know what I could tell you.'

'This other man, Wilby – what happened?'

'His throat was cut.'

'When?'

'He disappeared twenty days ago. Nobody knows what happened to him after that.'

'I heard the police arrested a man.'

'And let him go again. There was no evidence.'

'What are the police doing?'

'I'm not in their confidence.'

'They sent somebody out to see me yesterday.'

I suppose I should have expected that, but I was surprised they'd got round to it so quickly. 'Who?'

'An inspector. Wall, that's it. He asked me if I'd ever heard of a man named Sergeant Wilby. I hadn't. We'd heard about the body being found but we didn't know who it was. Then he asked me if Charles had ever mentioned the name Wilby or had anything to do with the military police. I didn't know. Charles was on all sorts of committees and there were all sorts of names, but I don't remember that one.'

'Did the inspector seem to think Wilby's death and your husband's were connected?'

'I asked him that. He said he didn't know and they were keeping an open mind. But how could it be?'

'Two days before the election you told me you'd decided that your husband's death was an accident after all. Do you still think that?'

She pulled off a glove, finger by finger, and stretched it out on the table. 'I don't know what to think.'

'When we first met, you were certain your husband was murdered. What made you change your mind?'

'I suppose . . . I was shocked. I didn't know what I was doing.'

And yet she'd seemed more in control the first time I'd met her than now. She had to play with the glove to stop her hands shaking.

'You accused Jonas Tedder.'

'I was wrong about that. I told you.'

'What made you decide you were wrong?'

'You know what.'

'The piano?'

She nodded.

'I think there's something else. Something happened at the bonfire party and you only found out about it much later. It made you decide that you didn't want anybody looking into things too closely.'

This time she didn't ask what I meant. She looked away from me, down at the glove.

I said, 'Peter wasn't at school that night. He came home. He met somebody in the barn.'

'Felicity Tedder.' She breathed the name like a curse. I'd intended to respect Felicity's confidence as far as I could and not mention it.

'So Peter told you?'

She nodded.

'When?'

'After your friend played that trick on him.'

So Lucinda, like me, had made the right interpretation of Fah, Lah, Soh, Te. Perhaps there'd been a suspicion at the back of her mind all along and Peter, with some of the awful confidence knocked out of him that night, had broken down and admitted it.

'And that made you decide to call off the investigation?'

'What good would it have done? It wouldn't bring Charles back and Peter would have got into such trouble.'

'For playing truant from school or meeting Felicity Tedder in secret?'

'It wasn't his fault. Nothing happened, not what you're implying. And anyway, she encouraged him.'

' "The serpent tempted me and I did eat"?'

She was glaring at me now. 'You're as foul-minded as everybody else. You can see what I wanted to protect him from. After all, he's Charles' nearest relative, practically his adopted son.'

'What exactly are you trying to protect him from – trouble at school, trouble from Jonas Tedder?' No answer. 'Or what?' Still no answer. 'When the inspector came to see you yesterday, did he speak to Peter?'

'He asked him the same questions he asked me. Had he heard of Wilby or heard Charles mention the name? He hadn't. He described the man and asked if Peter had seen him anywhere. He hadn't.'

'Did the inspector ask anything about the bonfire party.'

'No, and you're not to tell him. I forbid you to tell him about Peter. It's nothing to do with anyone else. Do you understand?'

'I can't make any promises.'

'I was the one who brought you here. You wouldn't have known about it if it weren't for me.'

'You can't stuff me back in the bottle like Aladdin's genie. I wish you'd never brought me here too.'

We glared at each other for a while, then tears came into her eyes and she looked away. I felt guilty, but could only give her half of what she wanted.

'I haven't said anything to the police yet and I won't unless it's absolutely necessary. But two people are dead.' And one of those was partly on my conscience for not asking the right questions earlier.

'I'm sorry,' she said.

I didn't ask what she was sorry for. She got up to go and I went with her to open the door and see her into her governess cart that was waiting outside in the charge of one of the farm boys. Just as they drove away a motor car arrived, driven by the police sergeant and bringing back Wilby's brother-in-law.

He wasn't as shaken as I'd expected, but his cough had got worse, probably from the disinfectant fumes in the mortuary. The sergeant seemed happy to confide him to my care, so I took him into the snug and went to the kitchen for a pot of tea. When I brought it back he was sitting there, still in his overcoat, muffler and gloves. He accepted the tea without asking who I was and had the soft air of a man who was used to women fussing over him. Halfway down the second cup he sat back, undid the top buttons of his overcoat, sighed and said it was a sad business.

'Did you meet my brother-in-law, Miss . . . ?'

I explained about the election, the car and so on. He seemed mildly interested, but distracted by his symptoms, streaming eyes and a nose that needed frequent wiping.

'I really shouldn't be here at all. I was in bed under the doctor when the policeman came. There was this knock on the door and Flora looked out of the bedroom window and said it was the police. Well, I knew at once it would be something happened to Stephen.'

'You expected something to happen to him?'

'Not like that. I mean, who'd expect anything like that? In the war, when he was out in France, Flora used to worry about him. I'd say to her she shouldn't worry, that the redcaps always looked after themselves alright and you wouldn't find Stephen where the fighting was thickest. Not that he wouldn't do his duty. He was a great one for doing his duty, Stephen was. That was part of his trouble.'

'What was his duty, exactly?'

'Like all the rest of the redcaps, directing traffic, stopping people from pinching rations, rounding up deserters.'

'And he was out in France?'

'From nineteen sixteen up to two months before the Armistice. That was when his trouble started.'

'I gather he was on sick leave.'

'It wasn't sick leave, at first. He just had normal leave and came home near the start of September. He hadn't any other relatives, so when he was on leave he always came to stay with us. To be honest, I wasn't always best pleased about that, but he was Flora's only brother after all and blood's thicker than water, or so they say.'

He took another sniff and another mournful gulp of tea.

'Didn't you get on with him very well, then?'

'Oh no, I won't say I didn't get with him. He was alright in his way, but he was always fussing about things. If there was a tap dripping he had to see to it, a fork got in with the knives in the cutlery drawer it had to go straight back with the other forks. Always trying to get things in order. Flora didn't mind it, but then she's a bit that way herself.'

238

'So he came home on leave normally in September and then . . . ?'

'He seemed much the same as usual to start with, maybe a bit quieter. Then when he did start talking it was always about the same thing. Well, I listened to him at first and some of it was quite interesting in its way, but Stephen just kept on and on.'

'What about?'

'Deserters. Always deserters. Fair enough, it was his job, but he wouldn't let go of it. He'd go on and on about how he couldn't stand them, about how they were the scum of the earth and a man who deserted was letting another man be killed in his place. Which I'm sure we'd all agree with, but he didn't need to keep on about it, did he?'

His watery eyes stared at me over a damp handkerchief. I asked why his brother-in-law had been given sick leave.

'After he accused the vicar we knew we had to do something about it.'

'Accused the vicar of what?'

'Of being a deserter. There he was, shaking people's hands after morning service, seventy-five if he's a day and can't get up and down from the pulpit without somebody helping him, and Stephen looks him in the face and says straight out that he's arresting him on suspicion of deserting from His Majesty's Service.'

'What happened?'

'Well, the vicar took it very well considering. Flora and I got Stephen home and calmed him down, but after that people started talking and it came out about other things.'

'More deserters?'

'A bus queue, the grocer's boy and the milkman. Mind you, Flora and I had wondered what the milkman was doing out of uniform but you can't go round accusing people like Stephen did.'

'So what did you do?'

'Flora made me go up to London to talk to somebody, then we took Stephen to see an Army doctor. Very nice gentleman. He reckoned there was nothing wrong with Stephen except nervous strain and overwork. He put him on indefinite sick leave and said we should take him home, keep him quiet and try to get him interested in other things.'

'But it didn't work?'

'It seemed to at first. We managed to get hold of some paint and he helped me doing out the kitchen. If paint hadn't been so short I could have got him on to the spare room and all of this might never have happened. But we finished the painting and then the Armistice came and seemed to unsettle him all over again. He went quiet, then one morning he said the military police wanted him back to join a special unit looking for deserters in this country.'

'Did you believe him?'

'Looking back, perhaps we shouldn't have, but it seemed sensible enough at the time.' He gave a deep sigh that set off another coughing fit. 'To tell the truth, I didn't ask too many questions because I was glad to get rid of him by then.'

'So he left. When?'

'Back at the start of this month.'

'Did he ever talk about this part of the world?'

'Not a word. When the policeman came to tell us on Sunday afternoon I said "Where's Duxbury?" I'd never heard the name till then.'

'Or King's Swinton?'

He shook his head.

'When he came home in September you say he kept talking about deserters and some of it was quite interesting. Do you remember any particular names or cases?'

'Not names, no.'

'Cases then?'

He considered. 'I can't say I remember any in particular. They all seemed to flow together in my head. There was one I remember got himself up as a French woman going to market, only they rumbled him because of his boots. Then there were some gruesome ones as well.'

'Such as?'

'There was a headless German. Yes, I remember. It was something that happened back in the summer, not long before he came on leave. Our lads were pushing forward then, re-taking some of the ground that the Jerries had taken off us, and there were all the corpses from both sides that nobody had been able to get out of no-man's-land until then. Stephen was with some of the redcaps trying to get things tidied up, you know, men who'd been listed as missing for months or years being moved over to the "Died in Action" list. You can imagine the state some of the bodies were in. They had to turn them over to get their papers out of their pockets to find out who they were. When you come to think of it, it was probably that that sent Stephen a bit, you know.'

'This headless German?'

'I'm trying to remember. He was at the bottom of a heap in a shell-hole, so he was in an even worse state than the rest. His uniform was so covered in mud they didn't know whether he was one of ours or one of theirs until they found the papers in his breast pocket. Definitely Jerry. Only there was a funny thing, Stephen said. They found another lot of papers in the pocket of his greatcoat and these belonged to one of our men. Stephen kept on about it. What would a dead Jerry be doing with one of our boy's identity papers?'

'Perhaps he'd found a dead body and taken the papers off him.'

'That's what I said, but Stephen said what would have been the point of that? He'd have enough to worry about out there in no-man's-land without collecting dead men's papers. Stephen reckoned they must have been put there by somebody after Jerry had his head blown off.'

'Why?'

'He was trying to work that out, worrying away at it. I just gave up listening in the end.'

'And he never said what name was on the British identity papers?'

'If he did, I wasn't listening.'

He squirmed sideways in his seat to look at the clock on the wall.

'The landlady said she'd get the pony cart out to take me to the station. I don't want another night away from home. Flora will be waiting. She was hoping against hope it wouldn't be him after all, but I knew it would be.' He stood up, stuffing the handkerchief into his pocket and buttoning his coat. 'I asked the police if he could have done it to himself, but they didn't think so.'

'No.'

They must have spared him the sight of that throat. No suicide, however determined, could have cut that

242

deeply. I walked with him out to the yard where the pony cart was waiting with his bag on board. The last I saw of him as they trotted down the road to the station was his back bent in another bout of coughing. I went inside and found Bill.

'I'm going to get some truth out of Peter Chivas if I have to shake it out of him. Do you want to come with me?'

He did.

Chapter Nineteen

I told Bill about Wilby's brother-in-law as we were walking through the town, dodging past groups of gossiping shoppers.

'You know the Army. Can you think of any good reason why a dead German would have British identity papers as well as his own?'

'Not in those circumstances. He'd hardly have been a spy, in uniform in the trenches, and it's not as if the Germans paid a bounty for dead British soldiers. I suppose he might have taken the man prisoner.'

'And searched him and taken his papers in the middle of no-man's-land? Wouldn't he just have marched him back?'

'So what are you suggesting?'

'I'll know better when we've got hold of Peter Chivas. I'd like to talk to him without Lucinda there to protect him.'

We discussed how we could do that, walking down the road to the bridge. As we passed Molly's house I wondered whether to go in and see if Annie were back, but I knew it would be a waste of time. In the end we decided that we'd have to be direct about it and tell Lucinda we wanted to talk to him on his own.

'He might refuse to talk at all,' Bill said.

'He might, but when you're in a state of panic, it's easier to talk than not talk.'

'You think he's panicking?'

'Yes, even before they found Wilby's body. Much more now.'

In the end, the question of how to get Peter on his own solved itself. Bill and I had just turned into the track that ran down to Whitehorn Hall. It had started raining with a breeze from the west herding clouds in from Wales and the light was bad even in the middle of the morning. We heard a buzzing sound from down at the hall then it got louder, coming up the track towards us. A motor bicycle came into view labouring along a muddy rut no faster than a moderate walking speed with the rider bent over the handlebars. He didn't look up and see us until he was about twenty yards away. The front wheel wobbled. He jabbed a foot down to steady himself. Bill and I moved over to the middle of the track. Bill shouted to him above the engine noise, 'We want to talk to you.' The engine noise turned to a roar and the bike came at us like a charging animal. Peter's mouth was open, yelling something we couldn't hear. We jumped aside. I landed in the ditch and felt water coming in over my boots and thorns digging into my back through the coat. Bill was in the hedge on the opposite side, also shouting something inaudible at Peter's retreating back. But the back wasn't there for long. The machine skidded in the mud, lurched sideways. Peter must have dragged it upright and tried to accelerate out of trouble because it kept going for a few heartbeats but the balance had gone. It tilted again and this time went over. The machine went flat into the mud with its engine whining like a giant mosquito and

Peter went headfirst into the ditch. Bill ran to it, did something to the engine and the whining stopped. I dragged myself out of my own bit of ditch and ran to Peter. He was moving, his back jerking and his legs in brown leather riding boots scrabbling. His face was down in the ditch, under several inches of muddy water. Bill joined me and we got down on either side of him, took his shoulders and managed to haul his face clear. A rhythmic moaning came from him. His eyes were closed and his face dead white, apart from a long and shallow gash across the forehead that was adding a wash of blood to the wet.

'Can you move your legs round?'

Considering how he felt about the boy, Bill's voice wasn't unkind but there was no response and Peter stayed a dead weight in our hands. Slowly we manoeuvred him out of the ditch and on to his back on the grass verge. This caused a few yells.

'My ankle. I've broken my ankle.'

My guess was that it was twisted rather than broken, but it was hard to tell with a boot on. In any case, best to leave it on for support and cut through it later. We did a quick check and apart from the cut and the ankle there seemed to be no serious damage. I dabbed at the cut with my handkerchief, clean luckily, and Bill took off his overcoat and spread it over Peter. All the time he kept on moaning.

'My ankle, oh my ankle.'

'You'll do.' Bill straightened up, the disgust back in his voice now he knew Peter was in no serious danger. 'Nell, I'm going down to the house to get some people to help carry him. Are you alright here with him?'

Over Peter's head, his eyes signalled to me that this was my chance and I shouldn't waste it. It was more callous than the Bill I thought I knew and I had to remind myself that in four years he'd seen a lot worse than a spoiled boy with a hurt ankle. I tried to signal back that yes, I understood and Bill nodded and started walking down the track, in no great hurry. Peter had his eyes closed.

I said, 'Since we've got to wait, you can answer a question or two.' After all, he had tried to run us down. He only groaned. 'I'm not going to ask you if you were here at home the night your uncle was killed. I know you were.'

'I didn't kill him. I didn't kill anybody.'

'You met somebody in the barn, just before the party started.'

His eyes opened, furious. 'Did she tell you that? She's a bitch.'

'Not very gallant, considering she was risking her reputation in meeting you at all.'

'I didn't ask her to. It was her idea. She wrote saying she couldn't live without me, that she'd kill herself.'

'She says you wrote asking her to meet you. One of you is lying. I know which one.'

Felicity was not only more than ten years older, there was a sense of self-preservation about her that would save her from losing her head over anyone, let alone a schoolboy. She might have been flattered enough and bored enough to flirt with him, but not to risk her comfortable marriage. He groaned something about not lying and his ankle hurting.

'Anyway, it doesn't matter. The point is that you were there in the barn. What happened afterwards?'

'I told her I didn't love her, I didn't want anything more to—'

'I'm not interested in your romances. What did you *do*?'

'Went away. Walked to the station. Caught a train, the late train. I had to sleep in a church in Shrewsbury all night because I couldn't get back into school.'

That at any rate sounded like the truth. When he talked about not getting back into school his voice went young and petulant, a long way from the attempt at a worldly tone.

'Did you see anybody before you went away from the farm?'

He shook his head.

'Nobody at all?'

'There were some of the boys carrying wood. I didn't talk to them.'

'Or to anyone else?'

'No.'

He was still moving his head from side to side, making faces, but at least he was getting into the habit of answering. Bill would be down at the house by now, soon on his way back with the stretcher party. Not much time.

'What happened before you saw Felicity Tedder in the barn?'

His head stopped moving and his body went rigid as if he expected a blow. 'Nothing. Nothing happened.'

'How did you get there?'

'Walked from the station.'

'Did you go straight to the barn?' It was a simple enough question, but I had to repeat it.

'I waited, to make sure there was nobody about.'

'Waited where?'

'There's a bit of wall near the barn. I waited there.'

'Did you see anybody.'

'It was dark.'

'Hear anybody?'

No answer.

'You kept her waiting in the barn. You were late.'

'She's a bitch.'

'Never mind that. You weren't only late, you were scared. Do you remember what you said to her?'

'No.'

'Of course you do. You told her you'd seen a ghost. She didn't believe you. She thought you were only making excuses and you were scared because you were playing truant.'

'Bitch, bitch, bitch.'

'She was wrong about that. You really believed what you were saying. You still believe it now.'

He was crying and shaking. Delayed shock possibly. 'Alright. It's true. He was dead and I saw him.'

'It was dark.'

'He struck a match. Struck a match to light a cigarette, standing there outside the barn. I saw his face. Then the match went out and he disappeared.'

'Disappeared or walked away?'

'Just disappeared, like ghosts do.'

I could hear voices coming up the track, Bill's and others.

'Whose ghost?'

The fear was real. He didn't want to tell me, as if naming it would somehow bring it back. In the end he squeezed a name out, hardly parting his lips. It was the name I expected but I made him say it again to be sure. As Bill came up with two of the farm lads carrying a hurdle for a stretcher I caught his eye and nodded.

We helped carry Peter back to the house. By the time we got there he was either unconscious or, more probably, pretending to be. Lucinda, waiting by the front door, gave a little cry when she saw him. Bill had told her that he'd had an accident on his motor bicycle but wasn't badly hurt, leaving out the fact that he'd tried to run us down. The housekeeper was with Lucinda and they'd already telephoned for a doctor. They wanted us to wait and fussed about our water-logged boots but there was nothing more we could do there and I needed to talk to Bill. We talked all the way back into Duxbury, walking fast and squishing ditchwater with every step, and this time I didn't keep anything from him.

'Wherever he is, Annie is.'

'Voluntarily?'

'Is anything voluntary in this situation? I'm surprised she hasn't gone mad as well.'

'Mad?'

'What else can you call it?'

Bill said, 'Do we tell the police?'

'I want to get her away first. They'd call her an accomplice.'

'Which she is.'

'Not to murder. I don't think she had anything to do with either of them.'

'How do we get her away if we don't know where she is.'

'She won't have gone far. He won't go far away and she'll stay with him. Bill, she's gone through so much. At least give me a chance to get her clear of it.'

We argued all the way into town. It was just past three o'clock by the time we got to the bridge but the light was going already. Last light of the old year. Last light of the strangest year I'd ever known.

'Alright Nell, until tomorrow. If nothing's happened by then, we go to the police and tell them everything we—'

'Know?'

'That's what I was going to say, but we *don't* know.'

'In that case, there's nothing to tell and one more night won't make much difference.'

I asked him if he knew from his chats with the police where Luke Dobbs lodged.

'Yes, a street just off to the left here. But you won't get anywhere talking to him.'

'I know that, but he's central to everything. He could tell us what we're only guessing.'

Then we would know. Did I want to know?

'He could, but he won't. The police didn't get much out of him and he's scared as well as angry.'

'Probably with reason.'

We crossed the bridge and the road, then turned up a narrow side street to the left. It was still within range of the tannery smell, which probably accounted for its run-down look. Almost all the streets in Duxbury ended with a view of fields and open sky but this one got there sooner than most. Two stubby lines of brick terraced houses ended abruptly at a broken wooden fence with pasture on the other side and brown bullocks grazing. The street was deserted apart from one man, too neatly dressed for his surroundings, walking slowly up the cobblestones with time to kill. When he saw us he said 'Good evening sir' to Bill and touched his cap to me. A more obvious plain-clothes man I'd never seen in all my life.

'Good evening. Has our friend come out yet?'

'He looked out half an hour ago. He had his hat and coat on and I thought he was going out, but he had a look around and scuttled back inside like a rabbit with a ferret after him.'

He and Bill were looking at a house in the middle of the row on the right, number six. It looked more decrepit than the rest, with a cracked window upstairs and paint flaking off the front door.

'Perhaps he saw you,' I said, though the man was too mild-looking to be a ferret.

'I don't think so, miss. He didn't even look my way.'

The three of us wandered over together to the house. There was a litter of straw and bits of newspaper blown against the worn sandstone doorstep and something else too solid to have been put there by the wind. It was a forked leafless branch from a small tree, about two foot long. It was beside the doorstep with its forked end resting against the wall in a place where somebody coming out could hardly fail to see it. I pointed it out to the plain-clothes man.

'Dobbs saw it too. He picked it up and put it down again.'

'Could that have been what made him scuttle back inside?'

I picked it up. The bark was ridged and soft like cork, surrounding a thin circle of wood and a core of white pith. The larger end of it had been newly cut from the tree with a sharp knife.

'Elder.'

Bill said, 'What's so alarming about an elder branch?'

'Don't you know the superstition? Judas hanged himself from an elder.'

Bill stared at me.

'So he did,' said the plain-clothes man.

'It was put there as a message to Luke Dobbs, and from the way he bolted back inside, he knows it was.'

I looked at the field and the bullocks grazing quietly in the dusk. Anybody could have come across the field and over the fence. Anybody could be out there still, watching and waiting.

I said to the plain-clothes man, 'When did you come on duty? Was it there then?'

'It must have been. I came on at one and nobody's been up or down the street since then.'

'Was there somebody on duty here all night?'

He didn't know for sure. He thought the men on patrol had probably been told to keep an eye out for Dobbs.

'So it was probably put there last night or this morning while it was still dark.'

After Dobbs had been questioned by the police and released. After somebody might have heard about that and believed he'd told the police more than he had.

'Somebody's telling Dobbs he's a traitor. A false friend.'

I gave the elder branch to the plain-clothes man. He took it uneasily, as if it really were tainted.

'I don't suppose he'll be coming out again today,' I said.

'I'd say you're wrong, miss. There's no power'll keep Luke Dobbs away from the Three Tuns especially on New Year's Eve.'

We said goodbye to him and walked slowly back to the centre of town. In the High Street the feeling of new year celebration was in the air, with lights on in the shop windows and women with full shopping baskets blocking the pavements as they stopped to talk. Most of the talk seemed cheerful. Wilby had been an outsider, after all, and probably none of them had even met him. The manner of his death was something to shudder and talk about, not something to spoil the first new year of the peace. But the person who'd come across the bullock field in the dark carrying a branch of traitor's tree would be out there somewhere with nothing to celebrate.

Chapter Twenty

'Life going on is what hurts. Haven't you ever felt that? Something dreadful happens and you feel the whole world should stop, but it won't.'

Bill didn't answer my question. With less than half an hour of the old year to go, he and I were walking slowly along a path behind the church between dark clumps of yew bushes. We'd done a lot of walking that evening, waiting for we didn't know what.

'The victory party was the first thing. Charles Sollers and the rest of them were saying it was all right, it was all over, they'd won. Only it wasn't all right and it wasn't all over. Then there we were with our election campaigning. Elections are about the future, they have to be. But perhaps things can be so bad that even people talking about a future are an obscenity.'

'You can't give reasons to madness.'

'You can in this case. That's why I know something's going to happen tonight.'

Welcoming the new year meant leaving the old year behind, but there was somebody who couldn't do that. Sometime before the celebrations were over, the violence would come. Only, I didn't know when or where which was why Bill and I had been walking and waiting. He still wasn't convinced, I knew that, but he wouldn't leave me on my own. Dutiful as ever. Every half hour or so our wanderings had taken us back to the square. The Three Tuns, like most of the other public houses, had an extension till midnight and was the focus of the celebrations of the rougher element of the town. Its walls were already bulging from age, but as the night went on they seemed to bulge more from the press of the men inside and rock with singing and the jangling of an old piano. A police constable was stationed in solitary sobriety outside. Inside Luke Dobbs hunched on the end of the settle near the fire, like a drone bee in the middle of a buzzing swarm, drinking steadily and not talking. We knew because Bill put his head into the bar to check. We knew too from the constable that Luke had eventually left his lodgings at around seven o'clock and scuttled to the pub so fast that the plain-clothes man could hardly keep up with him. The constable didn't seem to find it odd that Captain Musgrave should ask. Dobbs was everybody's business.

We'd checked on the pub a quarter of an hour or so before then strolled towards the church because that's where other people were going. The respectable element of Duxbury scorned the public houses, but were coming out of their houses to hear the bells ring in the new year. The bell-ringers were already arriving, passing us on the yew walk and slipping in at the lighted door of the vestry. Bill lit his pipe then struck another match to look at his watch.

'Ten to. I'm going to see the inspector tomorrow and ask if he still needs us here. If not, we could be on the midday train.'

'I'm not thinking about tomorrow.'

'You'll have to. It's nearly here.'

Another figure came hurrying along the path and went in at the vestry door. We walked round to the churchyard at the front. There were perhaps fifty people standing in little groups on the path and among the gravestones.

'Nell, Bill. Hello.'

Moira, with Morgan beside her, silent as usual. I hadn't seen her since my party, but she'd heard about discovering Wilby's body.

'So many terrible things. Did you hear that we'd been attacked?'

'You and Morgan?' That didn't fit at all.

'No, the memorial slab we were carving. Somebody got into Morgan's workshed last night and attacked it with a hammer.'

'What part of it?'

'Nell, what an odd question. The bottom of it. He'd smashed away at—'

Then the clock started striking and everybody went quiet. Twelve low, slow strokes clanging out over the town, probably audible in fields miles away. After the twelfth stroke there was a sigh from everybody standing among the gravestones, perfectly simultaneous as though they'd rehearsed it and then the bells started pealing, and people were wishing each other a happy new year. We stayed for a while with Moira and Morgan but I didn't ask her anything else. The last question had been answered now and I knew all I needed to know. Except where and when.

'Well, that's it,' Bill said. He sounded relieved, as if that midnight sigh had resolved something. 'We're into a new year.'

'Let's get back to the square.'

257

When we got there, groups of young men were standing around and more were coming out of the Three Tuns. One man was being sick on the cobblestones with a group of appreciative friends round him. Another lot were singing 'It's a long way to Tipperary' more or less in tune. They seemed to be making no movement towards home. In fact, although the turning of the year had come and gone, they still looked as if they were waiting for something. The same constable watched from the far side of the square with the sadness of a sober man among the cheerful. Bill and I went over to him.

'No sign of Dobbs?' Bill asked him.

'He's still inside, sir.'

As he said it a surge of men came out of the pub, talking and laughing. Tagging along behind them, not very steady on his feet, came Luke Dobbs. He didn't look as if he belonged with the rest and nobody spoke to him or looked at him, but he seemed determined not to be left behind. There were thirty or so young men in the square now and the group that had just come out must have included their leaders because they started forming up in something that was too informal to be called a procession, more like a herd movement. They moved out of the square, past the King's Head then into the High Street and turned south towards the tannery and the river bridge. There were no lights on in the shops and Duxbury didn't run to many street lamps so they were moving as a long dark shape. The singing had stopped when they left the square and there was mostly silence, apart from the tramp of feet and the occasional muttered remark. Bill and I fell in behind, alongside the constable.

'Where are they all going?'

'Nupp's farm, I expect, just the other side of the bridge. That's the nearest.'

'Nearest for what?'

'Burning the bush. It's the way they always used to see in the new year. They stopped it in the war, but I suppose now it's over they want to do it again.'

He seemed to assume we knew what he was talking about. It sounded as if we were in for some kind of ritual incendiarism and considering what had happened the last time Duxbury had a bonfire party the unease that had been nagging at me all evening got worse. Somewhere in the herd of young men was Luke Dobbs, not because he wanted to be there but because safety was in crowds. They left the narrow High Street and spread out in the broader road going down to the bridge, but still with the same slow sense of purpose. Over the bridge, lights were on in the tannery cottages and there was a little group of people waiting outside, all of them women. I went over to them.

'Is that you, Molly?'

'Yes. Annie's not come back yet.'

'What's going on?'

'It's only a thing the men do to bring good luck. The girls are waiting to see the lights up on the hill.'

The men walked past the women with a few shouts of 'Happy New Year'. They sounded to me a touch ill at ease, as if they weren't quite convinced by what they were doing but intended to go through with it anyway. Then they took a turning to the right into a narrow uphill road between high banks with hedges on top and just a narrow strip of sky visible overhead. Left again, through a gateway and into a farmyard. There was mud underfoot and a clucking of hens suddenly roused from sleep. The men stopped in the yard and started calling to come out and get started. A door in a barn opened and several more men came out with lanterns. Some of them were carrying stone cider jars like the one that had felled Prest. The tallest of them carried a pitchfork upright with a mass of sticks impaled on it, like a circular birdsnest.

'What's that?'

'The bush.'

I gave up trying to understand what they were at. In any case, heads turned towards us when I whispered to the constable. He hadn't been invited and neither had we. The men filed through the farmyard, along a track and out to a ploughed field, the man with the pitchfork in front and the carriers of the lanterns and the cider jars on either side. The mud was sticky and the field sloped steeply towards the town and the river, making walking difficult. The crowd began to fan out and individuals appeared as silhouettes against the lamplight or darker humps against the sky.

'There goes Dobbs,' Bill said.

There was a hunched-up look about him that you could pick out in silhouette. He was downslope with two or three other men, who didn't seem to be paying much attention to him. Without anything being said, Bill, the constable and I fell in behind the group.

'There it goes.'

A burst of cheering and shouting from higher up the slope. A small blob of fire was moving across the field a little higher than a man's height, bobbing up and down. As my eyes adjusted I could see the man carrying it on the pitchfork, running unsteadily over the heavy ploughland. There was more cheering, then the crackling and flare of a larger fire. As the bonfire took hold another sound started, a kind of male howling. Maybe husky dogs in Arctic wastes make the same kind of sound. It started quite low and long drawn-out, then a high staccato yap, then another long note, starting loud and dying away until it was no more than a throbbing in the air. Then before the throbbing died away the drawn-out howl started rising again. I found out later that what they were howling was 'Auld Ci-der', pouring the stuff out on the ploughland round the bonfire in a crop rite that went back goodness knows how long. It was not surprising that they'd been a little shame-faced about wanting to do it still in a world of motor cars and machine guns. At the time, all I knew was that cold crawled up my spine and the feeling of unease flared into a panic that made me want to shout out and run.

Then Bill said, 'Where's Dobbs?'

For a while, everybody's attention had been on the bonfire and howling. All the people who hadn't got there in time for the lighting were still plodding to it across the field, easier to see now the fire was flaring. The furthest group, and lowest down the field, was the one that had included Luke Dobbs. We managed to pick them out but couldn't see the familiar hunched figure.

'I'll go and see.'

Before I could say anything, Bill and the constable went running towards them. I thought of following, but it didn't need two of us and I was watching the bonfire. Fire and people celebrating. It was a magnet that had drawn a murderer once, and unless I was very wrong, would do it again. I started to move up the field towards the fire, sensing that women wouldn't be welcome there but it was no time to worry about that. I'd got about halfway there, finding it heavy going in town shoes over the plough, when there was a yell from somewhere below me.

There was nothing ritual about that yell. It was pure terror, like an animal. It can't have sounded so loud up by the bonfire, because the figures up there went on with whatever it was they were doing. I couldn't even see Bill and the constable, but it didn't come from the direction where they'd been going. It was almost directly below me, towards the bottom of the field.

I shouted to Bill and started running downslope. There were trees down there, I could see that much and, from what I remembered, the river. The cry came again, breathless now and faint, but closer to me than it had been.

'What's happening?'

A man's voice tried to answer but it wasn't coherent, just a babble of words, something about 'get me'.

I said, 'Is that you, Luke Dobbs?'

Then Bill's voice now, from some way off. 'Nell, what's happening?'

I called back, took another step downslope and practically fell over Luke Dobbs. We both staggered and had to prop each other up, with him puffing beer and terror into my face.

'. . . tried to drag me . . . down there by the willows . . . drown me.'

Even through my skirt I could feel that his trousers were soaking wet.

'Nell, where are you?'

'Over here.' I held on to Luke Dobbs with my face close to his, more or less willing words into his fuddled brain.

'You'll have to tell the police all about it. They won't shoot you. Even if they send you to prison for a while, you'll be safe there.'

'Assisting deserters. Gets you shot.'

'Nobody's going to shoot you. Anyway, it wasn't your fault.'

'Made me do it. Nothing in it for me. Tossed a coin to see which one of 'em was going to live. Didn't give me my chance.'

'I know. It really wasn't your fault.'

'Nell?' Bill and the constable, only yards away.

'Here's the constable now. Go back with him. Tell the inspector everything and he'll see you're locked up safely in a nice dry cell.'

'Is that him, miss?'

'Yes, it's Luke Dobbs. He's got a lot of things he wants to tell you, but I suggest you get him straight back to the station before he dies of cold.'

I still had my hands on Dobbs' shoulders and could feel the relief in him as he gave up at last. Luckily, the constable didn't argue. After all, keeping an eye on Luke Dobbs was what he was there to do. He unhitched Dobbs from me and hooked an arm through his.

'Come on, you.'

These words, probably familiar, seemed a comfort to Dobbs. He let himself be led away.

I said to Bill, 'You'd better go with them in case he needs help.'

'Dobbs or the constable? Anyway, I'm not going anywhere until you come with me.'

'I'm staying here for a while.'

'Then I'm staying here as well, until daylight or until you tell me what exactly's going on. Whichever comes sooner.'

'I'm looking for somebody.'

'Annie Carter?'

'Yes, and somebody else. Dobbs had been in the river. Somebody tried to drag him in.'

'You should have told the constable to send people back. I'll run after him.'

'No. Give her a chance at least.'

He drew a long deep breath, but when I started walking to the line of trees that I thought marked the river, he followed. On the hill up above us the howling had died away and there were more normal shouts and laughter coming from round the bonfire. None of them knew what had been happening half a field away. The trees were pollarded willows. We struggled through bramble stems and tussocks of dead grass to the nearest one and leaned against it, looking down. We could smell and hear the river, very close below us, but not see it. From the sound, it was flowing fast.

'That way first. Tree to tree.'

We moved carefully upriver, from one willow trunk to the next, waiting at each tree and listening. At one of them, just as we were about to move on, there was a little sound ahead that might have been a dog or an otter. We froze.

'Annie?'

It wasn't exactly a sound that told us she was so close, more a sudden absence of sound as if she'd stopped breathing.

'Annie, it's Nell Bray. The police have gone. I want to talk to you.'

The breathing started again, harsh and distressed. She was just the other side of the big willow trunk.

'I know what happened. The police don't yet, but they will any minute now.' As soon as Luke Dobbs got back to the station. 'Listen, I know there were the two of them, your brother and the man you were engaged to. That last time, when they were home on leave, they decided that one of them was going to survive at least. They tossed a coin for it.'

Beside me, Bill started to say something, then stopped as Annie's voice came out of the dark.

'It were for me. They said one of them should be left to look after me.'

I waited for her to say something else, but she let the words hang there.

'They kept to their agreement,' I said. 'The one who lost the toss went back to France with his friend's papers as well as his own. He answered for him at roll call. He must have needed some help there, which was probably why he told Luke Dobbs about it.'

Nothing in it for Dobbs, but he'd kept faith with his friends too, even though he was committing a serious offence by aiding desertion. It wouldn't have mattered much at the time. None of them expected to survive long.

'There was a plan of a kind. As soon as there was a chance, the one who lost the toss would find a dead body and plant his friend's papers on it so that it would look as if he'd been killed in action. He did it. He even found a body without a head. The only problem was, it was a German soldier's body.'

There was a sound on the other side of the tree. This time, I was sure it didn't come from Annie. I saw Bill's head go up.

'That didn't come out until months later, and poor Sergeant Wilby got obsessed with it. Meanwhile, the friend who stayed at home was having to live off the land. That's not too hard in summer for a countryman, but it got harder in the winter. He was still close enough to the town to know what was going on, even came in there sometimes at nights. He knew that his friend had been killed – and that it was his fault.'

'No, it weren't his fault.' The cry from Annie masked any other sound there might have been.

'He thought it was his fault and the guilt of it drove him half mad. I'm sure he must have wished that they'd never thought of it, that he'd just gone back and been killed like the rest. But he'd made his decision. He was an outcast with no more future than if he had been killed. He blamed everybody, especially Charles Sollers who could have saved them from it all.'

'He could have saved us with one stroke of his fucking pen.' Not Annie's voice this time. A man's voice. It came out in a low roar as if the tree itself had spoken. 'With just the one fucking stroke.'

'Simon Whittern,' I said.

There was a silence, then feet swishing in the grass. Bill was trying to move past me and round the tree trunk. I put out an arm to stop him and spoke at the tree.

'The police know now. Luke's talking to them. He only did that because you tried to drown him. He wasn't a traitor. He didn't tell them about the barn. I did.'

Silence, but I could feel the man listening on the other side of the trunk, as if the few yards of darkness between us had become a vibrating membrane.

'So the police know now, and there's nothing else to be done except one thing. Unless you want Annie arrested as an accessory to murder, you must tell them she didn't know anything about Sollers or Wilby.'

'She didn't know.'

Annie started saying, 'I don't want—'

But he cut across her. 'She didn't know. I'll tell the police and the judge and the whole fucking lot, she didn't know.'

'I believe you, but it's them you've got to convince. If you come back with us now—'

'No.' Annie, with a determination in her voice that I'd never heard before. 'No, 'e's not doing that. They'll 'ang him.' Then a silence, and her voice again, less certain, 'They'll 'ang him, won't they?'

Neither Bill nor I answered, but she must have read our silence. I said, as gently as I could, 'I think you should come back with us now, Annie.'

'No.'

'The police will come looking for him. If they find you together, they won't believe you had nothing to do with it.'

'You go back with them, Annie. There's no point in any of it if you don't.' Simon Whittern's voice, less harsh. Up till that point, I'd thought that self-preservation had had a lot more to do with it than love. I could be wrong.

'I'm staying with 'im. Whatever they do to 'im, I'm staying with 'im.'

Impasse. A bramble prickled my ankles. Up the field, things had gone quiet. The other men were probably going to their homes and their beds. Down at the station, Luke Dobbs would be telling the story. On the other side of the tree, Annie said something to him in a low voice I couldn't catch. There was silence for a while, then a rustling in the undergrowth.

Bill said, suddenly, 'He's getting away.'

He moved away from me, round the landward side of the tree. I stumbled over damp roots on the river side of it and we met in a trampled patch where Annie and Simon Whittern must have been standing.

'There they are.'

Two dark shapes were running along the edge of the field. The smaller one seemed to stumble, the larger one hesitated, took her hand perhaps, then they ran on together.

'Bill, no.'

I caught his right arm, with more force than I'd intended. He pulled away and we both lost balance, feet slipping on the dead wet grass. Then he was gone, with a cry and a splash into the river. At first I wasn't too worried. I knew Bill was a good swimmer and it was quite a small river. Then it dawned on me that nobody's a good swimmer with a broken elbow. I tore off my coat and shoes and let myself down into water I still couldn't see. The cold struck through to my bones.

'Bill?'

A shout from somewhere just ahead. I let the current take me, bouncing me into the bank and tree roots and off again, swimming when I could. After what seemed a long time something larger and darker than a tree came up on my right then there was total darkness overhead and a clammy smell. Stonework. A bridge. The lower stones were big and square cut. I managed to get my fingertips hooked on one of them.

'Nell?'

Bill's voice. I felt like crying with relief.

'Where are you?'

'Over here. It's not so deep. I just can't manage to get out.'

I flailed over to him. With three good arms between us we managed it and ended up like two beached fish on the pavement. It was the tannery bridge, deserted now. Bill could hardly stand. He was still in his sodden overcoat and would have been dragged down if the current had been less strong. It was too dark to see his face.

'I didn't push you,' I said.

'We'd better be getting back. Can you walk?'

'Of course I can walk.'

We slopped side by side through the empty town, hardly a light on anywhere, until a car carrying several uniformed policemen came down the street, headlamps blazing and swept past us without slowing down.

'At any rate,' Bill said, 'you gave her a chance.'

I knew he didn't believe me about not pushing him.

Chapter Twenty-one

The police must have been too busy with Luke Dobbs to worry about us that night. The call to the police station didn't come until eight o'clock the next morning. By then Bill had developed a streaming cold and his elbow was bad. I was afraid that the fracture had opened up again, but he refused to go to the doctor and I was in no position to insist on anything. The police station felt like a general's headquarters, with people rushing in and out, telephones ringing, a constable marking off sections of a big map on the wall. The inspector saw us together this time.

'I gather you were actually at the bush burning last night.'

We told him everything, except that neither of us mentioned Annie Carter. I was grateful to Bill for that.

'And you actually spoke to Whittern?'

'Yes,' I said.

'Do you know he's wanted in respect of the killings of Mr Sollers and Sergeant Wilby?'

'I didn't know he was wanted. You didn't know that yourselves until you spoke to Luke Dobbs.'

'But you suspected?'

Bill said to me, 'You don't have to answer that.'

'Yes, I suspected.'

The inspector gave me a long look.

'It's a pity you didn't manage to detain him last night.'

'Captain Musgrave tried to and fell in the river. I knew he couldn't swim with his broken elbow so I went after him.'

As I'd hoped, this touching combination of soldierly and womanly duty did its work. Inspector Wall looked pious and said he realised we'd done all that could be expected of us.

'In that case,' Bill said, 'I wonder if you'd have any objection if we leave tomorrow. I'm supposed to report back to hospital in Oxford and Miss Bray has her responsibilities in London.'

It sounded impressive, though for the moment I couldn't think of any. Again, it worked. No objection he could think of, provided we left addresses.

'One other thing, Whittern's fiancée, Annie Carter, has disappeared from her lodgings. I gather you knew her, Miss Bray.'

'Yes, she worked for me in my election campaign.'

'Have you any idea where she might be?'

'None.'

We got up and shook hands. At the door I said, 'Do I take it you haven't found Simon Whittern yet?'

'Oh we'll find him, have no fear of that.'

Back at the King's Head, Mrs Hincham took one look at Bill, called to young John to make up the fire in the snug and started concocting her own cold cure, involving whisky, honey and hot water. I went out and wandered round the town. Everywhere I went there were little knots of people talking about it, looking over their shoulders in case anybody was listening, and a general guarded atmosphere as if the place were closing up against outsiders. The odd thing was that there was no enthusiasm for the hunt that was going on in the barns and fields round the town, no sense of cheering on the police. These people knew the country and if they'd wanted Simon Whittern to be caught, they'd have got him before the new year was twelve hours old. I became convinced that some of them, at least, must have known about him all the time. To live off the land from spring through to winter a man would need some help, or at least the turning of a blind eye when potatoes disappeared from clamps or lambs from pastures. There was something old and stubborn in Duxbury that I'd caught glimpses of only now and then. It wasn't a lawlessness, exactly, more of a refusal to move to any other tune but their own. Charles Sollers, with his money from the Midlands, had been an outsider, poor Wilby even more so. Simon Whittern, whatever he'd done, was one of their own and they weren't going to show any unnecessary enthusiasm in getting him to the gallows.

Towards the end of the afternoon, I decided that I'd have to speak to Lucinda Sollers. I walked out to Whitehorn Hall along the road that had become so familiar, wondering why the prospect of being back in London by this time tomorrow seemed as bleak as the grey sky overhead. The housekeeper showed me in and Lucinda came into the hall when she heard our voices and drew me into her sitting-room.

'You were wrong, weren't you? You thought it was poor Peter.'

She looked tired, but less nervy than I'd seen her before, as if a crisis had come and passed.

'For a while I did, yes.' I didn't add, which would have been the truth, that there'd been a time when she thought it was Peter as well.

'And it was Simon Whittern all the time. The inspector told me when they came out this morning. They searched all the outhouses and barns.'

'I suppose they thought he'd come back to a place he knew.'

'Why did he do it?' There was no bitterness or anger in the question, just curiosity.

'He blamed your husband for not keeping him out of the Army in the first place, but it was worse than that. Simon Whittern deserted and Tom Carter went back, covered up for him and got killed. When Simon somehow heard about that he was already living as an outlaw, sleeping rough, stealing food where he could. Imagine him lying awake cold and hungry at nights with nothing to do but think about it. He must have felt guilt that he was alive and his friend was dead. After a while, it would feel as if Tom had died in his place – which in a way he had. Too much for him to bear all that guilt out there on his own, so he started to play the "if only" game. If only he hadn't deserted. If only he hadn't had to go into the Army in the first place. If only your husband had signed that piece of paper to keep him at home.'

She'd been listening quietly, head down. Now she looked up at me. 'Charles was only doing his duty. He died because he did his duty, like all those other men.'

If it comforted her to see it that way, I wasn't going to argue.

'Do you think they'll catch him?'

'Do you want them to?'

Very slowly, she shook her head. 'What good would it do? One more person dead, that's all.'

I regretted the times I'd been annoyed with her. There was more to Lucinda than I'd realised.

She said, 'There was something I didn't tell the police when they came this morning.'

'What was that?'

'Peter's motor bicycle's been stolen. After he had that accident on it I sent one of the boys to bring it back and clean it. It was in the barn. Last night, or rather early this morning, I heard somebody riding it away.'

'When was this?'

'Around three in the morning.'

A motor bicycle and clear roads. A man who was more than half-starved and a girl worn to a shadow. It would take them miles away from where the police were looking. They must have gone straight to Whitehorn Farm from the river bank, Whittern still sticking close to the places that he knew. Perhaps it had taken Annie to convince him that he must get right away at last.

'Did you decide not to tell the police, or did it just slip your mind?'

'I decided. Do you think I should have told them?'

'No.'

'I haven't told Peter yet. He hasn't asked about it.'

'He couldn't ride it with a bad ankle in any case. Did you know he saw Whittern in the yard the night your husband died?'

'No! Why didn't he say anything?'

'He thought he was seeing a ghost.'

'He does see ghosts sometimes.'

'That wasn't one.'

'Should I tell him?'

'That's up to you. I don't think he has a right to know.' Not after the piano business.

'He's better than you think he is. Peter's just at a difficult age.'

I thought but didn't say that Peter would probably be at a difficult age all his life. She needed something, after all.

She sighed. 'But perhaps I won't tell him. It might upset him, thinking he could have prevented it and he has to go back to school next week. I suppose you'll be going away too.'

'Tomorrow.'

Another sigh. Charles gone, Peter gone, the Tedders off triumphantly to Westminster and all her old circle of friends drawing away from Sollers' eccentric widow.

I said, 'I wonder if you'd do something for me?'

'What?'

'There's a woman who works at the tannery called Molly Davitt. She and her friends are going to lose their jobs when the men come home. They're thinking of setting up a leather workshop, only they need some advice and finance.'

Lucinda might be lonely, but she was a rich woman too. Luckily, I was wearing the belt that Molly had given me. I unclasped it from my waist and gave it to her. She looked at it and started tracing the pattern with her fingers.

'Good workmanship, don't you think?'

'Mmm, the buckle's too heavy.'

'That's the kind of thing you could help them with.'

That and a few hundred pounds. A hobby for Lucinda, a lifeline for Molly. It was the best I could do for both of them.

'May I tell her to come and see you?'

She nodded and started handing the belt back, reluctantly. She was taken with it in spite of her criticism.

'Keep it. It will look better on you than on me.'

She stood up and I fastened the buckle for her. Since she'd told me about the motor bicycle there was a feeling of conspiracy between us, a secret shared.

'I don't think you'll regret it,' I said, meaning Molly but thinking of Simon Whittern too.

She showed me to the front door. We shook hands on the step and she kept hold of mine for while.

'Good luck. And please give my regards to Mr Musgrave.'

Her tone showed that she still hadn't forgiven him for the Peter business, but I thought Bill would be able to bear that. When I looked back from the track up to the road she was still standing there at the half-open door, hand raised.

I met Molly when the tannery women came out of work to tell her that I might have found them a business partner. She seemed pleased and agreed to call on Mrs Sollers, but there were other things on her mind.

'Annie?'

'Gone with him. I tried to stop her, but I couldn't.'

'Silly little fool.'

'Brave though, and grateful. She thinks he did it for her. She might even be half right.'

'Silly fool.'

We shook hands on the pavement outside her house.

'I don't suppose we'll see you here again, will we?'

'Goodness knows.' I didn't know myself what I'd be doing.

'Thanks, anyway.'

She went inside. As I pulled my glove on I could smell a whiff of the tannery on my hand, along with a faint ghost of the scent Lucinda used. I walked slowly through the town by the back streets, noticing election posters wrinkled from the damp on blank walls and the doors of empty houses where they'd stay until the weather took them away altogether, some of theirs, some of mine, and thought that a murder investigation and an election campaign had things in common. In both of them you found yourself unmoored from your normal life, relying on people you'd never met before and sharing with them experiences more intense than with even your most trusted friends. Then one day it was all over and any mistakes you'd made were beyond correction and all you could do was clear up and go home. So I went back to the King's Head to pack.

Chapter Twenty-two

⊗

Bill and I caught the same train next morning, he making for Oxford and I for London. By the time we got to Worcester we'd spoken about two dozen words to each other. I'd offered to put his bag on the rack because he was struggling to do it one-handed and he said he could manage, thank you very much. Later he asked if I wanted *The Times* and I said no thank you, which was stupid because that left me with nothing to do but stare out of the window at the flanks of the Malvern Hills against a grey sky. We changed trains, getting a compartment to ourselves, and Bredon Hill in its turn disappeared into the misty west. The old man in the long black overcoat was out there picking Brussels sprouts again. Perhaps he hadn't stopped picking them all the time we'd been away. The sight of him standing on the damp earth reminded me of the scarecrow and I suppose I must have shuddered because Bill looked up from his paper.

'Anything wrong, Nell?'

'No.'

'There is, isn't there? You're looking out there wondering what's happening to Whittern and Annie Carter.'

'No.'

Not at that moment, although they were never far from my thoughts. Sometimes I imagined them in a city, like Manchester or Liverpool, looking for lodgings, living off the proceeds of the motor bicycle. Sometimes I thought Simon Whittern wouldn't know how to live except off the land and pictured them in a barn somewhere, like the one at World's End Farm.

'He killed two men, Nell. One of them was a poor dutiful blighter as mad as he was.'

'Neither of them would have been like that if it hadn't been for the war.'

'Well, don't blame me for that. I didn't start it.'

'I'm not blaming you.'

'Oh yes you are.'

'If anybody's blaming anyone, you're blaming me. You think I deliberately made you fall in the river.'

'Didn't you?'

'I told you at the time I didn't. Do you think I'm lying to you? For once and for all, I did not push you in.'

'But you did try to stop me getting Whittern?'

'Yes, I've never denied it. It wasn't so much for his sake as for Annie's. That girl had already had nearly everything that mattered to her taken away. It wasn't up to you or to me to take the last thing left.'

'You're quite right.'

'What?' I stared at him, expecting some kind of barrister's trick. 'Did you say I was right?'

'I did. Are you expecting me to put it in writing?'

'If you think I was right, why have you been sulking for the past two days?'

'For heaven's sake, woman, I've been wrenching my brain round to some ethical justification for what you did and you call it sulking. If you'd been Ophelia, you'd probably have offered Hamlet pills for his liver.'

'And probably saved a good deal of unpleasantness.'

'What I can't accept is that you didn't trust me. Once you'd started suspecting about Whittern, you had days to make up your mind what you were going to do.'

'Not days, but—'

'All you allowed me were a few confused seconds in the dark. Then you're blaming me because without your refined moral perceptions and acting with what you doubtless see as brutal military force, I tried to make a citizen's arrest of a double murderer.'

'If you wanted to see him hanged—'

'I don't want to see anybody hanged. I'm glad I fell in the bloody river. I was, believe it or not, working up to telling you that you were right to push me in. I'll quite probably get double pneumonia and— What's up now?'

I couldn't help it. All of a sudden, I was laughing in a way that I hadn't laughed for years. It was as if the Vote and peace, the election and all the things that had happened so fast over the past year that there was no time to be happy about them had all become real at once, as if the year had turned at last and was on its upward swing out of grey and cold.

'I'm sorry, I haven't said it yet.' I stood up. 'Happy New Year, Bill.'

And I kissed him. After all, it was easier for me. I didn't have a cold or a broken elbow. He didn't seem to mind.

After a while, when we were sitting side by side and his *Times* was scrumpled up on the floor he said, 'Resuming the conversation—'

'I thought we'd dealt with that.'

'Resuming the conversation we were having the morning we found poor Wilby . . .'

'Oh that.'

'Yes, that. The question of what you're going to do with yourself now. Journalism or translation work, you said.'

'Yes. A long time ago I thought I wanted to be a barrister . . .'

He shuddered. 'I doubt if the law could cope with your peculiar concept of justice.'

'Anyway, it's too late for that. I'll be forty-two this year.'

'Has it occurred to you to use your peculiar talent to make a living?'

'Which one of my peculiar talents have you in mind?'

'Detection.'

'For pay?'

'You were prepared to do it for election expenses.'

'That was different. Anyway, how could I be a professional detective with doubtful ethics and a peculiar concept of justice?'

'Very easily, I should think.'

I stared out of the window, turning over this unexpected picture of the future. We were labouring up a fold of the Cotswolds now, the engine smoke blowing back along the window.

'Of course,' Bill said, 'there is another possibility.'

'What?'

'You might consider marrying me.'

'Good heavens!'

'Well, that's very flattering. I realise that I'm merely a humble captain, shortly to change back into an even more humble barrister . . .'

'And I'm saving myself for a general or a law lord at the very least.'

'Nell, I wasn't joking.'

'I'm not joking either but . . . marriage.'

'An honourable estate, or so I'm told.'

'House-hunting and coal cellars and things. People coming to dinner and wondering if there are enough forks.'

I thought of a day on the moors in the last summer before the war, blue sky, the smell of peat in the sun and Bill lying back on a patch of dry grass among the heather.

'You know, there's a lot to be said for a dishonourable estate. In the right company.'

Soon after that the train stopped at Moreton-in-Marsh and a man and a woman got in, looking very married. Under their disapproving eyes we moved back to our seats facing each other and retrieved *The Times* from the floor. We didn't say anything else until the train slowed down alongside Port Meadow and Bill stood up to get his bag from the rack. This time he let me help. I went with him into the corridor.

'See you in London, Nell, as soon as they let me out. Think about it.'

The train stopped. He stepped on to the platform and I handed his bag down. Doors slammed. The train started moving. He was shouting something through the noise and the clouds of steam.

'. . . and a Happy New Year to you too.'

It sounded a lot better than his Happy Christmas. Not wanting to go back to the carriage, I stood there watching Oxford cemetery sliding past as the train gathered speed, enjoying the feeling of not thinking about Bill's 'it' or anything else at all. I think the feeling might be called peace.